The Wolf is at Your Door

Simon Maltman

Simon Maltman

Cover Design by Simon Maltman

Editing and Interior Design by Ivana Sanders

"A Wolf at your door. You give it all, he wants more.
There's a wolf at your door.
He says he's playin' for keeps. Breathin' down your neck.
Boy, it's sure hard to sleep.
With a wolf at your door."

Howlin' Wolf- 'The Wolf is at Your Door' 1952

PART I

SITTING ON TOP OF THE WORLD

CHAPTER I

New York City
June 1987

Rory scooped up a fry that was dripping with ketchup.

"You're full of shit, Jim," he declared with a smirk, before stuffing the fry into his mouth.

Jimmy rolled his eyes and took a bite of his mammoth burger. Relish soaked onion dripped off his bottom lip before he swiftly flicked it away.

"You a damn fool you know Rory?" he declared in-betweens chews.

The two men were seated in the Hard Rock Café on Times Square. It was approaching eleven o'clock and closing time. Their booth backed onto a large glass display case featuring a 1970's David Bowie jump suit and a pair of Roy Orbison's black sun-glasses. The walls either side boasted various sought after rare records, autographed posters and ticket stubs. Across the walkway was a sensory overload of roof-suspended cars, guitars on walls and noisy television sets cranked up to eleven. The Rolling Stones were performing their recent single in a music video interspersing animation with Mick Jagger swaggering about a studio set.

"This is total bullshit," Rory added, grimacing at Jagger. A drip of ketchup escaped and dropped onto his pale blue jeans.

"Shit."

He wiped at it with a napkin, creating a pink smear. He had a blue denim jacket on too, with a plain white shirt underneath. At forty two he was in good enough shape, handsome even. His shaggy black hair was yet to betray a single gray.

"Listen Rory man, you're a blues freak- how d'ya not dig *The Stones*?"

"Blues? They've not played blues for twenty years. This MTV shit? Leave it out."

"Bobby Womack's in it too. What's not to like?"

"All of it," guffawed Rory, "And it's even a bloody cover. They haven't written a decent tune in years."

Rory checked his watch. It was okay, they had a few minutes yet.

He felt a flutter of anticipation. He glanced toward the door.

"You're such an excitable motherfucker, I give up with ya!" Jimmy said laughing, leaning back against the spongy corner seat. He shot Rory a wide smile, Rory allowing a grudging smirk. Jimmy was dressed in a yellow t-shirt with blue jeans. He was black, thinly built, with round thin-rimmed glasses. A few years older than Rory, he presented as a few years his junior.

"Seriously though Jim," Rory started- chewing absently on a fry, "For me there's no Stones after Brian Jones."

"You a poet now *Irish*?"

"Fucksake," Rory said before wiping his chin, then he pushed his plate away, "Right, best get down to it, enough of this bollox." He had another quick glance around the sprawling restaurant. There were maybe two dozen people left; most on deserts and coffees. There were only a few hardened drinkers.

"You clear on everything Jim?" Rory said quietly, his eyes shifting back.

"Yeah, like sure we been through this like a thousand and twenty times."

"Aye, but I mean once we're past the first bit... when we need to get the items and the cash. You sure the safe's not gonna be a problem?"

Jimmy chewed his lip for a second, then leaned forwards and pulled out a pack of cigarettes.

"Yeah man, chill out. There ain't nothin' able to trouble me and my little bag of tools."

He nodded to the large sports bag on the booth beside him. There was a matching bag beside Rory, though his was empty. Rory ran a hand through his hair, scrolling the plan one more time through his mind. He felt tense, it was always the same as this point on a job. He was never a panicker, but neither did he enjoy this waiting just before, waiting and primed.

"Can I get you two folks anything else?"

"Em… I'd take another Pepsi cheers," Rory said, a little taken back by the waitress who abruptly appeared. Her smile widened at the sound of Rory's Belfast accent that she stifled, "And what about you sir?" she said turning to Jimmy.

"Well uh," he said pulling the remaining label off his bottle of Bud, "I might take another of these." He caught a look from Rory before adding, "Well ya know- we're kinda havin' a business meeting and all, so I'll maybe just take a Pepsi too."

"Be right with you," she said lifting their plates, "We'll be closing up in about fifteen minutes, I hope that's okay."

"Yeah, sure," said Rory, wondering what would happen if he said that it wasn't.

"So, Rory listen- remind me; what's the items you gettin' again?"

"Don't you worry about those," he said, plucking out a Marlborough Red from his own deck, "You just worry about that safe."

"I know, but I'm interested," he said adjusting his glasses, looking more serious.

"Okay, so first off," started Rory, lowering his voice, "There's the Elvis hat."

"The Fedora?"

"Aye, from one of his movies."

"Love Me Tender."

"Aye whatever…"

"You gonna dis Elvis now too?"

"Just his movies. Anyway, then we gotta get them Beatles suits."

"Fuckin' sweet. It's those grey ones over there ain't it?"

Rory looked over his shoulder towards another glass cabinet, this one containing the Fab Four's early trade-mark matching suits, with a signed photograph displayed beside.

"They're the ones we can fence for sure, but nothin' stopping us grabbing whatever else we can carry as well."

"Hold up- so you're not gonna dump on The Beatles?"

"They're okay."

Jimmy rolled his eyes and stubbed his smoke out. The waitress delivered the drinks and they each took a sip. In the background U2 now moodily played *With or Without You."*

"Not even get me started on those wankers," Rory said quickly, sharing a smile with Jimmy.

Jimmy gazed around the room "You got your eye on anything for yourself?"

"Aye," said Rory simply.

He couldn't see it from where he sat, but in his mind's eye saw the incomparable sunburst Epiphone Casino. The owner had once been one Chester Arthur Burnett, AKA Howlin' Wolf.

Chapter 2

Jimmy flicked through a newspaper as the minutes ticked down towards closing time. Rory sunk back the end of his cola.

"Anything about back home in it?" he asked, his leg jiggling.

"Nothing much different bud. Not good." He turned back a page, "The last week... let me see- nineteen dead, three IRA bombs."

"Fucksake," said Rory, shaking his head.

"Sorry bro," Jimmy said, straightening his glasses again.

Rory shrugged heavily, checked his watch, then he lit another cigarette. He accepted the paper as Jimmy rolled it up, passing it across.

Rory flicked across a few pages, trying to reduce his growing pulse-rate. He could start to feel it throbbing in his neck.

"Here Jimmy- did ya read about this supposed serial killer? This place just gets crazier the longer I stay."

"Where?"

"Here- New York."

"Well there's more than one murder in this town."

"Thanks for the heads up. This guy- says here he could've killed at least two or three already."

"Don't they know?" Jimmy said with a throaty chuckle.

"Thing is, there's no bodies. But they find these weird messages."

"What kind of messages?"

"Fuckin' poems written on plaques and stuck on benches in Central Park."

"What? That is some fucked up shit."

"Yeah- NYPD says it's BS, who knows. Papers are calling him *The Couplet Killer.*"

"What?"

"Writes his notes in rhyming couplets."

"Crazy. Isn't there that whole- 'adopt a bench' thing though they started last year?"

"Yeah, but these plaques sure aren't approved."

"Dunno Irish, sounds like a media hoax to me."

The main door swung open and a well built cop marched inside. Rory and Jimmy shared a look. The cop headed straight to the bar and up to the duty manager.

Rory glanced at his bag, then rubbed his hands together nervously. His leg continued to jiggle.

Keep it together Rory. Almost there.

He cast his eye over the rest of the place again. There were maybe twenty customers left and about ten staff. The cop ended his conversation with the manager and lit up a smoke. The manager; gray haired and gray faced, began talking urgently to the waiting staff. They in turn headed off around all of the occupied tables. The waitress from before was coming their way.

Rory cleared his throat and Jimmy stubbed out his smoke before flopping back against the cushion of the booth, awkwardly titling his head back.

"Excuse me sir," she said addressing Rory, her eyes flickering concern as they passed over Jimmy. "We are closing in a few minutes anyway, but … er… the police need everyone to leave. It's nothing to worry about, but if you wouldn't mind finishing up and squaring your bill."

Jimmy kept his eyes on the poster covered ceiling, blinking every few seconds.

"Yes, of course," said Rory.

"Thanks, sorry for the inconvenience." She paused, looked sideways at Rory, "Sir, is your friend okay?"

"Yes, he's okay. He's diabetic and I think me may need to up his blood sugar a little bit. Is it okay if I help him to the bathroom for a minute? I think we best get him his insulin shot."

"Um… yes, yes of course."

Jimmy made a show of apparent weakness and Rory helped him across the restaurant to the rest rooms. As they made their way, the remaining diners all started to exit. Rory held the cop's stare as he passed close by him.

The rest room was empty. They each took a moment and splashed water on their faces. Rory went into a cubicle to urinate, but nothing would come. His stomach did another final summersault. He pulled up his trousers and washed his hands at the sink.

"Right… we're almost there. You all good?"

"Yeah bro," Jimmy answered calmly, slipping on a plastic *Halloween* mask.

Rory took out his own mask and covered his face.

It looked like Mike Myers and his twin were staring into the Men's room mirror.

"Okay then, let's do this."

They didn't burst through the doors. Rather, they cautiously stepped through. Both now had a gun in their hands; Rory a Glock and Jimmy a 32 S & W. One of the staff had her back turned as she was flicking the security bar across the front door. Two staff standing near the manager both gasped when they saw them come in. The manager continued to look grey.

"Everybody be cool," commanded Rory.

"Y'all just put your hands in the air," added Jimmy.

They all did as they were told.

All accept the cop.

He had had his back turned too, looking out a side window.

He swivelled on his bar stool.

His hand hung down by his own weapon.

"Think carefully about your next move," he said, his voice hard.

Some of the waiting staff visibly tremored. A kitchen porter stumbled in from the kitchens and shot his hands in the air.

Rory and Jimmy both trained their guns on him. He released a tiny squeak.

Then Jimmy chuckled. He reached into his back pocket and pulled out another mask and threw it to the cop.

"Cheers buddy," he said, catching it and pulling it on. "Right all you lot- up against the bar."

Chapter 3

They took their time, making sure that they had everyone who was in the building together. The supposed cop- their partner Dave- did a final sweep through the building just to be sure.

"All clear," he announced on his return.

"Okay cheers. Right guys," Rory began, "We have no interest in hurting anyone here. We want the money and we want a few other things. Don't fuck us around and we won't fuck you around. Okay?"

There was a muted response and nodding heads from the small circle of staff. They had all been cable tied on wrists and ankles and made to sit in the middle of the room. They all were shocked, some looked terrified. Jimmy stood to the side, his gun hovering between them.

The three gunmen then came together in a huddle off to the side.

"Right Jim- you get started on the safe. Dave-you watch the staff. I'm gonna join the manager for a personal tour."

"Okay," said Dave. He was a big man with small movements. He nodded and walked off to the group. Jimmy patted Rory on the back and headed down towards the office and the safe.

"Okay big chief," said Rory helping the manager to his feet. He cut his tied ankles with a pocket knife. "You got your keys on ya?"

The squat man gave a curt little nod.

"Good, let's get crackin' then."

In less than ten minutes, Rory had the suits and the hat out of the glass cabinets and transferred to his large sports bag. Ten minutes after that and Jimmy had cracked the safe and he and Dave were stuffing bundles of cash wound with rubber bands, into the second bag.

Then Rory set his eyes on the Howlin' Wolf guitar, displayed on the wall. "One more key buddy," he said to the manager, a wide smile underneath his mask.

Thirty six minutes after donning the masks, the three robbers were driving away from the back of The Hard Rock Café' in the direction of Hell's Kitchen. Keeping to the limits but keen to get away from Manhattan. Eight minutes after that and they dumped the van. No sirens to be heard, all going to plan. They switched to their own blue Ford Transit, parked at the back of a disused pool hall. Leaving the security video tapes, masks and gloves inside; they threw petrol all over, then Jimmy tossed in the still lit end of a joint inside. The upholstery caught fire with a whoosh. Before the first siren sounded, they were safely back at Rory's apartment in Fort Greene.

CHAPTER 4

The Killer set the newspaper out in front of him, running a thick fingered hand over it, straightening out the creases. Then he leaned back into the tired, green upholstered chair and smiled. He stretched out his long, spindly legs in front of him, underneath the rectangular glass coffee table. He plucked out a piece of loose fabric from the armchair, his bushy eyebrows knitting, the smile still fixed on his face. He brushed the small tear flat with the back of his hand. Evening was setting in, but the determined evening sun was sending sheets of light into the room through the blinds, With it could be seen an army of dustmites, already having descended on most of the room. He stared down again at the news article. There was a decent sized write up this time. Good, but not too much. Yes, they were finally waking up to him weren't they? Those silly little worker bees. It took them long enough. No matter, things were working out just fine. He allowed himself a few moments to revel in how his planning was finally paying off.

The Killer laid out the tools he required across the glass table, carefully setting a leather mat across first to prevent any scuffing. Then he set down the hunting knife upon it, unravelling it from a strip of rough velvety cloth. With a six inch steel blade, it was at times quite difficult to conceal. Cutting, skinning, gutting; it could do it all with ease. How he adored its simple and efficient beauty. First he used a polishing agent, thoroughly drying it afterwards with an old dish towel. Then he lightly and meticulously oiled it, before wiping the blade down once more. Afterwards, he worked with a clean cloth, rubbing hard at the inset medallion in the black handle. He breathed on it, before giving it a final wipe. He held the blade aloft in front of himself proudly, pleased with his work. Excitement pulsed through him. Along with it were vivid memories of his recent kills.

He was already hard.

He lifted over a box of tissues and then one of his magazines that he had purchased at the grubby little newspaper stand off eleventh.

CHAPTER 5

"Play us some *Wolf* then- *Malted Milk maybe*," said Jimmy, sparking up fresh joint.

Rory scowled over the top of the unplugged Epiphone Casino. "That was Robert Johnson, you eeijit."

"Oh."

"I need to educate you."

"Are you even black at all?" chimed in Dave.

"Jesus, Dave," guffawed Rory.

"Da fuck you say homeboy?" Jimmy responded, putting on his best *ghetto* affectation.

"You know I'm just messin,'" Dave said. A smile curled at his lips. He looked back down at his comic book. They had been holed up so far for three hours. A game of Texas Holdum hadn't lasted long- nobody was much in the mood for it. The conversation had died down and they were each passing their time in their own way. Jimmy straightened out his neck, set down his paperback, taking in the sparse apartment. A lone painting hung on the wall, an uninspiring water colour of an Irish harbour town.

"What you reading anyways Dave?" he said.

"Huh? Oh- it's the new *Splendor*."

"Splendor?"

"*American Splendor*. Ya know- Harvey Pekar? He just writes about his day to day life. No superheroes, no big action. A working man's good philosophical shit right there."

"He the one Crumb did some of the drawing for?" Jimmy asked, before taking a long pull on his smoke.

Dave rolled his eyes. "He is one of the *artists* for the material, yes."

"Right you two big girls' blouses, settle down," said Rory setting his guitar gently over to the side of the living area. He gazed at it, barely able to believe that this blues relic was now resident at his place. The apartment was hot and as Summer threatened, it would soon become almost unbearable. He went over to the windows and pushed them open as far as they would go. His apartment was a run down, one bedroom Brownstone in Fort Greene. It wasn't the worst place by some standards, but it was no palace either. If he put more of an effort into it, that would have helped too. He had never planned on staying in it long to start with. He had hoped after a few jobs that he would have moved on by now. But it was rent controlled and it suited his needs. There was no girlfriend to tell him to smarten it up or move and his friends didn't care either way. One thing he should add though was an air conditioner. Both Jimmy and Dave lived less than a forty minute walk away at this time of night. They had all agreed to first wait things out at Rory's, then head their separate ways.

"Do youse wanna hang about for another half hour or so? I think we got away clean. Best to be certain. We'll check the news again in a minute, sure."

"That's 'cause we're legends us three," said Jimmy with a wink, licking the ridge of another joint, then rolling it over.

"I'd agree that things are looking good," added Dave in a measured tone, "So what about this *fence* of yours? He say he 'aint gonna have any trouble shifting this gear?"

"No, these items we took he's got buyers lined up and all. That's why there wasn't much point in nickin' anything much else. Just more chance of us getting caught with stolen shit."

"What about that there guitar?" Dave said wryly.

Rory smiled out the side of his mouth, "Well boys- that's different. Right- who wants another beer?"

Rory ignored the dirty dishes spread over his grotty little kitchenette and grabbed three bottle of Miller from the integrated little fridge.

"You two get started on these and I'll go ring him now actually?"

"Ring who?" asked Dave, looking up from his comic again, raising one eyebrow.

"The *fence*."

"Yeah I know- but what's his name?"

"You know it's better no names."

"Yeah, yeah- go and make your call Irish," said Jimmy, flicking the top off his beer.

He didn't have his own phone, so relied on the communal one across the floor. Out in the hallway, the air was colder and smoke free. Instead there was a dry mustiness there. Nobody was about and there was barely any noise, save for the sound of a sports repeat playing on a distant T.V set. Rory dropped in a few quarters. He took a slug of his beer, then punched in the number.

"Hi, it's me… yeah sorry it's late. Yes, no problems. Tomorrow? Aye, sure. We'll get a proper chat then. Yeah that's fine. And usual spot? Okay, see you then."

Rory walked the few steps back to his apartment, glugging back the rest of his beer. The scene that greeted him on the other side of the door made him question if he had just drank a case.

"Mother of God," he said, quickly closing the door behind.

Jimmy and Dave cracked up, falling about laughing.

Jimmy was dressed in one of the full Beatles suits and Dave had quiffed his hair forwards underneath Elvis's fedora.

Rory smiled. "Don't get any fuckin' ash or beer on those ya eeijits. Or we'll never get our money. Bloody half wits."

The two stood up and began strutting back and forth across the small living area. Dave curled his lip up and Jimmy smoked his joint, Bogart style, while rolling his shoulders in a half dance.

"So which Beatle are you?" Rory said shaking his head, starting on a fresh cigarette.

"I'm Billy Preston- the fifth Beatle."

"I thought that was George Martin."

"Lots of fuckers said they were the fifth Beatle," chimed in Dave, "Brian Epstein, Pete Best…"

"Jesus, I need another beer."

The tone in the room had lost its edge as they all settled in and began to enjoy a job gone well. They drank more beers, chatted, listened to the news.

"So Rory, is there another job?" asked Jimmy later, admiring himself in the small, dusty mirror above the T.V set.

"There's always another one," smirked Rory, with a knowing smile.

"A good one?" shouted Dave after him as Rory went to fetch another drink from the fridge."

"Well," said Rory, coming back in and flicking the screw lid free, "Let's just say this. You know how this job'll keep us sweet for a lot of months? How'd you like to not need to work for a few *years*?"

CHAPTER 6

The next morning, Rory hopped on the subway at Dekalb
Avenue. He spent the half hour train ride listening to his walkman.
He had picked up a bootleg cassette of a Muddy Waters concert from
1957. He was captivated. He didn't even notice the humidity, or the
sweating bodies crammed up close to him. He eased back against his
ripped seat and let Muddy's growl wash over him. With that and the
feeling of satisfaction after the job, he was on a high. It couldn't have
gone any better. Setting off on foot into Central Park, he flipped the
tape back to side one, rewound it and started it over again. He
smoked a couple of cigarettes as he walked. He wore a plain red polo
shirt and blue cords. The day was hot, dry- but not overpoweringly
so. He headed straight towards The Mall. Ever since arriving in town
in 1984, this is where he always met his *fence* when they were
discussing business after a job. It was funny really because they met
in plenty of other places, plenty of others time. But always here after
a job. Rory had first discovered the Elm lined path in the movie
Kramer Vs. Kramer. He had watched it with a girlfriend in a run
down cinema in Belfast. There's a scene when Dustin Hoffman is
trying to teach his kid to ride a bike. Rory had been thrilled coming
across the very place in his first week living in New York. Central
Park reminded him of the Botanic Gardens in his native Belfast, but
on a massive scale. Three years later and he still hadn't gotten used to
the city- the size of everything, the smog, the noise, the people.

Winston was seated on a bench, a half folded New York Times
across his knees. He had just struck a match and was dipping it into
the end of his pipe, grimacing as he made a quiet puffing noise.
Winston was fifty six years old, thin, with greying shaggy hair and
horn rimmed glasses. He always wore a suit, and it was always an old
one. He looked up, catching sight of Rory approaching along the
path. He smiled; thin laughter lines becoming more prominent either

side of his sparkling eyes. He considered the end of his pipe and nodded to himself, then blew out some smoke.

"Rory," he said, standing and offering his hand.

"Winston, great to see you."

They sat down together, with the bench to themselves. There was a pleasant hub-bub around them. A mild breeze tried to cool them as it gently rustled the summer leaves. Families were out for a stroll, young couples holding hands, a shell suit wearing few joggers.

"You made the headlines alright," Winston said still smiling, tapping the folded over paper.

"Can I've a wee read?" Rory asked, his face taking on a boyish look.

"Go on ahead."

Winston sat back, arms folded, the pipe bellowing like a little chimney. This always reminded Rory of the Popeye cartoons he'd watched as a kid.

Rory scrolled through the article. "Jesus," he said, unable to hide the giant grin on his face, "Holy shit!"

There was a half page story featuring the robbery on the front page of The New York Times.

"If you wanted fame young Rory- you might just have it."

"Er… I think in my line of work it'd be better to remain anonymous."

"Perhaps infamy will come after you're gone," he said with a chuckle.

"Yeah, I think I'd prefer not to be famous in my own lifetime."

Winston leaned forwards, peering over his glasses into Rory's eyes, "Seriously though, did it all go without a hitch?"

"Yeah… I mean- I think so. It was smooth enough- no real trouble."

"I see you got rid of the van good and proper," he said tapping the paper again, "You leave the tapes in there too?"

Rory nodded.

"Good," said Winston thoughtfully.

Simon Maltman

Winston's role was only that of a *fence*, taking a fair cut of whatever items he had agreed to move on to a buyer. His role by nature was *hand's off*. But he always had taken an active interest in the jobs, an interest in Rory. Maybe it was that both his own parents were Galway Irish. Or it could have been their mutual respect for The Blues. Maybe it was because of that first time Rory had come into his antique shop. Rory had attempted to sell Winston a genuine Civil War pistol, only asking for around a twentieth of its value. Winston couldn't bring himself to completely rip off this dumb Irish immigrant. They soon had formed an unlikely friendship. Winston had discovered that there was much more to Rory than that first exchange. It hadn't been long until they began working together on jobs, with Winston behind the scenes.

"D'ya want me to wait a week or two before passing you the stuff, Winston?"

"Yeah, maybe that'd be best. A few weeks, just to be sure. The buyer will understand that, he's in no rush. Are you good with keeping them in your apartment?"

"Aye, it's no problem. Sure, I'll call into the shop during the week- get another chat about it. So far it looks like there's no heat near us."

There were never many specifics discussed at these first meetings after a job, seated on The Mall. But they both enjoyed the routine and familiarity.

"Stay for another smoke?" Winston asked.

"Yeah, 'course," said Rory, fingering out a fresh Marlborough.

Winston set about loading another pipe.

"You hear about The Bosses today?" he asked.

"Not today, no," Rory said searching for the page, "What's happening now?"

"Samuel Davison- y'know one of their lawyers, listen to what he says- here pass us that Rory."

Rory passed the paper back over and Winston adjusted his glasses.

"Ahh yes, here we are. This is what he says in open court, 'Can you accept that just because a person is a member of the Mafia that doesn't mean he committed the crimes charged in this case?' Isn't that incredible?" Winston said, pulling off his glasses and slipping one leg over the other, "Jesus, the first time anyone's ever admitted the Mafia even exists."

"That's crazy, isn't it?" Rory said raising his eyebrows, "Bit like back home- nobody ever wants to admit they're in the paramilitaries. Except the nut jobs and cocky kids who aren't."

"Yeah. Speaking of nut jobs- what do you reckon to this *Couplet Killer*?" Winston said, absently scratching his neck.

"I dunno- Jimmy and me were taking about that yesterday. Seems a little far fetched."

"He part of your A-Team?" Winston asked, raising an eyebrow.

"Yeah- sorry I always forget you don't know those guys- it feels like you do. Aye- he's my BA Baracus. Oh wait… shit- that's maybe a bit racist is it? He can be Murdoch then. Aww heck I don't know," Rory said making a face, sucking on his smoke. "Oh yeah- that *Couplet* guy. I don't know- sounds to me like it's all hyped up by the press."

"Could be. I don't know there's much in it. It's a good story though. Here- they found another one of these poems it says here- another plaque on a bench. It was actually just down near Robbie Burns' statue," he said, gesturing along The Mall. "Anyway, listen to this- see what you think…

'The ground is damp and damper still,
By the time the sun has set.
The air is fresher from the scent of the kill,
Free and vital and wet.'

"What do you think?"

"I think his poetry is shite."

CHAPTER 7

"Please… please, you don't have to do this."

"I know I don't, you don't have to tell me that," he said, his voice almost bemused.

He returned the gag to her mouth, securing it tightly. Her eyes above danced dully. A death march.

He considered the knife in his hand and then rotated her slightly on the trolley. Now only dressed in her underwear, her torso and legs were covered with fresh superficial slices.

He had had enough fun with this one. There were always plenty of others to choose from.

The Killer was satisfied with his choice of angle, now he plunged the hunting knife deep within her side. She screamed from within her gag, spittle running out from underneath it. The gag certainly helped to muffle the noise. The sheetrock inner wall helped too. Before the first of the so called 'Couplet Killer' murders, he had built this inner room inside his basement. It wouldn't have made a huge difference to the noise, but he always thought it better to do something than to not. The more prepared you are, the more effort you put in; the better chance you have of success. It was one of the many lessons his mother had tried to drill into him. She tried her best not to show her disappointment in her son She thought she was being encouraging.

'You'll find something you're good at,' she'd say, with no
        thought of what that inferred.
'It's not your fault that you're different.'
But he felt it, he knew it. Her absence of malevolent motive
        almost made it worse.
'You'll find your place- I know you will,' she'd go on, 'In the
        kingdom of the blind, the one eyed man is king.'
Anyway. That was all history.

Simon Maltman

Killing number three would be completed any minute now. What was the rush? Nobody could be sure that she was missing. Nobody would find her here. And nobody would ever see her body again. He pulled the knife out and gazed at it, blood dripping in little pools over the well oiled hilt. Blood gushed from the wound in her side. He made no attempt to stem the flow. It amused him. She stopped screaming and her body heaved, her breathing racked.

Then he plunged the knife in again.

CHAPTER 8

Rory milled around for the few days afterwards. There was no particular place he was meant to be, nothing in particular he was meant to be doing. Technically, he was registered as working as a labourer for a large New York firm. But like plenty of the other *workers*, he had never actually been there. The weather had stayed good and he still got up early each day and pounded the streets. He would crack up staying inside for too long as well. It was always the same in-between jobs. He was never one for blowing his take and living it up for a few months. He liked walking around, directionless, smoking; letting his mind simmer a little on the next job. He enjoyed exploring it in his mind's eye, testing ideas out, trying out a few different paths. At this stage there was no pressure, it didn't matter if his mind ran down a few blind alleys. It was all part of feeling out the new job. It was like fixing a blindfold on and exploring a new building. The inside could be as grand as you wanted it to be. It could be a shack or a cathedral. He did his best thinking, walking around, sometimes with music playing loudly in his earphones. The buzz around him, the crush of people here actually helped his mind to focus all the better.

He turned up by Gramercy and headed towards Fifth Avenue. A huge poster that was being pasted on a massive billboard caught his eye- *The Living Daylights*. It was the new *Bond* movie. Rory had seen it already and thought it pretty good. A lot of the critics had given Timothy Dalton a hard time- but he had liked him. *Not as good as Connery*, they would always say that. Rory preferred him to the middle-aged cheese of the later Moore years anyway. He had also watched Connery's belated 007 return in the unofficial, *Never Say Never Again,* a few years before.

"It's like Sean decided to take a dump on his classic Bond movies and used the script to wipe his arse," he'd said to his girlfriend at the time. That had been back in Northern Ireland. Back in Belfast. Back in the troubled and poverty-stricken neighbourhood that was Ardoyne. That was a very different city from here; it felt more like a different planet. There was violence everywhere and if not actual, the threat was always there. If you walked down the wrong street, you were targeted and you may never make it home that night. Maybe your T-shirt was green or your eyes were 'too close together.' These were genuine reasons behind beatings, maiming's or worse. As a young Catholic, the hostile British Army and RUC Police were not his friends either. It didn't help that Rory sometimes found himself already on the wrong side of the law. That same year, thirty eight IRA prisoners had escaped from The Maze prison. The biggest breakout in UK history. He hadn't wanted to- but Rory had ended up playing a part in it. Three years now, he had been living in New York City. Three years since his heart had been broken and he had left everything he had ever known behind him. Flying half way around the world with the clothes on his back and a rucksack in the overhead locker, he had had no plan. In many ways he had landed on his feet. It had been sink or swim. He had been shown kindness, particularly from those who liked to hear his accent. And he had made the right connections. Very quickly he had put together a regular team and they were pulling jobs that were both smooth and lucrative.

The thought struck Rory that he had been living here, this Irish lad born into poverty, now resident in the most exciting city in the world, and he had never taken in the sights. Not properly. In the distance was The Empire State Building. He had passed by it many times, seen it from afar more times still. It had been the tallest skyscraper in New York for four decades for good reason. Maybe now he should take in some of the sights, act like a tourist. He never had done before. Do it right. Why not start there? He headed past The Rockerfeller and Saint Patrick's. Staring up to where King Kong climbed, roared and beat his chest, the urge to go inside dwindled. Seeing the queues, the whole sight-seeing notion evaporated. Maybe another time. Walking on, he lit up a cigarette and his mind drifted back to his plan.

Not much happened for a day or two, except the plan did begin to take shape in his mind. That was always one of his favourite parts of a job. It was still hazy, but he could begin to make out a little of the picture. A few days later he found himself on the southeast corner Fiftieth and Tenth. This time where his feet had taken him was by design. He headed on into Grogan's pub. He took a seat at the well-worn bar and ordered a pint of Guinness. It was two in the afternoon and just about an acceptable time of day for a pint of the black stuff. Scanning the room, most of the ramshackle bunch of characters were not anywhere near their first of the day. Many wouldn't have even remembered it. There was one middle aged guy at the bar sipping on a bottle of sparkling water. Now that was weird- it takes all sorts. Just as Rory was slipping into an empty booth with his pint, she walked in. A girl like her in a place like that. Now that made the sparkling water guy look inconspicuous.

"Alice!" Rory said warmly, sliding his legs back from under the table.

They hugged. "Rory, so good to see you."

"Messy pup," she said rubbing away a pot of foam off his chin with her finger.

"What're you drinkin'?" he asked.

"Oh, I don't know, sure as we're in an Irish pub- I'll have a Baillies. Thanks Rory."

Alice patted him on the arm and then took a seat at the booth. She was wearing a thin blue denim jacket over a red Led Zeppelin T-shirt. She pulled off the denim and set it on the seat beside her. Her short and spiky, died red hair flopped to one side. She flopped it back over again, out of her eyes. She was thirty seven years old, but her youthful skin and toned body meant she could have passed for ten years younger.

"There you are, one large Baillies." Rory said, setting the glass tumbler down.

"A large one?" she asked with mock horror, "Are you trying to get me drunk Mr Downie?"

"So what if I am?" he said grinning, "Slainte!"

"Bottoms up!"

"So how you been?"

Rory had first met Alice a year and half before, working on a job. He'd been brought in to help on someone else's plan- a small bank heist out on Staten. It had gone okay and Alice and he had fallen straight into an easy rapport. He had brought her in on two of his own jobs since then. He liked her. They hadn't met up socially before, it had all been about the jobs.

Rory filled her in on the Hard Rock robbery.

"Yeah, it worked out great to tell you the truth. Again though- I'm sorry that we couldn't bring you in on that one."

"No, don't be stressin'," she said waving the thought away with her hand, "Sure I only got back from my Mom's last week."

"I know. We were lucky to be sure- we could've done with another man… or woman. We couldn't wait much longer. If they'd that new safe put in- it might even have given Jimmy some trouble."

They took a sip of their drinks.

"Where abouts does she live- your mum?"

"Oh, we're from Pennsylvania, Scranton actually."

"Oh right."

She smirked, "You've absolutely no idea where that is do you?"

"I absolutely don't," he said with a laugh.

"You're not missing much, there's not much to tell."

"Okay, I'll take your word for it."

"So, what's new? Are you wanting my expertise on something, Rory?"

Rory loved the way her eyes gleamed and how her smile slipped off to the side.

"Yeah could be," he said raising a thick eyebrow. He plucked out a Marlborough. Alice took out one of her long tipped cigarettes, crossed her legs and lit up.

"So, yeah," he said leaning in, "I do have the start of something. Would you be interested?"

"Always. Yeah, I mean I ain't got much on. I always love workin' with you fellas."

"Well alright then, that's great. I don't have it all thought out yet- gimme a couple of weeks and I'll know if it's a goer."

"Is it a good one?"

"If I can get it all squared in my head, yeah the haul could be very nice."

"Ok cool. Well now we've settled that- another drink?"

"Why not?"

They whiled away an hour or more with ease, with a few more drinks inside the dilapidated old Irish pub.

"So hey, Rory- you got much on the rest of the day?"

"Hell, yeah," he said examining his cigarette packet closely, "I gotta get another deck of these soon and apart from that…" he shrugged, smiling widely.

"Good to hear", she said pushing a stray hair away from her eyes, "You fancy seeing a movie? I was thinking of going anyways. This is fun. No worries if you can't."

"Sounds great. Anything in particular?" He tried to sound casual, but actually he was very pleased that she'd asked.

"I heard that Lethal Weapon one's decent." She stubbed out her smoke, a dusting of ash landing on her red painted fingertips.

"That's what-do-you call him… Mel something?"

"Mel Gibson."

"Aye, that's the one. Yeah, it looks good."

A few minutes later and they were spilling out into the afternoon sun. They both shielded their eyes, now unprotected by smoke and darkness. Rory sniggered as he steadied himself. Alice started to laugh, then they both broke into a wrinkle. Rory stumbled forwards on the sidewalk a few steps, bumping into a well built jogger.

"Fuck man- watch it!" the guy shouted, stopping suddenly to shout into Rory's face.

Already in a too-tight red vest, the jogger flexed his arm muscles.

"Okay, Jesus like- I'm sorry," Rory said.

Alice put a hand to her face to hide her smirk.

"Watch your fuckin' way next time, *Paddy*."

On a dime Rory's good humour evaporated. His nostrils flared and he took a step forwards. A moment later, the jogger's own expression changed suddenly too from arrogant antagonist to meek little lamb. He swiftly jogged on. Alice was standing off to one side, now giggling. Rory looked quite pleased with himself. She gestured to behind Rory. Rory turned to see a huge hulk of a man behind him, just inside the open door.

So that's what he was afraid of.

"There surely are some gobshites around," the man said in a deep brogue, winking and walking back inside.

"C'mon lets go," said Alice laughing, grabbing Rory's arm and leading him away.

"I swear this country of yours is more fuckin' nuts than mine."

CHAPTER 9

"That was quare craic," said Rory as they came out of the small Cineplex. The sidewalk was even busier now that the sunlight had dwindled and the cooler evening had set in.

"English please?" Alice said putting on a vaguely European accent.

Rory gave her a pretend punch on the arm, "What the hell was that?"

She shrugged, "You started it with all your *Oirish* shit," she teased, now trying a full Brogue.

"It's like *The Quiet Man*, all over again." He grinned. "You Yanks can do a good Irish accent, never mind a Northern one. Anyhow, I thought it was class- a really good movie."

"It was pretty good. You boys love all the explosions and big guns though. Big kids. I'd be happy just with Mel Gibson."

"He your type then?"

"Yeah he's one of them," she said a little coyly.

"Drink?"

"Why not? One for the road."

They ended up in a little bar two blocks south. There was a singer songwriter earnestly singing his heart out, which may have contributed to the place being half empty. They found a snug corner, got a coffee each with chasers, then both lit up.

On the stereo system Neil Young sang how it's "better to burn out, than it is to rust," and Rory nodded to himself in appreciation of the music.

Not quite Blues, but what a song writer.

"This is the life ay?" said Rory, sitting back, relishing the cigarette.

"Oh my God- yeah- not a bad place to live sometimes. Different from back home I imagine?"

"You could say that. We only have like one and a half million people in the whole country. *The North* I mean. Jaysus- I'd get in trouble back home for saying that."

"What d'ya mean?"

"Aww the place is fucked. It's so messed up," he said, squinting as he inhaled a lungful of smoke, then leaning forwards, "It's difficult to explain. I'm Irish like- I don't like The Brits much. But I still see The North as my home whatever it is. It's Ireland to me. But some of my Nationalist friends wouldn't take kindly to me calling it a country."

"Shit- that is confusing," she said.

"Unionists say Northern Ireland. Nationalists call it *The North.*"

Her face creased in concentration. But all Rory could think of was how beautiful she looked. Maybe it was the drink, maybe it was dumping the stress from the last job, but he could imagine himself becoming quite smitten.

"And you were already doing jobs then?"

"Yeah, as Howlin' Wolf once said, 'I couldn't do no yodelin', so I turned to howlin'. And it's done me just fine.'"

She grinned at that. "Is that why you left there, Rory? Sick of all of the politics?"

Rory blew out his cheeks, "That's the sixty four thousand dollar question," he said raising his heavy eyebrows, then taking a sip of his coffee. It was hot, and tasted good. "The place is literally a bomb site. It brings you down, you know? Drags you in to it all as well."

"Did *you* ever… get dragged in?"

"You mean with the paramilitaries?" he said tilting his head.

"Well… yeah I guess…sorry- I maybe shouldn't of…"

"No, it's fine," he said raising a hand, trying a little too hard perhaps," I suppose the short answer is, no… well not really." He moved closer to her across the table. "I've no time for any of that shite. I never did. No one should kill anyone else- period. Especially not over two types of the same bloody religion. Doesn't matter if you're a Prod or a Catholic, we're just people; some good, some not so much.

"And which category do we fall into?"

We?

"I suppose the latter- not you. But yeah- there was one time I kinda was close to getting involved. It's tough growing up where I lived. There's no equality- still isn't now." He tipped the rest of his whiskey down his throat, his forehead wrinkling.

"You don't have to talk about it Rory," she said softly, moving closer to him.

"No, honestly. It's good to talk about it sometimes. I *should* talk about these things- I suppose I never have much. I don't wanna end up like most people here seem to do- visiting a shrink." He gave a little laugh. "So, yeah. There was one time I'd been working for some dodgy guys, pulling jobs. I suppose it was inevitable my path would cross with theirs at some point anyhow. I mean I'm from Ardoyne so I already knew who a lot of the *connected* guys were. So I ended up owing a fella a favour and he says I need to drive for a job. Not like I was really *asked*." He paused and blew out a plume of smoke. "You ever hear of the escape from The Maze?"

Her eyes narrowed. "A couple of years ago- the prison, right?"

"Yep- the biggest breakout in UK history. Well, I was roped in as the getaway driver."

At this he gave an incongruous chuckle.

"Fuck," said Alice putting a hand to her lips, "No way. I remember hearing about it, yeah"

"Yes pretty nuts really. The funny thing is there was a fuck up with the timings. We arrived like five minutes after they had broke out. By that time the Provos had run like fuck- nickin' cars, hiding out in the woods- allsorts."

"Fucking hell Rory!" she said breaking into a full wrinkle, "Crazy."

"Yeah, so I guess I dodged a bullet there. Quite literally possibly. That time anyhow."

Then a sadness drifted from somewhere inside him and crossed his face, ghosting his colouring.

"So I guess that sort of stuff puts you off a place? I understand why you'd look for a clean start." She said a little awkwardly.

"Yeah, you could say that." He took a last sip of his coffee, weighing up something in his mind. "There was more to it though."

Alice reached across the table and squeezed his hand for a moment, "Hey- it's alright."

"I... uh had been seeing a girl- for almost a year. Her name was Bronagh. We weren't engaged or anything but, you know- we were pretty serious." He gazed off towards the bar, licked his lips and then focused on Alice again. "We were out for a drink one night- a local dive in Belfast- not even as nice of this. Just an ordinary Friday night, not all that many in." He wiped the residue of the drinks from his lips, then fished out a cigarette, his hand displaying a minor shake. Alice kept her eyes on him; warm, concerned. Her feet were flat on the floor, leaning in; mirroring his own body language.

"About eleven that night, the doors burst open. Two gunmen marched in, straight away raining bullets all over the place. We all dove to the ground. Everyone screaming, glass exploding all around, some dead within seconds." Rory swallowed hard again, took a shaky draw of his smoke. "It felt like hours, but I suppose the whole thing was less than a minute. They ran out again over the broken glass. There was a screech of tyres outside and inside was left in carnage. Thirteen dead in all, twenty three injured."

Alice's own eyes were sparkling now and her voice was hoarse when she spoke, "That's terrible Rory. And Bronagh?" She searched out his hand again and gave it another squeeze.

He nodded. "We had hit the dirt together, I tried to cover her with myself. But somehow a stray bullet reached her. Went straight through her neck."

A tear dropped and he wiped it away, "I dunno how it happened- it makes no sense. I didn't even have a scratch on me. Made no sense why anyone was shot that night anyway. It was a tit for tat thing. They were just lookin' to shoot some Catholics. Senseless."

"God, that's tragic Rory," Alice said very quietly, welling up herself. She shuffled around the side of the booth and put an arm around him. The emotion of the story, tiredness and drink had transformed Rory's face. He looked gaunt, sallow.

"Thanks Alice. D'ya mind if we maybe call it a night?"

"Yeah, 'course."

"Another time?"

"Another time Rory."

CHAPTER 10

The skinful of drink was the first thing he remembered. That was due to the immediate hangover. He remembered the whiskeys he had sunk back at his apartment before he drifted off into a drunken sleep. His throat was raw with dog's breath and his head pounded. Sitting up in bed, his stomach joined the band of ailments. Then his brain finally kicked in. Why had he told er all of that the night before? It had all just came out.

Jesus. I'm such a div.

He ran a hand through his hair, then regarded the hand scornfully, along with the greasy, smoky residue now on it.

He had thought he had put all of that behind him. The notion that he hadn't properly dealt with it frightened him. He pulled himself out of bed and dragged his body into the shower. By the time he was dry, seated in his chair with a cup of coffee, he felt better. He pushed the feelings back again. Back where they belonged.

He had things to attend to. It took a fair amount of running around to tie up the last job. There was getting the merchandise to Winston and squaring all the takes, deducting the running costs. He never felt fully focused on the next job until the last one was completed, all the nickels and dimes split up. But he allowed himself just to dip his toe into the next one. At this point in tying up a job, planning for next one felt like a little treat to yourself. He spent a little time digging, research, talking to a few contacts. This is how it usually went. He'd take a sip, see if he got much of a taste for it. Then once he was free of the last job, he'd feel his way around the idea, commit only if it felt viable. If so, he'd jump right it- working on it 24/7.

A few more weeks passed, now the beginning of July and the city began to boil. Rory called a meeting at his apartment- just with

Jimmy and Dave. Jimmy was dressed in a striped, short sleeved shirt with jeans, Dave in a blue T-shirt and green combats.

"Here's your packets boys," Rory said, handing them each a brown envelope.

They took them, setting their beers down, their faces open.

"Ohhh, nice one Rory, fat," said Jimmy, rifling through it.

Dave kept a poker face, counting through each bill, mouthing the totals as he went. Rory and Jimmy exchanged an amused look.

"Much obliged Rory, that's a good score," he said eventually.

"I'm glad you reckon so," said Rory with an even smile.

"It all went smoothly with your here fence?" Asked Dave.

"Aye it was all grand. He's rid of them already and has his share. That's it all split now."

"Sweet, thanks man," said Jimmy.

"You fellas free for a bit longer?"

"Yeah, sure," said Jimmy.

"Can you put on *The Nicks* score first?" Dave said, reaching up his beer.

"I'm sure it could be arranged," Rory said, switching on the radio.

They listened for a few moments, then Dave groaned at the score, "You can turn that shit off now, thanks."

They moved from the small kitchen table and laid out on the old sofa and *almost* matching chair.

"You further on with this next job then, Rory?" Dave asked, extending out his substantial frame.

"Yeah, a wee bit."

"You're keeping us on tenders here," Jimmy said.

"I'm not committed to it just yet- but it's looking better all the time." He lit a cigarette and straightened up in his chair, "Okay, so it's a Bingo hall."

"Bingo?" broke in Jimmy, looking puzzled.

"Yeah, Bingo. But it's not like a church hall or some shit. Don't forget- there ain't no casinos allowed in New York. High rollers gotta spend their money some place. Anyhow- I gotta tip about a place- I been looking into it. It's looking better all the time. We hit it on the right night- it'd be a big score."

"Who was the tip from?"

"You remember Big Bobby?"

"From Queens?" said Dave.

"Aye- he did that job with us at the docks- must've been two years ago."

"Oh yeah I remember," said Jimmy. Dave nodded.

"He's moved out to Florida, but we'd talked about this place a few times. He used to work there- part time like. He owed me a favour and laid out an angle I could use. He said to hit it if I wanted, no strings."

"Fair enough," said Dave.

"I wanna bring Alice in on this one," Rory added, "We could do with having four and a girl- could be a bonus."

"Yeah- that girl got qualities we don't," said Jimmy with a wink, finishing off rolling a joint.

"Sounds fine Rory, she's always been solid." Agreed Dave.

They chatted some more, Rory not wanting to be drawn into too may specifics about the job just yet. They talked mostly about music and sports, had another beer each. Jimmy rolled another- Rory reflected how it never seemed to affect Jimmy any. He wondered why Jimmy even bothered with it.

"I sure do like the sound of this score," said Jimmy later, "Be nice to feel a bit more flush, keep the wolf from the door."

"Lift you out of the hood?" Dave said mockingly.

"What's that supposed ta mean?"

"It means you're from outside the fuckin' Village- you ain't from Harlem Jim." Dave rolled his eyes. It was hard to tell sometimes how much of what Dave says is in jest. Particularly after a few drinks have been taken.

"For fucks sake," said Jimmy.

"Come on you two," sighed Rory.

Half the time Dave and Jimmy were like two squabbling brothers. Even if their appearances and personalities couldn't have been more different.

"What? Come on Rory- we just playin'. What's it you say in the UK? Don't get your panties in a twist?"

"Well for a start I'm Irish, Dave," Rory replied, pressing his palm to his head. "Anyway let's just have a beer and chill."

"I haven't got my panties in a twist either Dave," started Jimmy, his face hardened. He adjusted his glasses back from the end of his nose. "It bugs me when you say shit like that. You don't know nothin' about me."

When he was verging on feeling angry, Dave's voice took on a monotone and mechanical sound, "I was merely pointing out that you had a pretty swell upbringing, Jim. I, on the other hand *did* grow up in Harlem in the fifties and sixties. It would have been better if I had been fuckin' black."

"Alright, alright- Jesus," said Rory standing up, "And I'm a Nationalist Catholic from the last fuckin' outpost of The British Empire. We've all had our problems, let's have another bloody drink."

"You're now in the good old U.S of A, Rory. The Free World's here- all are welcome. We already taught those Brits a lesson a few hundred years ago."

"Thanks for the history lesson, Dave. At least my country used to be an equal member of the United Kingdom and not just an uncivilised colony."

They did have another drink, and a whiskey to chase it away afterwards. The atmosphere gradually thawed. The talk that followed was more light-hearted, Jimmy and Dave even eventually sharing a hug.

"I'm gonna bounce now man," said Jimmy a few hours later, a little the worse for wear. A half smoked spliff sat smoldering in the ashtray.

"I'd better bail too, I promised my Mum I'd clean out her yard later," Dave chimed in, looking unimpressed at the idea.

"Take it easy guys, I'll be in touch."

After they left, the apartment was silent. Rory was left to his own private thoughts, alone again.

Chapter 11

It was hot in Central Park. The Killer didn't much care for the heat. He could never get used to the oppressive humidity of the city. Even so, he still wore a coat. It was an unfashionable green zip up with a hood. He wore a pair of black work trousers underneath it and plain white shirt. It was late morning and as he pressed on through the park, a smell of frankfurters and cooked onions hit him. He was hungry; he'd stop at a deli before heading back to work. The Killer almost walked straight into a group of students, them rushing past him towards seventy ninth street. He looked away. Irrespective, his natural form involved him hanging his head slightly down from his six-three height, his large, almost circular eyes also lowered. His gait was unusual; he always strode along in an awkward, but assertive manner. Sometimes it appeared as if he was working against the first steps of a descending escalator. His interpersonal skills were no better, often misjudging encounters being either awkward and standoffish, or over familiar and intense. He was somewhat aware that his outward projection was strange, or at the least eccentric. He didn't care much about that. It didn't worry him enough, he didn't much care how people viewed him. It never appeared to put him at any risk. And in fact it would more likely lead to underestimation. Perhaps that was why the anonymous recognition in the press pleased him so.

He crossed the Bow Bridge, then onto The Ramble. His eyes scrutinized a row of wood and concrete benches close by the water's edge. Only one was occupied- a young mother rocking her baby in a purple hooded pram. He sat down at the bench beside, attempting to give her a causal smile. Her smile back was brief and didn't get as far as her eyes. She left a minute later.

He looked out to the water, taking in a deep breath. He looked down at the bench, then nodded to himself.

Simon Maltman

His eyes sparkled, his nostrils flared. He shifted round in his seat and ran a hand over the wooden back. It would do fine, he decided.

CHAPTER 12

Three days later, Rory set off to the bingo hall for the first time. He took the train, this time listening to a cassette of the second album by the English jazz-blues fusion band, Back Door. He rode in, mute, immersing himself in the sax and electric bass grooves. It had been recorded ten years earlier in this very city. The thought struck him of how well they had captured a tiny part of its feel. He got off near The Upper East Side and walked along East Seventy Seventh. The building was on York Avenue. It was named Handy's Bar and Bingo. It was over a decade old and was a hotspot for daily gamblers who couldn't get a legal game of poker in New York. It was also popular with a wider audience at the quarterly big event games. It cost more to buy a few cards on those nights, but the winnings were considerably higher than at ordinary games. And during those nights, the stakes rose as competitors were weeded out and the rounds generated huge cash prizes. It was the next night like this that Rory had in his sights for the job.

He had arranged to meet Alice outside at quarter to three, ahead of the daily afternoon game. The street was busy with people passing in and out of other places on the block and a department store across the road. The actual pool hall was at the end of a traditional New York block and a few years ago, a mid sized mall had been constructed, attaching onto it. With a mostly glass exterior, it had been shoe horned onto the old brick structure. Handy's still had its own first floor entrance, but it could also be accessed from the second floor of the mall as well. Rory found a space to stand in between the various smokers outside and had one himself. Then, turning the corner was Alice. Walking along with an easy stride, she was dressed in a casual blue dress. Rory couldn't help but stare. She greeted him and gave him a hug, they they nodded to the two door men and headed inside.

Half an hour later and they'd finished their respective Guinness and glass of red wine. Alice was gazing intently at her bingo card, holding it aloft in her left hand.

"Stop and run- eighty one," announced the caller.

"Yes!" she shouted louder than intended, with genuine thrill.

Taking a draw, Rory almost spat the cigarette from his mouth. "You're enjoying yourself," he said with a mischievous smirk.

"Sorry," she said, pulling a face, "I guess I am." She placed a finger over her mouth and set the card back down on the table. That had been her third number to come up in five minutes.

The caller continued to shout out numbers. They mostly kept their eyes down towards the cards, while continuing to chit chat.

"You don't need to apologise. I'm glad." Rory said, still looking down, "Good that we blend in and all."

"Here we go folks… Kelly's eye! Number one!"

This time there was a gasp from the other side of the room.

"Bingo!" shouted a middle aged woman in a red suit. She hopped out of her seat and hurried up towards the caller.

"There's someone more excited than you are," teased Rory, raising a thick eyebrow.

"Way to you see me after a few more of these," she said, raising her glass towards a passing waiter.

"Yes Miss," he said approaching.

"Another of these house reds would be swell, Rory?"

"Er… yeah- another stout please buddy."

The waiter scuttled away, Rory's eyes following him while he took another scan of the building. It reminded Rory of a slightly more upmarket version of the gaudy GAA clubs that he had frequented back home. Tables were spread throughout, cabaret style. There was a small stage at the front where The Caller stood. Off to one side was a bigger stage that would house bands on the event nights. Along another wall was a long bar with four serving areas and clusters of pumps. Tom's eyes swept back and forth noting the rest rooms and the other doors. There was a large door at one end that led into the mall. They had entered through the main door on the first floor. From ground level customers entered up a large metal staircase. The other door down there was always locked; leading to the store room underneath the actual bingo hall. His eyes glazed over thinking hard, visualising the various entrances and exits. He plucked out a fresh Marlborough Red.

"You still in there?" said Alice waving a hand in front of his face.

"Yeah, sorry Alice." He kept his voice low, "I reckon it all tallies up okay with the map I've got. My info's good."

In the background the game continued, but they both were now distracted from their cards.

"Good stuff. So what's the plan look like?"

He blew out his cheeks, then raised a half smile.

"Well, I've still a bit to get ironed out. It's not gonna be as straight forward as some of the other ones. I mean- that Hard Rock one for instance- we knew they were down on security staff and that they were due an upgrade to their systems too. They were due to get a better safe the next week. Timing is everything. For this job- it has to be on a big night- or it wouldn't be worth the risk."

"You think it's a risky one?"

He considered this for a moment, his eyes wandering past her, hovering on a light fitting on the wall.

"Yeah- I'd say it's riskier. But then the pay out rises in relation to it too. And I haven't worked it all out yet. But when I do, it'll be solid. Solid as it can ever be. I wouldn't work it otherwise. How do you feel about it?"

She shrugged, "I feel good, well from what I know. I got a good feeling. I trust you Rory. Look out- here comes our drinks."

They stayed another hour and Rory went over the plan, such as it was at that early stage. They kept the drinking to a more reasonable level and he began to enjoy himself. Mostly, he was glad that there was no awkwardness between them. He knew it was unwise to mix business and pleasure. But he just might.

Chapter 13

"You want a beer or something Dave?" asked Rory.

Dave unfolded the newspaper on his lap while pursing his lips. He checked his watch. It was ten after midday.

"Yeah, thanks Rory- I think I will."

It was a week later and they were in Rory's apartment, waiting on the other two to start the meeting. Rory pushed the window out further, the traffic noise all the worse, but little breeze sweeping in with it.

Dave flicked to the Sports while Rory went over to the fridge. Dave pulled a few faces and shook his head at one point, muttering about "the fuckin *Nets*." Then he leafed back to the start of the paper. Four pages in there was another article about 'The Couplet Killer.' A third unauthorised and unusual plaque on a bench had been discovered in Central Park. It read:

> *"Just lay still, allow it all to happen,*
> *There's nothing to do or try.*
> *No longer the queen of all Manhattan,*
> *We are all just born to die."*

Again there was the speculation that this could be linked to a missing girl. A few names were suggested by the journalist of known missing persons. They made no mention that ten thousand people go missing in New York every year. Dave shook his head again and turned back a page. Rory came and sat down opposite, setting down two tins.

"Hey Rory- did you read about Hess?"

"Oh aye- I saw that. Good riddance- 'bout fuckin' time. What age was he?"

Dave searched down the page, scratching the stubble on his chin with his other hand, "… Ninety three- Christ. The bastard got to a right old age."

"Yeah well- fuck him."

"Agreed. Right-wing Nazi, mother fuckin douche bag."

Rory smiled at that. "Fuckin' weird though killing yourself at that age. What you say- ninety three? Why bother?"

"Fuck knows."

Just then Jimmy arrived and the buzzer went a second time a few minutes later.

"Damn nice seeing you again Alice," said Jimmy taking her hand, "makes a change from looking at all them ugly faces."

"And you Jimmy, Hiya fellas," she said giving a little wave.

Rory guided her around to the little kitchen area and chatted with her, asked if she wanted a drink. She smiled warmly, with a touch of apprehension. Perhaps she felt a little out of place. She asked for a beer. Everyone got comfy and settled down. The four of them sat with their cold beers, each can with beads of perspiration dripping down the sides. It was another hot day and Rory's new but ancient air-con unit barely worked.

"Okay, so here's the long and short of it. You all know we wanna hit it on a big day. Well, actually- the night before a big day."

He noticed Alice frown on the sofa beside him. "It's 'cause they have a big money reserve in the night before," he explained, "And less security than afterwards. After they'll worry more about protection. Seems like the sweet spot for a group our size. Saturday the 15th August is the big game- so we'll hit it the night before. Yeah?"

They all nodded and Alice kicked off her shoes before curling her feet up under herself.

"Our way in is gonna have to be to do it quiet. I've a few ideas. That's our best bet. And we don't want to make trouble if we can help it. That's where Alice comes in. She'll use her womanly charms on the small amount of security guards while we come in from the other side."

Alice gave Rory a playful slap on the leg.

"How's that go exactly Ror?" asked Jimmy, licking the gum on a fresh rolling paper.

Rory smiled, scratched his neck.

"Yeah I still gotta work that out."

Chapter 14

The Killer's eyes narrowed.

"It's quite alright. I just need some directions."

He recognised clearly the fear that flickered across her face. But she took a step forwards, still uncertain.

"Sure- lemme see that map you have there," she said stretching out her arm.

He had approached her just off Eleventh in Queens. She had crossed at a Stop/Go onto the sidewalk by a quiet entry behind a narrow row of shops. It was a little after ten at night.

"Where is it you're looking for?" she said, placing her fingers on one side of the map.

"It's em… Sorry, I can't quite make it out," he said squinting and holding the map close to his long, pointed nose. He shuffled back towards the street light, also towards the mouth of the dark road. It's a small hotel… em." He continued to make a display of trying to focus on the map. Her eyes moved up from the map and stared into his face. She was in her twenties, in good shape and most importantly; she was street wise. She didn't move any closer to the black alley, she didn't have a good feeling.

He glanced up, irritated that she had stopped moving with him. There were few people out on foot and the roads were quiet too.

"My car's just down here- could I give you a lift somewhere on my way to finding it? This bloody city- it's so confusing." He attempted a friendly chuckle.

She chewed her lip for a moment, taking in his formal though colourless and old fashioned suit, and his curious transatlantic accent. He wasn't a hobo, he didn't look like a thief either, but there was something off about him.

"No, sorry I oughta get going."

"Please," he hissed, suddenly grasping her wrist.

He had played it all wrong.

"Hey!" she shouted, instantly angry, no hesitation.

He had chosen wrong too.

He yanked her arm hard, making her yell out in pain. He swung her round towards him- the momentum catching her off guard. He rotated around. Now she was backed onto the dark road and he stood blocking her exit.

She stood, actually petrified, unable to move. The controlled expression on his face had evaporated. His eyes were wild, his thin and rubbery face cocked to one side. He flicked hair away from his eyes,

"I should have known you'd be trouble. Now don't make this any harder on yourself." His grin was cold and unpleasant.

He reached inside his jacket pocket. He never usually killed with a gun, but it had its uses. Regaining her senses, she bolted down the alley away from him. He ran after her, shuffling along fast, despite his uneven gait. The small snub-nosed revolver in his left hand.

"Help, help me!" she screamed, passing a shuttered up mechanic's garage.

Her two inch heels clicked along the sidewalk as The Killer came ambling after her. "Help, Please… someone!"

"Hey bitch- shut up- stop running. I've got a gun." His deep voice sounded strange to him, cracked maybe; especially saying these words. He was almost amused at the absurdity of the situation. Perhaps Dirty Harry would stride around the corner and they could have a Hollywood shoot-out.

She ran across to the other side of the road, squeezing between the cars. That side had a residential block backing onto it. The Killer jammed in behind her, lumbering ever closer.

This would never do. He didn't want to shoot her now- where would be the fun in that?

She shrieked. "Get the fuck away from me!"

"Fucking stop!" he screamed back.

The Wolf is at Your Door

A window opened somewhere. A dog barked. A light went on across the way shooting a new stripe of white across the black top. He shoved the gun back inside his coat, the light dripping across his face. He quickened his step and lunged after her, grabbing the back of her arm.

"Get the fuck off me!" she yelled.

His eyes raged and he squeezed harder, digging in his fingertips. His right arm swung back to his coat, to search out his knife.

The game was lost now with this one. He may as well kill her and be done with it.

Before he could try, she spun around and clawed at his face-scratching him across the eyes. She dragged herself free and sprinted desperately away, back towards the main road and to safety.. He put a hand to his face, cursing her. More lights came on. He stared after her, fury filling every inch of him. He had been watching her for days. Now it had been worthless. And he had been put at risk.

The sound of her shoes echoed into the distance, towards the light of the intersect. There were more noises now in this street, other lights blinking on. He jogged off towards his car, his breathing already strained. His heart hammered inside him.

Such anger bubbled through him. How could he have been so careless?

Chapter 15

Rory had agreed to go to a gig with Dave at The Wetlands Preserve. Dave was a big fan of the punk/ blues band The Gun Club. He'd played some records to Rory and he liked it. Rory tried to get to as much live music as he could. Coming from a place with a very limited music scene and a curfew due to bombs and bullets, he was still lapping it all up. They'd all talked about it at the meet at Rory's place. Jimmy hadn't fancied it, but Alice had said she'd like to come along too. Rory had tried to conceal his delight at this.

Dave and Rory had got the train down together. Alice had said she'd meet them outside- she was joining a friend for dinner that night.

"You want one?" asked Rory, offering his cigarette packet.

"No, no- my body's a temple- except for the drink. I'm tryin' to keep off 'em," said Dave.

"No probs mate- very sensible."

They stood further along the road on Hudson Street, in Lower Manhattan, just up from *Wetlands.* The two story and rather scuzzy venue had only recently opened up. There was a buzz outside the venue, a small queue snaking back from the main entrance.

"I gotta say- I'm fuckin' made up 'bout this gig- it's gonna be boss."

Rory raised a non committed eyebrow, "Yeah, should be pretty cool."

"You not convinced Ror?"

"Well- I liked their first album. I knew that one before you played me some of the other stuff. It was a cool mix. I mean it was punky, but had a sweet blues thing going on too."

Rory looked past him, his eyes searching through the stragglers, looking for Alice.

"Yeah, it's class and all," Dave said nodding, "But like, you need to get into *Miami*- such cool fucking vibes man."

Dave always stuck out a little bit, he was tall and had an awkward manner. He had a confidence that at times didn't appear to be well placed. Clothes seemed to hang on him in an odd way too. He was just an oddball, but who wasn't? But Rory thought there was something else different tonight. Something else. He moved closer, being sure to blow his cigarette smoke away from him.

"Were you on the piss earlier already?"

"No."

"Did you take something Dave?"

Dave's face flickered worry, then a smirk.

"I might have."

"Jesus- what happened to your body being a temple?" Rory asked with a wink.

"Well…"

"What did you take?"

"Just one wee acid tab."

"Jesus wept- you'll be trippin' balls in there."

"Sounds like a plan," said Dave with a goofy grin.

Rory threw down his cigarette and trod on it. He scanned up and down the street again. No sign of Alice. Rory checked his watch. Dave did the same, squinting his eyes up as he did so.

"Shit- it's gonna start in a minute," he said, "First band is Masters of Reality. You heard them?"

"Just a track or two," Rory said distracted.

"Such good stoner blues stuff."

"Cool."

"Will we head in- Alice can find us?"

"I don't know- it's pretty busy- she should be here, she's maybe here already."

Dave smiled wildly and shook his head, "Aww shit- you've got it bad."

"Shut up Dave."

"You do!"

"Whatever. Listen- you head in and I'll wait a few more minutes- I'll have another smoke- okay?"

"If you say so, catch you inside."

Dave joined the queue of mostly sweaty t-shirt and shorts clad twenty somethings. Most were already in a worse state than he was.

In the end Rory stood outside during the whole first set. He smoked another three cigarettes and kicked a few loose stones around the sidewalk. The music sounded good from what he could hear pulsing through the brickwork. He was asked by a variety of strangers for smokes, drugs and money. He declined them all. Only when he heard The Gun Club had taken the stage and were blasting through a storming rendition of *She's like heroin to me,* did he grudgingly venture inside. He enjoyed the gig- but only on a level.

Why had she stood us up? What if she did this on the job?

Even when the band worked up their Howlin' Wolf inspired *I asked for water*, Rory still couldn't raise a smile. Dave was stood beside him; sweating bullets, swaying, bug eyed. Rory left after a few songs.

CHAPTER 16

Rory had a quiet few days afterwards. He worked on his plans for the job. He spent a lot of his time in his apartment. He slept late and worked on the plans late. He worked his way through a fresh bottle of Jamesons, but didn't line his stomach with all that much food. He wondered about Alice. *Brooded*, may have been more accurate. He hadn't heard from her. Apart from her missing the gig, there was nothing unusual about that. He'd go months without speaking to her sometimes. Even when setting up a job, she didn't get involved much in the main planning. She'd always be attentive at the start, then come in near the end and do her part and do it well. There was no need for him to be thinking about her so much now. But he did you feel like he had been beginning to form a different connection with her.

On one of these days, Rory passed much of it smoking a half deck of Marlborough reds, watching Dallas and The Cosby Show. He even spent an hour on an early morning re-run of Wrestlemania 12. But most importantly, he had made progress with the job. He couldn't let it slip away from him. He needed to get stuck into the logistics, and he was doing. A finer level of detail was the next step. And that's what he now had. It was how he worked. He was constantly layering it up a level. Right up close to the very end he'd always tinker with it. He was fussy to a level, but never *fussed* by it. He approached it like a proud mechanic- with the intention of doing a thoroughly good job. One where nobody would get hurt, that was always important to him. But he only needed for it to run smoothly. Just that and no more would do fine.

On the Thursday he arranged to meet Johnny and Dave at a diner on West 16th. They agreed to spend it as a shopping day.

"Yeah, I'll take another cup thanks," Johnny said after Rory passed.

"How about you big fella?" asked the olive skinned and personable waitress.

"Yeah, perfect, thank you," said Dave with his most pleasant smile. She was older than any of them and had a slightly weathered face that may once have been beautiful. Dave looked smitten.

"You want any milk honey?"

"No thanks, I prefer it black."

He kept smiling and she creased her brow before breezily leaving with a brief, "Enjoy your meal."

He stared after her as Rory and Jimmy both cracked up.

"Shut up," he said grumpily.

"What the fuck was that?" sniggered Rory.

"Oh man. *I like it black*? Christ." Jimmy slapped his own leg and laughed loud and long.

"Alright, alright fuck you guys. So tell us what we doing first Rory."

He busiest himself with his pancake and maple stack. Rory and Jimmy both tucked into plates of waffles with bacon.

Dave folded over his newspaper, with the picture on the cover of the frigate USS Stark listing towards port. It had been hit twice by Iraqi missiles, apparently by mistake.

"Fuckin' Arabs trying to sink our ships now. And what does Reagan do? Pretty much just bends over."

"You'd prefer World War Three?" said Jimmy.

"No, but like we're meant to be *America*! Jesus- the guy's a joke."

"Okay guys, let's get down to it, so first off…"

"Aww shit- there's the new one from Prince," he said gesturing towards the radio speakers, "Sorry man- so fuckin' cool though man- what you reckon Rory?"

He shrugged, a little irritated by the interruption.

"*You got the look*," sang Jimmy under his breath, with a little bop in his chair.

"It's okay, like." said Dave.

"Alright fucksake, you guys are missing out, you no taste mother fuckers." Jimmy smiled and forked a large slice waffle with bacon on it.

"Okay if I go on?" Rory said, gritting his teeth good-humouredly.

"Yes massa," Jimmy said with his ghetto affectation.

Before he could start, Dave gestured to the radio, "I mean he's a, like 'star' or whatever, but where's the soul? Where's the fuckin' grit? I mean- he's from the streets- he knows what shit's like."

"That mean he can't play popular music then?" said Jimmy, rubbing the steam off his lenses with a napkin.

"He can play whatever he likes, but I'm just sayin' for me- there's more truth elsewhere. Take The Gun Club the other night. *The Masters* too. I mean- this shit- it's raw…"

He got a look from Rory. It wasn't often that he looked thoroughly pissed off. This was one of those times.

Everyone quietened down and Rory took a long sip of his coffee.

"Okay children, here we go. So, today is officially *shopping day*. But we're not getting no new duds, no new cassettes. Ge prepared to be busy. We're gonna get us some of the main things that we're gonna need for this thing."

They all nodded, in between mouthfuls of food.

"Dave's found us a van- a block from here?"

Dave nodded again, a drip of syrup dripping off his lip onto the table.

"That'll be our first stop. Then we need a shitload of hardware type shit. Ropes, saws, tools- all that. I gotta list. We can buck all that in the van afterwards. Then we gotta call at a few music stores."

"Music stores?" asked Jimmy.

"Yeah- I forgot I hadn't told you guys that bit yet. That's gonna be our 'in'. We'll start the night on the inside. Posing as a band will give us the chance to be in there and we can leave whatever we want behind after the job. We can also start drilling from the mall side. One of us just blatters the drums while it's going on. Then we finish going through from the other side, crack the safe, get our cash. Easy. While that's going on- Alice is in working her magic on the guards. We're in and out and nobody even knows it 'till the morning, maybe a little before. Safer all round."

The other two nodded along in agreement, finishing off their breakfasts.

"Oh yeah- just one thing- we'll need to kidnap the real band."

CHAPTER 17

The killer lay back on his bed, panting. He finally had his 'number four'. It had taken a few more days of perseverance after a false start, but now it was done. He had already been keeping an eye on her as a potential. She was downstairs now- in the basement. This time it had gone smoothly- not like with that other silly bitch. No, she was safely tied up down there and now he could relax. Perhaps he had rushed it with the last girl- not taken the usual precautions. Now wasn't the time to get careless. There was still so much work left to do.

Now that the mouse was in its house, it would be best if he took a little time out. A short sleep and then he would go out for daily his walk in Central Park. It had become a crucial part of his overriding and all encompassing dark routine. It was where he went to let his mind linger on the acts he had done and would still do. It was where he both relived and acted out again in his mind, the worst parts of his nature. And it all was done as he slipped by the drones of the city carrying on with their gray, pointless existences. He would visit the benches he had adorned and would think of the girls they related to. It excited him so and brought so much pleasure. He often thought it must be like an architect standing in front of a skyscraper they had designed. Or an author, quietly leafing through a bookshop shelf where his novels were on display. For him, it was like walking through a graveyard. A graveyard that he alone had created.

The dagger lay on his bedside table. He ran his fingers over it, while stretching out on the bed. This had once been his parent's master bedroom. Not much had changed in the years since their deaths. A hospital bed had been moved in for a time while he nursed his sick mother. An oxygen tank too and those horrible stacks of incontinence pads. It had taken weeks to rid the place of that awful smell. It had long since been expelled, though there remained a mustiness, a fug. It was somewhere in the old linen, the faded cream drapes on the windows, accompanying the woodworm in the old wicker chair perhaps. But he liked it. This was the smell of 'home'. It had always smelled this way. But now he was the man of the house and this was 'his' room. He had cast off his old room with its childish wallpaper, second-hand toys and posters of Adam West's Batman.

Life had evolved and so had the secret part of his life. His 'work'. This was one of his favourite parts of it all. The thrill of the capture had come and now he had his prey. And it was all up to him what would happen next and for how long.

The satisfaction of a job well done.

But so much more than that.

It was the sensation of anticipation and endless possibility.

He felt a stirring. He unzipped his flies. He kept hold of the knife in his other hand, while he dealt with his urges.

CHAPTER 18

"I wanna be the drummer," said Jimmy.

They were inside a used musical instrument shop, off Perry Street. The air conditioning was broken and it was incredibly stuffy inside. Jimmy was seated behind an old Pearl kit. Rory was looking at a bulky looking PA unit in the corner- measuring it out roughly with his hands. Dave was deep in conservation with the middle aged Hispanic guy behind the counter. He was a large man and had a big smile and an even bigger laugh besides. They had discovered a shared dislike of hair metal. He and Dave were enjoying themselves making fun of Kiss and Motley Crue.

"What you reckon?" asked Jimmy, half successfully attempting a rudimentary fill on the kit.

Rory smiled, walking over to him and whispering,

"I reckon as long as you can whack it enough to mask a big fuckin' drill."

"What do you think of that cabinet?" asked Rory, nodding to the speaker part of the PA system. It was a wooden cabinet around four square yards.

"Pretty sweet. Tell ya what- your Howlin' Wolf guitar would sound so fuckin' cool through it."

"You're right about that," Rory said, his mouth curling at the side, "But do you think you could fit inside it?"

"The fuck?"

...

They drove along Hudson Street, in their newly purchased twelve year old white transit van. In the back were the drums, PA and a small mixing desk. Beside it was everything else on the shopping list they'd bought from a large hardware store. It was ten minutes after five. Rory was driving, the other two riding up alongside him.

"You know it'd be kinda cool to call in on Alice- show her all of the gear. What do youse reckon?"

"Yeah, cool with me," said Jimmy.

Dave turned to look out the window, a smirk crossing his lips, "No sweat."

"Okay, dead on, let's do it."

"She up in Queens ain't she?" asked Jimmy.

"Yeah, I think I remember the place."

The traffic was wild getting across the city. There was no point in trying to battle against it. They stopped for a Wimpy and the flow was better when they were back on the road again. They made it to her block before seven.

"I'll go check if she's in sure," Rory said hopping out of the van and shoving a fresh cigarette in his mouth. He jogged up the metal stair case to the fourth floor. It wasn't the nastiest of blocks. He'd seen plenty with a worse smell, more graffiti and even rougher looking characters. His own block for a start.

He found her place easily enough. No doorbell. He hammered twice on the door with his fist. No response. He tried again, before squatting down and pushing open the mailbox with two fingers. Inside was in darkness, blinds drawn. There were a few letters piled up on the mat. He stood back and chewed his lip for a moment, then hammered again.

The door of the flat beside swung open suddenly, making him bounce on his heels for a second. No sign of Alice, but instead there was a tall African American woman in a grey track suit, with her hair tied back, peering out inquisitively.

"Can I help you?" she asked, her accent sounding somewhere to Rory close to Texan.

"Hi, yeah- sorry if I knocked too hard- I'm a friend of Alice's."

She took a step towards him, "Oh yeah- I think we met at Alice's one time- probably around Christmas. I remember your accent."

"Oh yeah- you're right. Er... Charlotte?"

"Crystal."

"Of course, sorry- I'm Rory. I was just looking to catch up with Alice- she about do you know?"

"No, sorry hun I ain't seen her in a few days. I don't think she's been around all that much come to think of it."

"When did you see her last?" Rory asked suddenly. He couldn't quite understand why an uneasy feeling had began forming in the pit of his stomach.

She thought about it, looking up at the grubby hall ceiling, pulling at one of her hooped earrings.

"Come to thing of it I don't suppose I've seen her all week. She'd been at her Mom's for a while before, then she was round again for a week or two. But, no not this week."

"It's just about a bit of work I've got going and I don't have her Mum's number. It's alright, don't worry."

Crystal began rubbing a finger over a recently plucked eyebrow. "Yeah, I guess I ain't seen her for a week more or less."

"Is that unusual?"

"She usually tells me if she's going away somewhere for more than a night. Yeah, I guess it is unusual."

Chapter 19

The Killer cleaned up after his dinner. The baking tray was scrubbed clean with a Brillo pad. His plate and cutlery were washed and dried. He used the toilet, watered the plant pots out the front and then locked up the house. He lifted the keys for the basement and his knife.

Alice had been drifting in and out of a dreamless sleep filled with shadows and despair. The door swung open. There was a shadeless bulb in the hall that cast The Killer backlit in a mixture of light and shadow. He was grinning, his rubbery face taken over by it. The eyes above were deep set, huge and glowing. Alice gasped and let out a whimper beneath her gag. He shut the door and the room returned to a semi darkness, only lit by the small lamp in the corner. He moved towards her, slowly.

Then his hands were suddenly down around her face and he undid the gag with a swift flurry.

"We don't really need that now do we? It's only you and I down here. Besides- even if you screamed- nobody would hear you. For being in a big city, we are quite isolated out here."

He carefully placed the gag at the end of the bed, beside her bound legs. She was dressed in a tight pink T-shirt with blue jeans. She had been wearing sandals, one of them had dropped onto the floor.

"Please, please… let me go- I don't know who you are, what you want. I'll give you anything you like. Please… just let me go. I won't tell anyone."

He smiled almost benevolently at her. "You wouldn't believe how much you are all so alike. Really- you all sound exactly the same." His eyes narrowed with his grin and many thin laughter lines appeared around his eyes, like little arrows pointing inwards.

"Of course, I'm not going to let you go."

The Wolf is at Your Door

She dry wretched, more painful for being strapped tightly to the bed. "Please," she said helplessly.

"Now that's enough of that. Surely you must know how this is going to go… how it will end?" He looked at her severely, as if he was a headmaster scolding a misbehaving pupil.

She began to weep, accompanied by a terrible keening sound from the back of her throat.

"Now that's enough, don't be a baby," he said sharply.

He set about delicately examining her bare arms. This was the third time he had visited her down here. There were recent cuts up and down her arms and one slash across her face. None were very deep and several were already changing colour and wanting to scab over. He lifted up a bottle of antiseptic from the table beside them. He poured a little into a small blue dish. He set in a piece of ripped cotton wool and let in expand in the liquid.

"There now. Shush, shush," he said in a sing-song voice over the sound of her sobs.

He squeezed the cotton wool, then set began dabbing her gently, almost tenderly on her various wounds.

Alice flinched as he did so. She bit her lip and strained her head back, screwing up her eyes.

"Please," she whispered again, "I can get you anything you want. Money… I can get you money- I know people."

He jumped up, pressing a finger clumsily against her mouth. The cotton wool in his other hand, left dripping over her legs.

"Shhhhh."

His eyes danced inches from her own. He forced his finger to slip inside her mouth for a moment, then he pulled abruptly away and returned to his work.

"Yes, I think I'll keep you about for a while. Good news for you- you won't die tonight."

Suddenly she screamed. As loud as she could muster she let out an almighty, primitive howl. Then she cried out, "Help, Help me! Help!"

The Killer straightened up. Speaking coldly and firmly, but quietly too, he said, "Now I've told you that no one can hear you. But that doesn't mean I want to listen to that racket."

She continued to scream and shout, the veins her neck rigid above her skin..

His eyes hardened. He leaned his left arm down, then drew back his right arm and punched her hard in the face.

She stopped shouting and let out a pained cry. Her cheek flushed. Tears streamed down her face, rolling freely into her mouth. She blew away the salty tears, groaning, her tightly bound body heaving as much as it could do.

"Well now- look what you made me do. And here I was looking after you. I was being gentle, wasn't I? You'll have to learn some manners. Now… you brought this on yourself, silly girl."

He unexpectedly pulled off her other sandal and threw it across the room. Then he reached for a leather bag from the ground, that looked much like a doctor's visiting bag. He flicked open the clasp, before pulling out a thick pair of pliers. The Killer held them up, the light bouncing off, casting a huge shadow across the bare wall.

"Now then- you get to choose. I'm still trying to be reasonable here. Which toe will I take?"

Alice's eyes bulged, her face tremored. "No… no!" She cried uncontrollably, straining at her bonds, twisting her head back and forth.

"Come on now- I won't wait on an answer forever… alright then I'm choosing this one here," he said grabbing her right foot.

"No! No… please… please don't."

"I'll just take the little one. You'll hardly even miss it. I mean, it's not like you'll be walking out of here anytime."

He grabbed hold of her little toe. There was a residue of pink nail polish still remaining on the nail, underneath the dirt. He held the pliers in his other hand, hovering them above her. He squinted; his eyes in concentration, bringing his head in close. Alice continued *to scream, trying desperately, but unsuccessfully to move her foot away.*

"Now I'm afraid, this is going to hurt. It'll hurt quite a lot."

CHAPTER 20

Rory didn't sleep well that night. They had left the van and new purchases in a lock up that one of Jimmy's relatives leased. Then they had gone their separate ways. Rory had poured two fingers of whiskey before bed, but it hadn't sat well in his stomach. And it hadn't aided his sleeping any. He felt tense, worked up. His mind was now fully engaged with the next job, maybe it was only that. He had tried some late night T.V as well. He had zero interest in the sports highlights- especially as there was no rugby or *real* football in sight. There was an old and very serious looking James Mason film that he wasn't in the mood for. He clicked off the T.V and padded off to his stuffy and overheated bedroom.

He didn't do much with the day that followed. A bad mood cloud floated above him. He went for a walk, smoked a lot of cigarettes. He had gone from feeling pleased with their previous day's efforts to having an oppressive sense of worry. He knew there was no good reason for it. He also couldn't quite place what it was that was bothering him. It may have been annoyance that she had stood him up and may have even gone off without warning. Especially after he had opened up to her. But he also found it strange that she had gone away so suddenly, which was unnerving within itself. Alice's movements were no business of his anyway. They were barely friends, more like work associates. Nevertheless he felt odd, the feelings grating and very real. He stopped off at the small movie house a few blocks from his apartment. He needed a simple distraction. Beverly Hills Cop 2 was playing and it offered just that.

Rory came back from his walk around three. Almost immediately, there was a rap on his door.

"Hey Rory, heard you come in there."

"Alright Lee, what about you?"

Lee was his next door neighbour. He was tall, black and athletic. Lee was a personal trainer who had never convinced Rory to go for a run or to work out since he'd moved in two years earlier.

"There was a call for you when you were out. Some girl- sounded nice," he said with a wink.

He handed over a scrap of paper with 'Crystal Morgan' written on it and a phone number. Rory looked confused for a moment. Then it clicked.

Alice's neighbour.

"Ahh right- cheers- I couldn't think there."

"You Irish wide boys- too many dames to keep of track of ay?"

"Yeah- you know it Lee," he said ironically, forcing a smile.

Why was she ringing me?

"Cheers for taking the message, Lee. Must get a drink one night."

"Sure thing. No problem buddy."

Rory made himself a cup of coffee and stared at the scrap of paper on his kitchen counter as his drink cooled. He felt uneasy. What did she want? He grabbed a few quarters from the jar and went out into the hall.

Answered on the third ring.

"Hello?"

"Hello- Crystal?"

"Oh hi, is that Rory?"

"Yeah, I got your message there. Sorry I missed you."

"I hope you don't mind my ringing, I didn't know who else to call. I found your number in the book. It's just… I've been thinking about Alice. Bernard down the hall- do you know him?"

"I don't think so."

"Well, we were chattin' down at the Seven- Eleven- I mentioned about Alice going AWOL. How I was a little worried. He says he saw her down the street- just half a block- about a week ago. She was by herself one night with a bag of groceries. She stopped to talk to some guy at the top of the alleyway, down by the shops.

"What happened?"

"Well that was it…" she paused, her voice uncertain, "Except… It's probably nothing- it's just that nobody seems to have seen her since. I don't know- I thought you'd want to know." She gave an unsure little laugh.

Rory was conscious of a growing sense of dread within himself. It still didn't really seem justified and the clinical part of his brain tried to push the feeling away. He found himself staring at a gray and moulding patch of damp in the corner of the ceiling above the phone.

"Yeah… no, I appreciate it- thanks," he said finally.

"The other thing is… well- Alice gave me a spare key a while ago. I thought maybe I'd have a look in her apartment. If nothing's wrong- she wouldn't mind. I've watered her plants an' all before when she's been at her Mum's. And if there is something wrong… well…"

"Yeah- I mean… I think you should."

She was silent, save for her shallow breaths, "I was thinking you might want to go in with me?"

"Yeah? Yeah, okay, thanks." Rory pulled his eyes away from the damp patch, focusing instead on the greasy receiver in his hands, "When suits you?"

"I'm free now if you like."

"Okay great- I'll be over in half an hour."

He hung up the phone heavily. It caused an echo around the dank hallway. He rubbed at his chin, then regarded the phone with suspicion and wiped his hands on his jeans. There was music coming from Lee's apartment and he could hear an argument from some apartment below. It was comforting to hear people around him, because his mind had began to wander to some dark places.

···

It was about forty five minutes by the time Rory had taken the subway and then walked up to the apartment block. He had necked his coffee and then headed straight out. He didn't bother with his Walkman, instead he sat like a zombie, lost in thought on the journey. The hubbub around him- the laughter, the raised voices, platform announcements- it all synced together into white noise.

He wished the knot in his stomach would break loose.

Rory didn't need to knock when he got there. Crystal came straight out with her own front door key and Alice's, pulling her own door closed. She was dressed in a tight white vest and blue baggy pantaloons. Her medium length tight curls were bunched up into a bun. She had a little more make up on than the last time and he took the time to notice that she was quite stunning. Aside from that brief moment, he was gripped by anxiousness. He kept having the stupid fear that they would get inside and find Alice in there, cold and dead.

They chatted for a moments, both chatting more animatedly than their usual style. Then Crystal put the key in the lock, one click for the deadbolt, one for the secondary lock. Rory pushed the door open. There was a vague mustiness and odour of stale tobacco smoke. They gingerly stepped in and Rory closed the door after them. It was a clean and tidy apartment, looking much the same as had done when Rory was there before- just without all the people and the music. They moved slowly around it, feeling like intruders. They opened the doors to the small bathroom and bedroom and peered inside.

Nothing.

Then they stopped in the kitchen/ living room- a similar set up in layout to Rory's.

Rory realised he had been holding his breath intermittently, "Nothing looks too out of place. Does it?"

"No," agreed Crystal, picking at a piece of fluff on the sofa and running it through her fingers.

Rory picked up a diary from the work top, bent flat, its spine facing upwards. The pages were open on the previous week. There were a few entries in it- nothing much that stood out. He turned to the next page. There was an entry for that very morning- a hair appointment for a salon in The Village. There was also an appointment for the previous day with a loan company.

"It was turned to last week's pages," he said holding it aloft with a shrug.

"Oh?" she said, striding across and accepting the little green book into her hands. She leafed through it making a little humming noise. She set it back down onto the counter with a shrug, raising an eyebrow.

"I don't know. What do you think?" She began to say, picking at a rag nail.

Rory puffed out his cheeks and stepped over to the sink. There were dirty breakfast dishes with a thin skin on both the cereal bowl and coffee cup.

He turned to look at her, "She's not been here for a while, I think. I don't know what that means. I don't think she'd usually leave town leaving these things like this… and her diary too. It doesn't feel like she was planning a trip."

"And there were appointments for this week."

"Yeah. That as well."

"Here… let me try something."

Crystal picked up the diary, reading it as she walked across to the hall. She put a finger holding the page, then lifted the receiver and plugged in the number.

"Oh hello, yes- I think I missed an appointment yesterday by mistake. Yes, I can hold."

Two phone calls and few minutes later, she had discovered that Alice hadn't made it to either appointment, or cancelled them.

"Nice work," Rory said, impressed. He also felt ever more fearful for Alice's wellbeing.

"D'ya think we should say anything to the cops?"

"I dunno," he said blowing out his cheeks, "I mean… I'm not sure there's enough to say. Maybe."

"D'ya want a drink?"

"I sure would."

They sat next to each other on the sofa of the apartment next door. A similar apartment in all but style. Crystal's place was cosier, filled with colourful cushions, throws and the walls covered with a range of vivid canvases. She poured them both a large measure of Jack Daniels.

"I'm sorry I've nothing Irish."

"That's alright. When in Rome."

"Jesus," she said after a sip, running a hand through her hair, "I feel so weird. I just don't surely know what to think of any of that."

"Got me," Rory said shaking his head. He felt some of the weight lift after leaving Alice's apartment. But there was still the continued sense of dread. At least the whiskey felt warm and welcomed, as it ran down his throat.

"I hope she's okay," Crystal said, curling a strand of hair absently around a finger.

"Me too. And she probably is. Maybe we'll leave it a few days and then see?"

"Yeah, sounds good. Rory… are you and Alice er…"

"No, nothing like that. We're just friends."

Rory couldn't place why he felt a little pang of guilt.

They chatted easily. The oddness of the situation, along with the whiskey; offered them a camaraderie, made them feel like old friends. She poured them another and they eased all the more, changing subjects to brighter areas. They chatted about movies, life in the city and Rory told her a little about back home. An hour passed and Rory found his mood much improved and that he was actually enjoying himself.

"Another?"

"Sure- why not? Thanks."

She came back from the kitchen with two glasses of ice, swaying slightly.

"You don't gotta be up early in the morning or anything?"

"Nope," he said, having a stretch, "Don't need to be in bed too early."

"You don't need to be in bed early," she repeated, nodding, putting the drinks down, before sitting back next to him.

"No."

She paused, rubbing her fingers delicately around her glass.

"You wanna maybe go to bed with *me*?"

Rory swallowed down a gulp of whiskey with a start, trying not to cough.

"Yeah. Yeah, I would."

CHAPTER 21

Rory woke early. He hadn't meant to stay there, but sleep had grabbed him and thrown him into the darkness. With the drink and the urgent, passionate sex, he had slept like a log. His head was already pounding whenever he found her clock and saw that it was only half six. The hot light coming through Crystal's thin drapes made it appear more like midday. Rory found his clothes, then his boots and wallet with relative ease. It helped that Crystal was still out cold, lying silently on her back. The sheet had fallen away, exposing one of her breasts. He leaned over and pulled up the sheet before quietly shutting the door behind him. He padded through the apartment and was especially careful closing the apartment door. Outside, walking past Alice's front door made his stomach flip.

Back in his own apartment, Rory got undressed and back into bed. There had been little point. His head was all over the place. His thoughts were dashing off in all directions. He sat up in bed and lit a cigarette. He had picked up a new packet and a copy of the *Post* on the way.

His eyes burned. He was agitated. The comfort brought from Crystal's embrace and the whiskey now was lost.

What about Alice? Has something happened to her?

He couldn't get it straight. And what was he thinking, sleeping with Crystal? He liked her, but it had come out of nowhere. It was messy- she was Alice's next door neighbour after all. And then first thing he had scurried off. He cringed at himself.

"Not gonna fuckin' sleep now," he muttered, heaving himself up and heading for the bathroom.

Feeling a little more human after washing and brushing his teeth, he got another coffee going and banged back two paracetamol. He lay out on his sofa, fired on a Muddy Waters record and opened up the newspaper. There was more about the Mafia bosses, a coming heat-wave and the political kidnapping of someone from England called Terry Waite. But it was a half page article on page five that stopped him in his tracks. He sat up and abruptly pulled the needle off of Muddy singing about *Champagne and Reefer*.

'Was This Another Target of The Couplet Killer?'
'Woman narrowly escapes. Where will he strike next?'

He read on. A girl had been attacked the previous week and had anonymously come forwards to the paper. She'd been attacked in Queens- two blocks from Alice's place.

"Jesus, fuck," Rory said aloud, reaching for his Marlborough Reds.

Some guy had dragged her into an alley and at gun point tried to force her into a car. She'd just managed to get away apparently. There was only a very brief statement from the police to say, "We continue to serve and protect our fine city and fight to protect its citizens from any form of attack. We have not received a complaint or report from this woman. Furthermore, there is no such investigation regarding whom the media has dubbed 'The Couplet Killer.'" The reporter went on to speculate that alongside 'anonymous sources' in the NYPD and with 'expert advice,' that it was thought that a killer was targeting young, white women and was then successfully disposing of their bodies.

Rory scratched at his brow, fumbled for his coffee, then immediately started reading the story again from start to finish. If he was honest, the notion had already crossed his mind that Alice could been a victim of something like this. But he had tried to push the notion away as something foolish. It was like adding two and two and coming up with 'x'.

Why would someone want to hurt Alice?
But if it was a serial killer…

No, that's silly.

Though...maybe this girl had escaped and he had gone after Alice instead. It would explain why Alice seemed to just vanish in a hurry. What if she's there now? Taken.

No, how many people are attacked in the city every week-dozens? Hundreds? It could have been about anything, could have been a hoax.

And the police don't believe there's a killer out there.

But... still.

...

"Yeah, Jesus I'll take another coffee."

Rory was finishing a second cup in a diner across from the NYPD's 65th precinct. He'd been sitting there already for quite a while. Before that he had walked the legs off himself, his mind running overtime.

"I'll have a coffee too please," said Winston to the waitress in his usual steady and even voice. He slid into the blue plastic booth, ducking to avoid the low hanging strip light.

"Well, how you been?"

Rory ran the back of his hand across the green and red striped table cloth.

"That's a tricky question, it truly is. Depending on how this conversation goes, I might be heading in there afterwards," Rory said gesturing across to the precinct.

"Oh, shame really," Winston said, raising an eyebrow. "Hand yourself in if you must- just leave me out of it, won't you?"

"Very funny. I actually have a dilemma."

"But not a guilty conscience?"

"Not about this."

"Okay then, I'm a fairly good listener, despite what my ex-wives might say."

Rory couldn't believe what he was thinking about doing. Since
he was 'knee high to a grasshopper,' it'd been drilled into
him that the police were not to be trusted. 'Pigs', 'the hun,'
'the filth'; he'd heard them called it all. He remembered
sitting on his Gran's cold kitchen floor as she stirred a pot of
her homemade and delicious fudge. "Never go near them
uniformed Brits, Ror," she'd said, "They'd skin ya, soon as
look at ye."

Rory explained all of his suspicions to Winston. He told him
about Alice not showing up to the concert. He told him about then
man in the alley, the dishes, the diary- the missed appointments. He
even talked about the woman in the paper. Winston listened to it all,
nodding and sipping from his coffee.

"Well, what dy'a reckon? Am I mad Winston?"

"Mmmm, that remains to be disproved, but it may make two of
us."

"You think that it's possible?"

"I think that it is not *impossible*. Besides, it's not me that you
would need to convince," he said squinting past the backwards
window writing and across to the station.

Rory leaned back against the weathered plastic booth. "Jesus,
I'm not sure what I was hoping for. I suppose I kinda thought you'd
tell me I was nuts."

"No, I don't think that. I think a lotta fellas in this city probably
are nuts. And I think it's a fact that sometimes one of them does some
very bad things. Is there one more who's doing like you say? I don't
know- there certainly could be."

Rory downed the rest of his coffee, swallowed hard, blew out his
cheeks. His heart was hammering- not helped by an overload of
caffeine shooting through his veins.

"So, do you think I should go talk with them?"

"I think you've already decided that."

CHAPTER 22

"Please take a seat over there."

The middle aged Asian-American woman in uniform behind the counter had taken a few notes, before disappearing back behind the cluttered desk.

The precinct was one of the smaller ones in the city. Even so, it was a hive of activity. Rory sat down next to a scantily clad young woman. It was so hot there, he almost envied her, her attire. On his other side was an elderly man with receded hair, long at the back in filthy clothes, doubled over. He may have already vomited, and it wouldn't be long until he did so again. Police officers marched through the hallway with men in handcuffs. Some of their prisoners were noisier than others. One spat on the ground near Rory's feet and received a cuff round the ear from a cop for it. A few groups of men and women in suits with briefcases walked back and forth to a corridor down to the left. Rory sat with his knees apart, his head down, right leg jiggling.

After ten minutes or so, Rory searched his jacket for his cigarettes, stuck one of his mouth and began clicking his lighter, shaking it hard as the oil was running low.

"You can't do that in here," the woman at the desk shouted across the hallway- tapping a finger on a 'no smoking sign' stuck against the glass.

"Oh right, sorry."

He shoved the packet back in his pockets, before leaning forwards again and fidgeting with his lighter. Twenty minutes later and he was reading a notice about the dangers of STD's and unprotected sex on the wall. The hall had quietened down some, the solid floor streaked with more dirt and what looked like the remanence of a few drops of blood.

"Rory Downie," announced a voice from behind him.

"Yes… that's me," he said turning. His stomach was pulling somersaults as he stood up. He suddenly felt incredibly stupid for coming at all. Stupid too that as a criminal, one who was planning a new job; that here he was voluntarily dandering into talk with the NYPD. He'd managed to keep off their radar for the last few years, and now he was presenting himself to them.

"Come with me, please."

He was led down a grubby hall, brightly lit by harsh overhead tube lights. The man walked at a pace ahead of him. He was maybe early fifties, short with graying black hair. As he held the door to a small interview room, Rory got a good look at the heavy-set sharp eyes and pencil moustache.

"Take a seat."

The man sat down heavily, flinging down a notebook in front of him. He flicked to a new page and took out a blue biro.

"Okay then. I'm Detective Greg Richmond, I believe you've come into make some kind of statement?"

"Em, well yeah. I suppose I want to report a missing person."

"Are you a relative?"

"No."

"Boyfriend?"

"Er, no- not really."

"Okay, what's the name?" he said with an irritable sigh.

"Rory Downie."

He stopped writing and looked up from the table, his impatient eyes set on Rory's, "The name of the missing person."

"Oh right, sorry. Alice Turner."

"Address?"

He gave it.

"Right, so what's the story?"

Rory told him how Alice was a friend of his and how she'd missed the concert, then about her abrupt absence from the flat. He told him how she was spotted talking with a stranger and that it was the last she had been seen.

"Well listen son. You're not a relative of this girl for a start. If everyone reported a *friend* they hadn't kept track of for a few days, well heck, we'd never get anything done."

"I understand that, but like I said- her next door neighbour's worried too. She let us in and we looked about the place. It was weird- seemed like she expected to be coming back."

"Hold on a second," he said resting his pen again and looking up at Rory, "You went snoopin' round this girl's place without her say so?"

Rory could feel is temper simmering. The room was getting to him. The amount of times he'd been hauled into Castlereagh R.U.C station in Belfast; those had been tough nights. Most of the time he hadn't done anything wrong. Nothing other than his being a Catholic.

"I didn't go *snoopin'*. Her neighbour asked me to come with her and have a look around. She had permission, I went with her."

"So *you* say."

"What the fuck is this? I'm here to report…"

"Watch your fuckin' mouth, Mick," said Richmond slamming down his fist. "This Alice never gave either of you her permission. We ran a search on you. Some interesting reading- were you casin' this girl's place out?"

"Fuck you!" spat Rory, standing up, the plastic chair skidding back against the wall.

"I'm not done here," said Richmond firmly, standing too. His yellow shirt had sweat patches forming under the arms and a vein was pulsing hard in his neck, "Sit-down."

Rory grudgingly pulled his chair back up and sat down. He took out his cigarettes and yanked out his lighter.

"You're not meant to smoke in here."

"I could give a fuck," he said lighting up.

Richmond scowled, shook his head.

"So, what you find in her place- anything?" He went back to making short, neat notes in his book.

Rory blew out a plume of smoke, shuffled in his chair. "A few things, yeah. There were dishes in the sink," he looked at the ground, frustrated, angry, "Her diary was left open at the week before- things like that."

Richmond stopped writing, wiped a hand over his face. "I'd better scramble a task force immediately."

"Look- I know they're all only wee things- but together it all is out of character. Crystal- the next door neighbour- she rang some of the places where Alice was meant to keep engagements and she never turned up."

Richmond ran his fingers over his moustache, absently looking towards the door, "And my colleague tells me you think the so called 'Couplet Killer' has got her?"

"I don't know, I mean not necessarily… I thought you'd want to know…"

"There is no investigation into this supposed killer. There aren't even any bodies for fucksake."

"Right well." Rory stood again, just about keeping his temper in check, "I've done my part as a citizen, it's up to you if you want to do yours."

"You're a citizen are you? We'll see about that. Maybe I'll *do my job* and have a word with immigration- IRS too."

"Fuck you!" shouted Rory, jabbing a finger out towards him.

Richmond jumped up, a dark expression on his face,

"You be very careful son- I'll have you out on your ear and back on the first boat back to your shithole country."

"Fuckin' redneck," Rory said under his breath, opening, then storming through the door. He marched back along the hall and through reception, barely able to keep the red mist at bay. He brushed past a few drunks, almost shouldered a beat cop out the way, he didn't care.

The fresh air outside was welcome, even if it was humid and tainted with smog.

What the fuck! I get all this shit for trying to do the right thing?

He lit up another cigarette and turned the corner, walking towards the subway entrance.

"Hey wait!" came a voice from behind. A man was jogging along the sidewalk, away from the precinct. "Hold up there." He placed a hand on Rory's shoulder. Rory swung around and shoved the arm away.

"Get off of me!"

The man flipped Rory's arm round and twisted it up his back.

"Assaulting a police officer now?" he asked, out of breath. A half smile was on his lips.

The man was around the same age as Rory. He was average height, broad shouldered and solid, with thick black hair coming down just below his ears. He was dressed in a grey suit and a white short sleeved shirt. He had intelligent eyes and a controlled movement to his body.

"Get the fuck off me- I haven't done anything," Rory said, "Jesus- you people."

"Alright- I just wanted to talk to ya- take it easy."

The man released Rory's arm and took a step away, brushing a hand down his shirt.

"I'm Detective Michael Kelly, you were speakin' with my partner in there."

"He's a prick."

"Well, yeah he is a bit of a prick at times. Listen- I was interested in what you had to say... about the girl."

"Your partner wasn't."

"Well, I'm not him."

Rory rubbed a hand up his arm, flexing his fingers.

"Another time maybe."

"Here's my card," he said passing it to him, "Sorry 'bout your arm."

Rory pocketed the card, shrugged and walked away.

CHAPTER 23

Alice wasn't sure if she'd been asleep. Had she slept at all in days? She couldn't be certain. It always felt like night there. She was aware of how badly she needed to urinate. She couldn't face the indignity each time of the bed pan and his eyes… his leer.

Then her thoughts returned to the thin rope on her hand.

She must have slept, her thoughts unclear.

After the last time he was in with her, he had bound her right wrist looser- presumably not be design. Before she had drifted off she had managed to wriggle the rope partially over her hand. It was too narrow to force over her it no matter how hard she had tried. Alice hadn't given up at that. She had began to scrape at the tightly wound threads with her finger nails. One nail had broken and the other was now filed into a point. She had made some progress in cutting through it. Hours it must have been before she gave into exhaustion.

But it wasn't enough.

She started back into it again immediately.

Soon enough a ragged and incredibly thin strand broke through. It was the smallest of progress, but it spurred it on.

She looked down towards her feet. Thankfully she only had to see the thick bandage covering where one of her toes had been taken from her. The lamp illuminated the yellowing bandage and the streak of dried scarlet.

How long ago had he done that to her? Maybe two days. He truly was a monster.

Her empty stomach was filled with nausea at the thought. Whatever he had injected her with had removed most of the pain, but there remained a dull ache.

Would he take her a piece at a time?

The Wolf is at Your Door

She winced at the thought of it.

Her mind swept back to only a few weeks before. That night with Rory. She had felt something. What she would give to be back with him, away from this nightmare.

She worked on, harder. Her wrist cramped and the rope cut into her, but she didn't care. This was her only chance. If she could free one hand, she could surely reach over to the table and grab one of his 'tools'. Then she would be free and could lie in wait for him.

Another hour passed and more strands broke. Just a little more time and it might be loose enough to pull her wrist free.

What was that?

He was home again. What time was it? Afternoon?

Footsteps creaked above her. She carried on frantically. It was now or never. She had no idea how long he would keep her there. But she knew how it would end. And he had said as much.

Click.

The light flicked on outside, creeping underneath the door. Then the inevitable footsteps trod down the stairs towards her. She turned her wrist inwards so she might be able to keep on working at it, even with him there.

"Did you miss me?" he said, as the door swung open.

"I'm thirsty," she said weakly.

"Oh," he said irritably, "I brought you something to eat."

He set a plate down on the floor- a sandwich with three slices of cucumber on the side.

"Please… I'm so thirsty."

"You said that. Alright- just a minute. Don't go anywhere," he added with a slanty smile. His footsteps climbed away again and she worked more furiously than ever.

Yes, yes! It could actually work. Another strip of twine snapped.

She heard the pipes rattle as a tap went on in the kitchen upstairs.

Come on!

Another two thin strands broke free.

She squeezed her wrist with everything she had.

Footsteps crossed the landing.

With one final pull, it was off.

She gasped. Her heart rattled unevenly in her chest.

Footsteps on the wood of the stairs again.

She lay the rope over her wrist so the break wouldn't be obvious.

"Your water madam," he said sourly, striding in and setting it down on the table.

He stared at her, his eyes huge and filled with evil.

Then he trained his eyes on her feet.

"I've been thinking. My little... amputation... went rather well. No? It's something I'm... learning. It would be a shame to leave you unsymmetrical; I thought I could even things up a little."

"No- please... don't."

"Come on now, don't be a big baby."

He bent down and unzipped his leather bag, rummaging inside it.

Her eyes set on the table. It was if her arm was still bound. Now it was bound by a sickening dread. But she broke through the fear and dived a hand out at the table, grabbing up a scalpel.

"What..." he started, shooting up off his knees, turning all at once.

He was only inches away from her. She lunged at him with all of her strength, plunging the knife into his side.

He shrieked.

"Ahhhhh! You little bitch!"

She pulled the narrow blade free and blood seeped out over his white shirt.

She went to cut him again, but he batted her hand away, instead his arm receiving a superficial slice.

In one movement his other hand went into his pocket and it came out with the hunting knife. He swung around and leaped on to the bed on top of her. She plunged the scalpol into his other side and he screamed again- his foul breath blown into her mouth.. He raised his arm and brought the dagger down into her chest. A rib shattered and the blade sank in deeply. She cried out. The shock was worse than the pain.

She choked and blood spilled from her mouth. She managed to pull the scalpel from him as they groaned in tandem. But he grabbed her wrist with his other hand, plucking the scalpel from her like an iced lolly from a child. It was thrown away beyond the bed. He wrapped both sets of fingers around the dagger.

Her eyes glazed over.

"I was hoping to keep you around for a while longer. Shame."

He primed himself, then forced the blade in again as deep as he could manage.

She exhaled softly and then she was gone.

PART 2

KILLING FLOOR

CHAPTER 24

Rory pounded the streets for half an hour, walking on past a number of subway stations. He needed to walk it off. It wasn't often that he *lost it*. He was close to it now. But when he did, it could take him a long time to calm down. Right now he just needed to walk a mile or two and smoke a few cigarettes.

Fucking dick heads!

He couldn't believe how he'd been treated. It reminded him of back home again. No respect- just being talked to as if he was dumb and ignorant. Something might well have happened to Alice and here he was being treated like a wanker.

Once he had a calmed a little, he threw down his current smoke and stepped into a phone booth outside a McDonalds. He rang both Jimmy and Dave and asked if they could meet him. They said they could. He fumbled in his pockets and found a few more quarters. Rory knew he should tell Crystal about talking to the cops, they may even want to talk to her. That other one at least seemed interested. Even if he did bend up his fuckin' arm. He knew he needed to tell her about the cops, but he also didn't know what to say to her. He had never meant to sleep with her the night before. He was awash with guilt and confliction. When did things get so complicated?

Fuck.

"Hello?"

"Hi Crystal, it's Rory."

"Oh Hi." Her voice went up a notch.

"Listen, I'm sorry for running off earlier…"

"No… I mean- it's fine."

"It's just you were sleeping so soundly, I hadn't wanted to wake you." He stumbled over his words. "I had an appointment first things," he lied.

"I hope I wasn't snoring like a hog," she said with an uncertain giggle.

He was relieved she wasn't pissed with him.

"No, no of course not. But I wanted to talk to you, I... er went to see the cops earlier."

"You did?"

"Yeah, I just sort of... you know- I thought I should."

"Okay, yeah- what did they say?"

"Well," he paused to exhale, his breathing blowing back at him through the receiver, "They didn't want to know."

"Oh."

"Yeah- I told them the stuff we'd talked about and to be honest- they treated me like a dick."

"Shit- that's the fucking NYPD for you."

"Yeah, I guess so. I just thought you should know."

He considered telling her about the 'Couplet Killer' part, but thought better of it. Maybe it *was* stupid. Alice was probably sitting in her mum's living room with a cigarette and a cup of coffee.

"It's good you reported it. So, uh... are you busy later?"

"Later, em... well actually I'm tied up the rest of the day. I'm sorry"

"Course... sure- I just wondered that's all."

"Another day? *Rain check* as you say over here?"

"Yeah, sure."

"Okay well, take care Crystal."

"Bye Rory."

He hung up the receiver with a click and breathed heavily again. *Fuck, fuck, fuck!*

His chest was tight and he realised his cheeks had gone red. Why was nothing ever straight forward? He searched for his smokes.

Rory arranged to meet Jimmy and Dave in a bar on Forty Sixth Avenue, He'd been there once before- it had only been open a year and was a little soulless and decked out in pine. The music was as bland- currently playing something by Madonna. But it should be quiet enough for them to talk privately and it was. It was hot inside, so he opted for an early evening pint of cider. He lit up yet another smoke, noting that he'd need to stop for another pack on his way home later.

"Hey lads," he said as Jimmy and Dave arrived in together.

Dave was in a black Metallica top and dark jeans, Jimmy in an orange t-shirt and yellow shorts.

"He's bringing the sunshine inside with him," Dave said nudging Jimmy.

"Just 'cause you're a miserable old metaller motherfucker."

They got their drinks and settled down to a conversation. Jimmy rolled himself up a regular cigarette.

"So, what's up Irish?"

"Okay, well- I'll get straight down to it. I'm worried about Alice."

They both nodded. "'Bout her skipping out on the concert and all?" said Jimmy.

"Yeah, that and a few other things. First off it was strange her disappearing off and not telling anyone. You know how I was talking to her neighbour?"

"What you call her…" said Dave… "Crystal?"

"Yeah that's her."

"Damn fine piece of ass," added Dave, lighting his smoke.

Rory winced, "Okay, well she had a key for Alice's place and we went round. Was weird as hell- neat place save for real old dishes in her sink, diary left out at a week before- appointments not kept… never cancelled. And she was seen with some guy by an alley before she disappeared."

"Disappeared?" asked Dave sceptically, "Aren't we making a bit of a leap there?"

"She did go to her Mum's for a while last time at short notice," suggested Jimmy.

"It's not a leap- I mean nobody knows where she's at. She's gone off grid."

"She's a free agent, sure it's only you and the neighbour don't know where she is. We don't rightly know what friends she has or how she spends her days," said Dave, beginning to look irritable.

"I don't know Rory. I wouldn't worry too much." said Jimmy.

"Yeah… it just don't seem right." Rory paused, squirming uncomfortably in his wooden chair, "It's just I… I do think something's happened. I went to see the cops about it."

"The cops!" Dave's eyes widened.

"Ya did?" said Jimmy.

"Yeah- I was worried about her. I… though that I should."

"What they say then?" Dave said curtly, chewing on his cigarette. His health kick hadn't lasted long.

"They didn't wanna know."

"No surprise there," said Dave sourly.

"It just seemed, I don't know- the right thing."

"When we're just in the middle of planning a heist you're worried about 'the right thing?' Jesus Christ."

"Fuck the heist Dave! If she's hurt- then I'd wanna know."

Dave took a slug of his beer, unimpressed.

"Alright guys, take it easy," said Jimmy.

"I'm sorry for shouting, okay- but my mind's been working overtime, I don't know. Then you read all this stuff about this killer pickin' up women and all."

"Wait up- now you think a serial killer's got her?" Dave said with a snort.

"Go easy, now," Jimmy said patting his arm.

"No, I mean come on for fucksake." Dave crushed his cigarette into the ash tray. "She blows you off for one date and so a serial killer must of got her?"

"It's not like that," Rory said gripping the table, his teeth clenched. He sensed that the earlier anger bubbling inside, hadn't died down much. "I just thought youse would want to know."

"Okay Ror, I get it," said Jimmy, glaring at Dave.

"Right, well at least that's the end of it then I trust?" Dave fixed his eyes on Rory and Rory stared back. "Look- I was meant to be somewhere this evening so I'm gonna split. We'll talk soon." He necked the last of his drink, stood up.

"Alright Dave, catch you soon," said Jimmy.

"I'll ring you in a couple days," Rory said as Dave began walking away.

They supped their drinks quietly for a few moments.

"You wanted another, Irish?"

"I sure fuckin' do."

...

Three drinks in and the tension in Rory's body began to ease.

"I mean- he just didn't need to be a dick about it."

"Yeah well bro- that's Dave for ya- some of the time he can be a douche."

They both lit another smoke, it was after eight and the bar had filled up. Fleetwood Mac pounded through the speakers. The stereo had been cranked up to compete with hubbub and their voices had risen along with it all.

"I dunno- maybe I am crazy Jimmy?"

"You're not crazy bro… just maybe a little, well just a bit off your game on this one."

"It just feels like there's really something there. Something not right. I dunno."

"I think you've been thrown a bad pitch. Things maybe just look that way to you, bro. You've had a few troubles in the past and it makes your thinking off."

Rory smiled, "Shit, is that meant to make me feel better?"

"Maybe- I dunno- do it?"

"No."

Jimmy shrugged, a wide smile across his face, "More drinks."

The evening was in full flow when they switched to shots. Outside was darkening and inside drinkers were well on their way to the road leading away from sobriety.

Rory squinted up his eyes, trying to focus on the green digits of his watch.

"Bugger, I'd better be getting to bed soon. I'm meant to be looking into more of the stuff we need to buy in the morning for… well you know."

"Yeah, cool." Jimmy was starting to slouch back in the seat, his eyes behind his lenses taking on their own glassy effect. "And you'll try and calm down about this Alice thing? Least to see if she swings back home in the next few days."

"Yeah, yeah I'll try Jim. Been good talkin' to you."

"You too Irish." Jimmy rolled his narrow shoulders with a sigh, then tipped a cigarette out of his pack.

"Last smoke then home?"

"Sound like a plan."

"Say bud, you had much of a go on that Wolf guitar yet?"

"Fuck- no not really. It's been kinda busy I suppose. It's in my bedroom, like. I've had a few wee strums here and there for sure, but yeah I suppose I've neglected it so far."

"Plenty of time to make it right."

"One thing is every time I walk in the room and set eyes on her, it brings a smile to my face."

"I'll get practicing them drums, then we can start ourselves a band."

"Aye, maybe it's time for a change in career."

CHAPTER 25

The Killer rolled off Alice onto the floor. He was panting, sweating, drops of blood dripping from his wounds. He clutched his side. One gash was pumping out blood worse than the other. He managed to rotate himself onto his knees, breathing hard, struggling to stay conscious. He began to tear at his shirt, ripping it in pieces from his torso, groaning from the effort. Cradling himself as best he could with one arm, he crawled across to the table with his supplies. He grabbed up the roll of bandages and began awkwardly wrapping it around himself. It was slow, painful work. He stopped at one point to turn to the side and vomit over the floor. Then he continued the laborious process of pulling it tight and passing it under his arm and around. Once he felt there was enough and a decent amount of pressure, he tied it off and plastered a strip of tape onto his skin. Exhausted, he dropped his back against the bed, managing to avoid the acrid vomit. His wounds pulsed, but the flow was stifled. His head hung back awkwardly, swimming, dizzy. He tilted his neck and could see the side of Alice's blood soaked body and her lifeless arm hanging over the side. Her blood seeped from above and some pooled on the floor with his own. The Killer closed his eyes and went to sleep.

CHAPTER 26

The night was filled with shadowy figures and unfinished thoughts. The figures blurred into one another; shapes disappeared into the darkness beyond. A solitary figure was sat in a field, strumming an acoustic guitar. Rory couldn't hear the music. Only the sound of a harvester making its way in the distance. Then the noise became a roar and he could see its many sharp teeth. It was upon him. He tried to scramble away, but his his legs were already being chewed up. His eardrums burst with the noise, blood dripping from his ears.

He screamed.

Then he woke up, still screaming.

Rory pulled the covers off, sweating badly beneath them- his T-shirt and boxer shorts both damp. He placed a hand against his ear instinctively. There was no blood there, only a few further beads of sweat. He calmed his breathing, ran a hand through his moist hair. It was almost eight. Padding through to the living room, his feet made clammy marks on the floor. He turned on CNN and allowed himself to fully awaken. Shortly, he washed and dressed; his stomach too delicate for breakfast. Rory walked to the subway and smoked his first cigarette of the day. It tasted rancid, but he had another one before jogging down the steps to the station.

There was a guy he'd been introduced to a few years before who could get him the more difficult items he needed for the job; unregistered guns and the like. Rumour had it that he had connections to the Mob, but Rory didn't know if there was any truth in it, nor did it matter much to him. He met his contact and had a good meeting in an Italian café on Forty Second street. The coffee was good too. He had two cups and managed to secure some of the more niche items he needed for the job. They'd be delivered to Jimmy's lock up the following week. He stayed on for a third cup by himself and tried to push thoughts of Alice away. But he couldn't do it. Rory knew it was in him to be obsessive at times, even pedantic. But he also knew that many times he had followed his gut and it hadn't usually let him down.

The rest of the day stretched out in front of him, directionless. He didn't know what he was going to do with it. Then he had an idea.

Chapter 27

The Killer had awoken in a daze of confusion and pain. In a messy heap on the floor. He was incredibly weak. He had no idea how long he had slept for, but it had in fact been almost four hours. He checked his bandage. The blood was dry. That was a good sign. The Killer pulled himself up and his head swam. He rested his head back against the metal leg of the bed. He concentrated on his breathing before gripping the bed and pulling himself up. He grunted as he made it onto his feet, as unsteady as Bambi. His own tall body loomed over Alice's dead body. There was blood everywhere; he'd have much cleaning up to do before the next one. Her eyes stared into nothingness. She was already quite rigid. But her body would have to wait. He wouldn't be strong enough to dispose of her for some time. He turned to the door and the now formidable flight of stairs. He spurred himself on slowly with each step. For who else had he to rely on? As he sluggishly exited the room and began dragging himself up the stairs. He thought of his parents, both now many years dead. His father was the longest deceased. What would he have said when he himself had been unwell or injured? Not much. He was practically monosyllabic at the best of times, stoic with it. And what if his son had something wrong with him? He may have attempted a rushed sympathetic word before closing himself into his small study with his pipe, tobacco and books. Such care would have been left to his mother. Yes, mother always understood. She would have lavished concern upon him, albeit an overreaction to the scale of whatever the illness was that had presented itself. She would smother him with affection at once welcomed by him, but if in company- cuttingly embarrassing. If in bed with a fever, she would stroke and mop his brow and tell him everything would be alright. Soup and cold drinks would be set beside him. But she would do nothing to hide the fear and anxiety in her own face. If he had scraped a knee in the park, the solution would be never to return to there. If he had swallowed too much water in the swimming pool, the answer was that he didn't need to learn to swim. And so he never had done.

What would she have made of the injuries he had now?

He dropped to his knees. A flashing pain from the wound on his left side.

Even she wouldn't have understood 'his work.'

A day or two's rest; that's what he needed. That's all. He was strong. He was the man of the house now after all.

Just a little rest. Then he would be able to attend to the usual routine. The plan. There was no rush.

First the body, then the plaque, and then on to the next one.

He made it into the bedroom, formerly belonging to his parents. He lay down on top of the warm sheets. He was so damned hot already.

His eyes grew heavy.

This was just a blip in the plan. He would get back on track, but first he needed to rest.

CHAPTER 28

Rory stood in front of The New York Public Library on Fifth Avenue. Gazing at the finely honed marble of the exterior, he was resolute in his decision. As he passed through the huge double doors, he felt good, he had to try something. Rory crossed the huge hallway and found a sign to direct him through the mass of reading wings, studies and collections. His decision had been simply to trust himself. He had felt at odds within his own mind now for days. It was bad enough to try and convince othhers that there was something very wrong. But at the same time he had been struggling to convince himself.

Fuck it.

Now he had decided just to go with it. He could keep it to himself. None of them needed to know. If he was crazy, well where was the harm? He had to try. He found the location he needed on the map before waiting on an elevator, joining six others inside. First he had to make one quick stop off, seeing as he was there. He may as well have a look at the most notorious part- famous from movie and T.V shows. Rory peered through into Room 315, commonly known as the Rose Main Reading Room. It was indeed impressive. It was sprawling, yet containing a grand and striking uniformity. He nodded to himself, then continued on. Entering another large public gallery, he smiled. He had never visited any of the building before. The last time he'd seen it on screen was when it was plagued by a haunting in *Ghostbusters*. The building was seriously impressive. It prompted him again to appreciate the kind of city he was living in. New York! Sometimes he'd wake up and it would just hit him again. A lad from the roughest of estates in Belfast. But it was very easy to forget where he was a lot of the time. He just caught up in himself too much, he knew that. Perhaps Rory spent too long in the dark side of the city.

Rory found the reading room he was looking for. It didn't take him long to find the bunch of newspapers that he needed as well. The library stored all of the last year's local editions on site. The rest were on microfilm. He secured the end of a table to himself and began searching for the correct weeks. He peered over the top of a broadsheet, noting how everyone else looked like they belonged there. Maybe they weren't, but to him everybody else looked to be an academic or student. It took him half an hour to scan through the last half year of papers. He found the main articles dealing with the plaques left in Central Park. It had begun as something very vague, a fluff piece in the middle of an edition. Then it had become a regular article. He also discovered a few recent substantial pieces with various speculations about 'The Couplet Killer.' It wasn't until the second plaque that the press had made it into a real story, one that could be as mysterious and melodramatic as they cared to make it. Of course, it was all conjecture- but it made for a good sensational story, particularly for the tabloids. Of course there were no bodies found, no defined victims, but that didn't stop them. Rory wondered if the plaques had since been removed. What did the City officials make of it? He supposed not a lot. He was sure they had plenty of other things to worry about. The NYPD said there was no case and the bureaucrats might be too scared to remove any plaques for fear of offence. Having no record, didn't mean there hadn't been a clerical oversite. There was nothing explicit as such in the poems. There were now dozens if not hundreds of deceased New Yorkers who had had a bench inscribed with whatever their favourite poem or line from a movie might have been. As Rory read on, flicking back and forth, making notes, he considered that it wasn't until the third plaque that the poems became more pronounced.

> *"Just lay still, allow it all to happen.*
> *There's nothing left to do or try.*
> *No longer the queen of all Manhattan,*
> *We are all just born to die."*

A chill ran up his back and he folded the paper over. *What the fuck?*

He had been making notes in his little pocket book. He jotted down the poem and added in this question. If not something sinister then what would this mean? He double checked the last few day's papers, his stomach tight. Nothing new had appeared, just a few of the papers still trying to wring a story out of what had gone before. How would he feel if a new plaque appeared? What would he think then? He noted in his book the name of Vicki Gibson. She worked for The Post and seemed to be at the forefront of the 'Couplet Killer' theories. He wondered to himself what the actual plaques looked like and if they were consistent with the others in the park. Were there no clues? Had the cops even taken a look? Maybe that guy Kelly would have. He'd have to go and see. But first he had another part of the library he'd in mind to visit. He located the 'Human Science' and 'Psychology' section a floor down and set about leafing through the shelves. He was beginning to think like he did when on a job. Making his notes, building an idea, testing out ideas. If he wanted to rob a place- he needed to find out as much as he could about it. Everything. No detail was useless. If it was a robbery like the next job- he had to discover every aspect of how the business worked. What are the weaknesses, where are the angles hidden. If he needed to break a safe he had to learn how to do it himself, or recruit someone like Jimmy to do it for him. He figured that this research wasn't much different. This theory was that maybe there was a serial killer out there and maybe he had Alice. Just like a potential job, maybe there was nothing in it. But he had to put the effort in to find out. So he needed to find out about serial killers. He'd seen *Psycho* and *Manhunter*, but that was about the height of his knowledge. He picked out a few volumes and found a free desk and began flicking through pages. The time passed easily and quickly. It was nearly dinner time and the library had grown quieter. He was craving a smoke, but could wait a little longer. No smoking signs were everywhere in the reading rooms. He decided on taking four books with him; *Helter Skelter- The True Story of The Manson Murders,*

Psychopathia Sexualis, Jack The Ripper: A Theory and *The Stranger Beside Me: Ted Bundy.*

He took his books up to the librarian who regarded both him and the books with mild disdain. She peered over her spectacles at him as she ran the little scamming pen over the front pages. There was something comforting in the faint squidgy sound. It reminded him as his first trip to a new library opened up near his housing estate. Rory thanked her with an almost ironically exuberant smile and crossed back to the elevators. He was glad to be outside again and smoking. The heat had reduced a little. There was even some fresh air hanging under the smog. As he jogged away down the steps, his stomach complained that it needed feeding. He found a McDonalds on the next corner and did just that.

CHAPTER 29

The rest had done The Killer good. He slept most of the day. He'd needed some water to quench his ravenous thirst, but hadn't tried to eat much. The second day he had felt much better. He had changed his dressings twice. The wounds weren't particularly deep, he'd had worse before from his father's strap. They had weeped a little and he applied an antiseptic ointment. He also took a course of antibiotics that he always kept a supply of, just in case. By the third day he felt stronger, just some minor aches. He had been able to return to work. His other work. He had made excuses of a virus- but then he did have the advantage of being the boss. Why have employees if they couldn't run things for a day or two? He was strong enough to dispose of the body in the usual way. It went perfectly as usual. Then he set to work on the latest plaque. After dinner that evening he ventured out to Central Park.

He drove and parked up near The Museum of Arts and Design on West Fifty Ninth. He entered the park, carrying his little leather bag with him. This time it contained his new plaque and the tools he needed to fix it in place. He walked for twenty minutes, casting his eye over the various benches as he went. He was dressed in an official Central Park worker's blue T-shirt, with a blue baseball hat and blue waterproof trousers. The Killer noted a few benches already with official plaques and walked on. He decided on a wooden bench under a tree alongside two others, about three hundred yards from the skating rink. The park was quiet. It was a mild evening, going on for eight, but there weren't any large groups of people. Nobody was near to the set of benches. He started work making holes with the small manual drill. In no time he was lining up the plaque and fixing the four black coated screws into place. He glanced around him, then stood up and admired his work. One of his wounds throbbed a little, but other than that he felt good. He took out a white cloth and wiped the plaque down, before cleaning down anywhere else his hands had been near as well. The Killer stood up again, pleased. He stretched, the pulsing in his side had settled down. He checked his watch.

It was still early, especially for a night owl.

Or a wolf.

Nowhere to be.

He'd go and visit his other works of art.

CHAPTER 30

Fed and watered, Rory took the subway to the side of East Sixtieth on the edge of the bottom right hand corner of Central Park. A nervousness entered him as he passed through the gates. He stopped near a drinks kiosk closing up for the night and lit up a cigarette. He consulted his notebook. The first plaque had been left west from there, on the Broadway side. He headed off at a good pace, pushing his nerves aside.

What am I nervous about?

He knew that these plaques existed. But maybe seeing them would bring a new reality to the whole thing. Perhaps he was more worried that he *wasn't* crazy.

The path was quiet; a few couples, joggers and solitary ramblers. There were one or two drunks on benches, in various states of inebriation and consciousness. He hoped that nobody was sleeping on any of the benches that he was looking for. Rory planned on visiting all three of the plaques- he could be back on the train again in an hour.

Once he was fairly sure he was roughly around the right area, he began checking over benches for the plaques. Most of them had none, out of the first dozen or so he only found one memorial, that was an official one. It was dedicated to a certain Alan Grofield, an amateur actor apparently. He walked up a short incline, stopping at the bin at the top. He stood and puffed the remaining tobacco from his cigarette. A few yards ahead of him were two black metal benches. A worker, dressed all in blue was polishing something on one of them with a cloth. Rory stubbed out his cigarette on the grill on the top of the bin, then poked the butt through with the other trash. The worker titled his head to the side, still facing away from him. He shoved the cloth into his trouser pocket, then picked up a leather bag. The man moved to the side of the bench, then walked steadily away towards Heckscher Ball fields. He had an unusual gait; lumbering off up the path. Rory started off towards the benches, watching the man disappear into the distance. He approached the bench in question, his heart beginning to race as the shiny silver plaque winked at him in the evening sun. He had found one. He gave the now faraway figure a last glance, then began to read.

He read it over and over. It might have been for the twentieth time that day, but the first at the source. He was too mesmerised to hear the steps approaching from behind.

"Good night for it, Rory."

"Shit," Rory said, startled.

He turned.

"Oh, officer, er Detective…"

"Kelly."

The large detective was stood behind in a white shirt with thin red stripes and black trousers. His shirt sleeves were rolled up and his wavy hair looked like it hadn't been brushed since the morning. He was chewing a piece of gum. His smile was level, but at least there was one there.

Rory took a breath, smiled and took a step back. "Well Detective Kelly- you managed to scare the absolute shite clean out of me just now. Thanks for that."

"I'm sorry Rory. Us Irish must be jumpy."

"*Us* Irish?"

"My parents. They both hailed from Sligo, Yeats country folk."

Rory nodded, "Aye, not far from the six counties. So, what brings you here? As in right now, tonight."

"Same as you I guess. There's a lot of benches to choose from in Central Park and we both ended up here." He pulled out his lighter and began rolling it around between his fingers.

Rory narrowed his eyes, wrinkles formed on his forehead.

"Yeah, true enough. You've been following me though haven't you?"

Rory's voice was now clipped, guarded.

It was Kelly's turn to furrow his brow. He shrugged dramatically. He reminded Rory of a younger Columbo, but without the trench coat.

"You got me Rory," he said raising his hands in mock defence. Read much of those library books yet?" he said gesturing to the books under Rory's arm.

"How d'ya know they're library books? Been fuckin' following me all day?" Rory said, his voice hardened.

"Some interesting books you picked out there."

"Yeah? Well maybe I thought I'd do a little research, seeing as the NYPD aren't wanting to bother."

Rory felt panic creep through him.

What the fuck are they doing trailing me? How much do they know about me?

Then a worse thought struck.

Had they been following him that morning when he was out sorting things for the heist? That could cause a real problem. His contact wouldn't be happy for a start.

Kelly pursed his lips, then he fumbled in his pocket for a cigarette. He pulled one out of a cheap gold-plated cigarette case.

"I told you already- I *am* interested."

"So interested that you follow me around New York all day?"

Kelly relaxed his shoulders, scuffed his foot aimlessly against a few loose stones as he inhaled smoke deeply. "I think you might have some credible ideas, Rory forget about my partner for the minute. I'm sorry that he pissed you off, but I'm my own man. I gotta arrangement in place at the libraries. A guy picking out certain kinds of books at the minute- I get a call, 'specially a white guy in his twenties, thirties."

"I'm in my forties."

"Well then- take it as a compliment. I'm being straight with you, I can't do any more than that. I think we should have a proper talk, grab a coffee sometime. Talk about all this," he said gesturing his cigarette at the bench.

"Yeah, maybe."

"You still got my card?"

"Yeah, I got it."

"Gimme a call then."

"Yeah, maybe, sure we'll see."

"Alright then. But I won't wait around forever Rory."

...

Back in his apartment, Rory picked away at the *Wolf* guitar, sitting, one leg under the other on his sofa. It was almost ten. A half drunk Jamesons and ice sat on the little table beside. He let his left hand run aimlessly up and down the neck, picking out a lazy lick or two. The guitar sounded lovely, but he barely noticed it. At least the feeling of holding it was comforting.

Why hadn't he said more to Kelly? Surely that was what he had wanted.

You're a stubborn idiot Downie.

Maybe it was the surprise at seeing him. And the fear of letting a cop get too near. The idea of him following him about more than rattled him. Or maybe it was just his stubbornness. He was still pissed off at how he'd been made a fool of at the station. And he had been further infuriated by Dave. But he should have talked to Kelly.

This guy shows an interest and I jerk him about. Stupid.

He set the guitar down, shaking his head, then sank the rest of the whiskey.

Turning the light off, he went to the bathroom, brushed his teeth, took his T-shirt and jeans off. It was so warm- he pushed his bedroom window out. He got on top of the bed covers, bringing his borrowed books with him. He flicked through a few of them for almost an hour, then fell asleep reading, the books piled around him.

Chapter 31

Winston was sipping from a steaming coffee when he arrived.

"Folks are gonna start talking about you and me."

"Hiya Winston, cheers for coming out again."

"It's alright- guess it's just as well I took on some help in the shop. I seem to be becoming rather social. Maybe up just preparing for my retirement." He looked kindly over the top of his thin round glasses.

It was the next day and Rory had went to meet Winston in a little café near to his antique shop. It was a Portuguese place with excellent coffee and delicious pastries.

Rory filled him in on what had happened at the police precinct.

"Well, I'm sorry fella, but I can't say I'm surprised. God-damned police 'round here. You'd go through twenty before catching a decent natured one."

"Yeah, I suppose you're right."

"I'm serious Rory. You'd be hard pressed to find one not on the take, not a thug or not stuffing powder up their nose."

Rory nodded, savouring a slurp of his coffee.

Winston was being guarded about his own opinion on Rory's theory and Rory had no urge to press hin on it.

"Listen, I uh… have a proposal for you."

"Oh, sounds serious young fella," he said wrinkling his nose before taking a bite from a crisp apple puff.

"Well, I've been thinking. This job we're gonna do," he leaned over the table, setting his mug down carefully, "It's all cash- should be around thirty- forty thousand total score. We obviously don't know where Alice is right now. Maybe she won't be back for the job, maybe she's got some troubles we don't know about. I dunno. Maybe she'll turn up tomorrow. Things is- she was gonna be the straight guy for this thing. The *in.* Y'know- chatting to the security guards- a distraction. I had a wee set up all worked out. It's kinda of an important key to it all. A layer of cover for the rest of us."

"Okay," Winston said slowly, "Not sure where you're going with this."

"Well…" Rory laughed nervously, rubbing his hands together, "I wanted to sound you out. This job is going to need to go ahead either way. I have a date for the good score and I have a solid plan. I wondered if you'd maybe be up for stepping in… if needs be."

"Oh… right." Winston blinked a few times. He began to fill his pipe and flattened the tobacco down with a little tool, "I wasn't expecting that I must say. You know I've never really been what you might call, a *field man*?"

"Yeah, but you know what you're at. You've lived in *the life*. I mean- you're a cool customer. It would just be playing a part, nothing heavy. I've an idea already for how we could work it."

"Mmmmm." Winston struck a match and began puffing on his pipe, watching the tobacco take, peering over his glasses. His eyes sparkled, "I must say I'm actually quite flattered. At my age you, don't expect a career change. Sure there was me talking about my retirement." He gave a throaty chuckle.

"Jesus- you're still a young man Winston. You're not much more than ten years older than me. And I'm in my prime!"

"Well young fella, can I think about it?"

"'Course you can. So you wouldn't write it off out of hand?"

"No. No, I guess I wouldn't."

…

Outside, the humid afternoon sun hit Rory like an impenetrable wall. Before moving to New York he'd never experienced heat like it. It was getting to Summer becoming his least favourite season. And this coming from a country where the seasons were only distinct from one another by if the rain was cold, warm or windy. Rory stopped at a street vendor to pick up a newspaper and a Diet Coke on the way to catch the subway. He was feeling better, he had a new plan for the job and he had something to focus on with the library books. He hadn't really expected there to be anything inside that would shock him.

But there it was.

Page 2.

The headline asked, "Has *The Couplet Killer* Struck Once Again?"

It sent an electric jolt through him. He instantly had to sit down on the edge of nearby café's bench. He read on. Another plaque had been found. There was a metallic taste in his mouth.

Jesus.

Alice?

The poem made his anxiety swell all the more.

> **"What fun we had the night we met.**
> **Your hair and the town were painted red.**
> **The only thing left was your debt.**
> **That was paid, as to death you were led."**

Fuck.

This was by far the most explicit one yet.

And red hair too.

He gripped the edge of the table, his knuckles white, just like his face.

Rory found the closest bar and strode inside and ordered a double. The whiskey hit the back of his throat before either ice cube had the chance to melt.

"Another please. Just a single."

He nursed that one. His insides had already been warmed. The discreet barman went about polishing an ash tray and attending to other customers. It was dark inside. Light crept in whenever the door swung open or closed. Rory stared down at the heavily scored bar, flicking his lighter nervously, before lighting up a Marlborough.

He couldn't actually believe it.

He felt fear, he felt panic. But he also felt a strange resignation. Surely this affirmed his feelings. But still- who would believe him?

Or was he still mistaken? Caught up in this theory, interpreting only what confirmed his fears?

He spread the paper out in front of him, flicking a stray sprinkling of ash away. He read it again, slowly. He nodded to himself. The story was convincing, the poem seemed to confirm it.

What if it *was* true? Poor, sweet natured Alice. Could she really be dead?

He folder up the paper, ran his finger across the now beer soaked print.

Vicki Gibson.

She might believe him.

CHAPTER 32

The Killer, was back at his day job, but had finished for the day. He lay back in his favourite armchair in his living room. He pulled up his shirt and had a look at his bandages. There was a small amount of yellow weeping again, but no blood. It had felt good to be back at work, having already tied up the previous killing the day before. Once again, things were as they should be. He despised when things did not go to plan. That was certainly true with the Alice girl. But now he had remedied things. He had faced the adversity confronting him and come through the other side. He sipped his cup of tea, almost chewing each sup. He stared at his newly oiled blade, wrapped in cloth on the table. This was probably one of the times when other people enjoyed something alcoholic. His parents had never drank and he had never been tempted to. Why would he want to feel out of control? Or queasy even? It wasn't for him.

It had done him good to visit his plaques. He had missed his daily ritual. But now he felt strong again. Not only strong; powerful. He indulgently set his feet up on his Father's old foot stool and spread out the newspaper across his lap. He read slowly, moving his lips. He switched his feet over one another.

He folded it over and set it on the chair arm, then picked up his cup and drained his tea. Not bad. It would do just fine. He didn't want things to become too rushed, he couldn't afford any more errors of judgement. The article was fine. It had gained more momentum than he would necessarily have wanted yet. But still, it would do alright. He would continue with his plan. And besides, as much as he would hate to admit it, the notoriety felt good. It was all unproven. If it was true, the police were still cautiously sceptical. That was good. But there were those now who knew something of what he was doing.

But only something.

And sure that was the most delightful part.

CHAPTER 33

1211 Avenue of the Americas: The New York Post. Rory pushed open the front door, filling his lungs first with a mix of fresh air and a draw of tobacco. A door man stepped to the side, giving him a vaguely suspicious look. Inside was a large, airy reception room with high glass windows. At the rear was a curved desk with two women in smart clothes speaking on the phones. There were a number of other people scattered around the room, seated on chairs. Some were waiting patently while one man was scribbling furiously in a notebook and another was speaking loudly into a phone, the long lead trailing back from the reception. Rory approached the desk, looking up at the walls ordained with front covers of famous events; The Moon Landing, Watergate, Reagan entering The Whitehouse.

"Hi, how can I help ya?"

"Yeah, Hi… I'm looking to see… er someone."

"Okay." The young woman's wide smile failed a little. "Have you got an appointment?"

"No, no I don't." Rory was suddenly aware how out of his depth he was. Here he was in the middle of a massive newspaper office in New York, half drunk, feeling all eyes were on him. He pulled at his T-shirt collar. He wished he owned a suit. Thank God the air-con was good- but it was still stifling in there.

"Listen, I gotta story. I have information."

"Oh Okay." She looked unimpressed. "Is it someone in particular you wanted to see?"

"Yeah, 'course, sorry. Vicki Gibson."

She pursed her lips. She held his stare for a moment. Other eyes were now on him too. Pater Gabriel sang quietly in the background about a sledgehammer.

She shrugged, smiled. "Okay, I'll ring up to her, but no promises honey."

He gave the girl some more details and she took more of an interest then. She even brought him a coffee, which he sipped for twenty minutes, before being told that Ms Gibson could see him briefly.

Vicki Gibson let her eyes linger a moment on Rory as he plonked himself down in one of her leather chairs. She shut the glass panelled door closed. Rory stared out of the window at its third floor prime view over the city, as she then gathered herself behind her desk. The office was on the small side, but it was neat, functional and contained expensive, utilitarian furnishings. He wondered what the view alone would have cost.

"So, ahem, Mr Downey is it?"

"Yeah, but call me Rory."

"You have some information you wish to share?"

"Yeah, I do, that's right. Thanks for seeing me."

She raised a heavy eyebrow. Her makeup was pronounced, but her features were of a strong contoured, natural beauty. Mid thirties, she had died blonde hair and her expensive blouse and skirt clung to her complimentarily.

"Okay then Rory," she continued in an affirmed and upper class Midwest accent, "Go ahead, I'm listening."

"First I'd better tell you what I want." He tried to sound confident, comfortable.

"What you would want? Right… you mean you want some kind of payment? That's something we can arrange, but it'd need to be for something substantial."

"It's about *The Couplet Killer*. I know who his last victim is. Well, I think I do."

She made an involuntary 'o' with her mouth, then wiped her hand across her face. She nodded. "We could pay pretty well for that type of thing."

"I don't want any money."

"Sorry?"

The Wolf is at Your Door

"I don't want any money. And I'd prefer not to be named. I want to speak to that girl. The one who got away. You could arrange it maybe?"

"That would all be rather irregular. Well, I don't know if we could do that. All I could do was ask her I guess. Why would you want that?" she asked sceptically.

"Because I wanna find this fuckin' guy."

"Alright then, tell me why." She reached into her drawer and pulled out a packet of Marlborough Reds. Rory gave a little smile.

He tried his best now to sound charming, he let the drink help relax him. It in fact slipped closer to shambolic. His thinking was all over the place, he hadn't had time to plan this out. Rory wasn't one usually for knee jerk reactions. He began to explain about Alice, trying to be as clear as possible- making sure to mention all of the supporting facts. As his mind became involved again in the actual words that he was saying, he relaxed a little. His demeanour changed to something very honest and sincere.

Vicki listened attentively. Her eyes disappeared over his head a few times, looking as if she was thinking things through. When he had finished, she traced a finger over her eyelashes a few times, plucked a stray one out.

"I'll be straight with you Rory." She stubbed out her cigarette, leaned backwards in her comfortable chair and glanced out the window briefly at the view. Hot and weary New York commuters passed back and forth, unaware that they were being watched. Rory followed her gaze and he wondered where the hell this killer was right now

"Have you anything concrete? No. Am I even convinced your friend has been taken? No, I'm not. Not totally." She picked a piece of chewing gum from a pack and tossed it into her mouth. "But, could I run a story about it?" She smiled, showing bright, perfect teeth, "Yeah, maybe I could."

"So… what happens now?"

"Now I speak to my editor. I see if we can work something out. Then I talk to you again. You gotta phone?"

"Just one in my building."

"Okay- come back in tomorrow about this time and I'll have an answer for you either way then. Fair enough?"

"Fair enough."

Back on the streets, the heat was blistering. Even the shade was hot. He needed a drink, another proper drink. And Rory felt drawn back to Central Park too. He needed to see the new plaque, perhaps Alice's plaque. He swallowed hard. He was getting somewhere, he was sure of it. He needed to go back there, he needed to think. But first- that drink.

CHAPTER 34

Back in Central Park, Rory hunted for a tree to sit under for a minute. He'd had two beers in a bar near to the museum. It had been too warm for Guinness, so he'd taken a Bud. It tasted bitter but did the two things it needed to do; it cooled him down and kept his buzz on. Rory needed to go and look at that plaque for himself, but he was nervous. He was nervous as hell.

Rory forced himself up and began to walk along towards the lower west side. He smoked a cigarette, concentrated on the inhaling and exhaling, ignoring the dog walkers and sweating joggers that he passed. The skyscrapers loomed heavily in the background, seeming to look down accusingly on him and the park. Rory made his way along Terrace Drive, the trees all around looking so healthy and green, he wondered how it was possible in all of this heat. Then he spotted a group of benches.

Could that be the one?

There was a park worker standing beside it in the usual attire and baseball cap. The man produced a cloth from his pocket and began to polish the plaque. There was a little leather bag at his feet. Rory's eyes narrowed.

Is that the same worker as the last time? Who was at the other bench.

Rory kept walking towards him.

The worker cocked his ear, still turned away, then slipped the cloth back in his pocket and straightened up.

"Excuse me," Rory shouted from a few feet away.

The man quickly bent down again and picked up his bag and began to walk away.

Maybe this worker could tell him something about the plaques.

"Hey there, excuse me…" Rory said again, quickening his pace.

The man continued to hurry away, his head looking left and right as he did so. There was no one else nearby.

"Hey," Rory said once more, catching up with the man. He reached forward and placed a hand on the man's shoulder.

The man turned.

The face before him frightened him.

He could have walked past this man on the street and thought nothing of him. But in this moment, the face told him everything. A long, gaunt and rubbery countenance stared back at him. The red rimmed eyes were huge and bore into Rory. There was a cruel twist to the curve of the mouth. There was something else in that face too; fear.

Rory's heart hammered in his chest, his mouth ran dry. He removed his hand from the shoulder and just stood and stared. It seemed like an eternity, but was only seconds. An animal scurried through a tree nearby. Then all at once, the man rotated his body away, put his head down and ran.

Stunned for a moment, Rory pulled his jaw off the ground and burst after him.

It's fucking him! Come to gloat over his work.

The man lumbered along the path at speed, almost careering into an elderly man. Rory flew around the other side of the old man, brushing past a jagged hedge. The Killer raced on, his long legs carrying him quickly, but awkwardly away. He tore around a corner, off towards Cherry Hill Fountain. Rory focused on his breathing, told his chest to keep up with him. They both tore into the little seated area, then The Killer cut off through the trees. Rory followed, only seconds behind. People began taking notice, stopping and staring. Those closer by, ducked out of their way, a few muttering obscenities. The Killer carried on through the undergrowth, towards Wagner Cove, dodging trees and hedges. He kept glancing back, his little leather bag swinging at his side. The Killer pressed on, then came through the clearing and found himself at the waters edge. He doubled back as Rory came crashing through. Rory launched himself at him. The Killer sidestepped and batted Rory's arms away. His eyes were wild for a moment and then he lunged at Rory. They fell onto the dusty stone path, grappling with each other. The man's hands wrapped around Rory's throat. Rory's already struggling respiratory system seemed to go into shock before Rory managed to lift an arm in defence. Then he made a fist and smacked The Killer three times in the side of his head. The grip lessoned, but he didn't let go. Rory saw some blood seeping in the man's side. Rory dug in his fingers and squeezed as tightly as he could. The Killer cried out and released his choke hold, clambering off of Rory. Staggering for a few paces, The Killer regained his senses and shot off back along the path. Wheezing, hacking, Rory dragged himself up off the ground and made after him, much slower then before. He heard a voice shout, "They're over that way," as he picked up his pace, The Killer disappearing around a corner and out of view. Rory skidded to a stop as he burst out the end of the path and onto Terrace Drive. Panting, his chest burning, he searched for where he had gone. Then he made out the blue shirt disappearing into the undergrowth below Frisbee Hill.

"Hey you! Stop!"

It was a cop. He came tumbling through the hedges beside Rory, looking very pissed, his gun drawn.

Rory looked towards the cop, then to the figure vanishing into the trees.

"Fuck!"

He raised his hands.

CHAPTER 35

"I keep telling you- the guy didn't work there. He tried to fucking strangle me for Christ-sakes."

Rory was in a little interview room in the 22nd Precinct, his hands cuffed together. The cop who had hauled him in was standing by the door. Opposite him was a Detective Bridges- a thin man in middle age, with a tight suit and thin lips. He tried a smile, but it wasn't convincing.

"Come, come now Mr Downey. You stink of drink, you've been seen acting, well… pretty erratic in Central Park by at least a dozen witnesses. And now you've spun us a yarn that Hans Christian Anderson would deem too fanciful. Come on now."

"Fucksake!" Rory shouted, exasperated. He banged his bound hands down on the table. "You let him get away!" he shouted at the cop by the door.

"Fuckin' nut job," the cop muttered in a heavy Brooklyn accent.

"Fuckin' idiots," Rory muttered.

"We've got you for drunk and disorderly Rory," continued Bridges, "We got you for disturbing the peace. If we find this gardener, I'm damn sure we'll have you for assault and battery. You were god-damned close to assaulting an officer as well. It's in your best interests to cooperate."

Rory blew out his cheeks, closed his eyes.

"I want my phone call."

Bridges rolled his eyes and stood, pushing his plastic green chair back. "Get him his call will you?" he said before opening the door and striding away.

"C'mon then," said the cop at the door.

He led him along the hall, past a few noisy groups of drunks, down to a payphone at the end. The cop dumped a few quarters into the machine, then passed over the receiver.

Who the fuck am I meant to call?

My Mum back in Belfast? Nope. Jimmy or Winston? They wouldn't thank me for calling them from the NYPD. Shit.

He bit on his lip, then punched in the number.

"Hello?"

"Hi… Crystal?"

"Yeah, Hi Rory."

"I… uh," he cradled the receiver in his cuffed hands, "I wanted to see how you are."

"Yeah… okay Rory, fine. What about you- you sound strange?"

"Yeah… sorry I'm just out and about on a street phone."

The burly cop beside him raised an eyebrow.

"Oh, okay. There's been nothing more about Alice… if that's why you're calling."

"Oh, right- I was wondering, but…"

The pips began to sound, telling him the money was running out, "But can we meet up- I'm not sure if I can make it later but, but…"

The line went dead.

"Shite!" he said, slamming the receiver down, "Can I not get any longer?"

"Nope," said the deadpan cop, leading him back towards the interview room.

Bridges was standing in the doorway with a steaming cup of coffee in a plastic cup. He sipped it as Rory walked back inside again and sat down. He was asked pretty much the same questions again and Rory gave pretty much the same answers. He also told them how he had talked to officers at the other precinct just days before. Eventually they offered him a drink. By that time his shirt was even more soaked with sweat and his face felt oily. Now his hangover was coming on early too. They left him alone for half an hour with his luke-warm tea. It gave him a chance to gather his thoughts, to try and process it all.

Why the fuck am I sitting here handcuffed?

He took another drink of his tea, then tipping the rest down. He was stil thirsty. Any alcohol buzz was long gone. But he could taste a bitterness left behind and if anything it had made him thirstier. They had left a plastic cup of water and he drank that down too.

His eyes.

The image gave him a shudder.

That was him. That was fucking him.

He shook his head. It was all too much to take in. What a day.

Rory was just about to knock the door and ask for a cigarette when it opened and Bridges walked in smoking one himself.

"Well son, it looks like you've leaving us."

"Aye? Can I go?"

"No, afraid not. Our colleagues over in 65th want a word with you. I guess you're their problem now," he said and shut the door again.

CHAPTER 36

Rory was marched off to a waiting yellow and blue and then driven across town. Within half an hour he was being bundled through the familiar reception area which again seemed to have the same quota of misfits and degenerates as the last time. Then he was sat down in another interview room and they closed the door.

Alone again. Naturally.

He looked around- lime green walls, cheap plastic chairs, an idle tape recorder. It looked much like the last one and he couldn't be certain it wasn't actually the last one. A lot had happened since then.

He was struggling to keep his temper in check. He couldn't believe this was happening. Tiredness, frustration, anger- it all fizzed through his veins. He hadn't done anything wrong! Not anything they knew about. His shirt was now incredibly uncomfortable- some of the sweat had died and was stinging his arm pits. His throat hurt from where he had been choked and he had small cuts from they had rolled about on the ground. He was hungry, in the middle of an early hangover and most urgently he was craving a cigarette.

Then the door opened and in stepped Lieutenants Richmond and Kelly.

"So we meet again Paddy," announced Richmond coming in first and sitting down across the table. He laid out a bundle of pages in front of him. Kelly closed the door behind him and crossed the small room. He looked at Rory, but didn't make eye contact.

"Rory," he said nodding, taking a seat beside his partner.

"And this time you're in handcuffs," Richmond said dryly, shuffling his pages.

"Nothing gets past the NYPD." Rory said irritably.

Richmond shared a look with his colleague and rolled his eyes. Kelly looked down at the stained table.

"So, do you wanna tell us what you've been up to exactly Rory?"

"Did your friends across town not fill you in? Are you all that inept?"

"Aye they did Rory," broke in Kelly evenly, "But we wanna hear it from the horse's mouth."

Rory blew out his cheeks. "I haven't had a smoke in a couple hours, can I've my cigarettes first?"

"All in good time," started Richmond.

"You can have one of mine," said Kelly taking out his deck and offering one across.

Kelly lit them both one, then passed another to Richmond too. They all smoked for a few moments, then Rory leaned his hands across and flicked the ash end into the overflowing ash tray. The nicotine hit the spot, making him lightheaded for a moment. His stomach rumbled inside. It wanted something more substantial. It would have to wait.

"So what d'ya wanna know?"

"How about you tell us what you were doing in Central Park this evening," said Richmond rocking back in his chair. He was wearing a dark blue shirt, tighter than the last one. Rory realised that the man was very thin for someone his age. No middle-aged spread. His face was just as sallow and Rory noticed the brittleness of his thin crop of hair. Kelly leaned back in his own chair, he was wearing a white shirt and trousers, inhaling deeply on his smoke. They both had sweat marks under the arms too. They'd probably been in those clothes throughout the long hot day. The room reeked of sweat; theirs and that of all of the others unfortunate enough to have been in the room. It mixed with the smoke into a nasty stench.

"I went to look at the bench- the new plaque. I guess you heard about it."

Richmond shrugged.

"I think the killer left it for Alice. My friend Alice- the one I told you about."

"Killer?" said Richmond shaking his head, looking at Kelly.

Kelly kept his eyes on Rory, now making eye contact.

"What makes you think it's about Alice?" Kelly asked.

Rory took in a breath, adjusted himself in his hard, uncomfortable chair.

"It matches. Don't you see? It's appeared a week or two after she vanished- it's clearly another message from the killer, it's got her red hair too, it…"

"I told you last time," said Richmond grinding his cigarette butt into dust, there's no killer."

Rory noticed Kelly wince for a second.

"What do you think Lieutenant Kelly?" asked Rory, tapping the last drop of ash gently off his cigarette, not wanting to stub it out just yet. "Do you think there's no killer?"

Kelly shifted in his seat, glanced briefly at his partner, then met Rory's stare again. "There's no official investigation at this time." He clapped his hands, making his partner flinch, then spread them out on the table, "Officially- there's no killer."

"But you think there might be."

"A lot of people go missing in this city every month- a hell of a lot of people. A lot of people get killed too. It's not what I'd want but it's true. Listen, tell us exactly what happened in the park."

Rory had wrung all of the nicotine from his cigarette and tossed it into the tray.

"Okay- but your partner here isn't gonna want to hear it."

"Try me," said Richmond, looking up from his papers.

Rory gripped the edge of the table with his cuffed hands, staring through it as he spoke. "Alright then. I wanted to see the plaque. I found it easy enough. There was a guy at it- dressed up like a gardener. He was standing over it, polishing it. I think I saw him a few days before too." He glanced up at Kelly. He looked away. "I went to talk to him… then… well basically he started to run."

"You crept up behind some guy and made him jumpy?" said Richmond.

"No, it wasn't that. He… he wasn't right."

"A guy dressed in park maintenance clothes working on maintenance in the park. Real strange."

"No, fucksake." Rory forced himself to keep his cool, "You should have seen him. He gave me the weirdest look, his eyes were like fuckin' saucers. He wasn't right, I'm tellin' you. Then he bolted."

"And what did you do?" asked Kelly.

"I just… I ran after him. I mean- I knew right away. It's him. It's fuckin' him."

Richmond finished making some notes, then flicked over a page, not looking up, "So you chased this *gardener*, then what happened?"

Rory ignored that and carried on, "I caught up with him and we… scuffled. The next thing I knew and he was on me- wild eyed- trying to fucking choke me. Two hands 'round my neck- you can see the marks."

Rory pulled awkwardly at his shirt collar to show the faded red marks up each side.

"That could have happened anywhere. You'd been out drinking in the bars hadn't you? God-damned steaming drunk so we heard."

"I wasn't drunk," Rory said gritting his teeth, "I'd had a couple drinks- no crime in that I know of? Prohibition isn't still a thing is it?"

"Might be better if it was; keep some of you Paddies from losing their shit."

Rory shot out of his chair. "What the fuck? What the fuck is this?"

"Si-down," roared Richmond, also standing.

"C'mon Rory, get in your chair," said Kelly.

"This 'good cop bad cop' is it?" Rory said, easing himself back down.

"Something like that," said Kelly, lighting them both another cigarette. "Alright Rory, then what happened?"

"Then your fuckin' beat cop pulls a gun on me and lets the killer go- that's what."

"You're lucky if we don't hear from the worker," said Richmond," He comes into make a statement about you assaulting him and you're in even deeper shit."

Rory took in a draw, shook his head, "Jesus- I thought the fuzz were bad back home, but you guys take the biscuit. Prejudiced *and* stupid."

Richmond's nostrils flared. He pressed his hands down so hard on the table that the table creaked.

"Let's take a break- will we?" Kelly said quietly to Richmond.

"Sure," he said standing abruptly, his eyes trained on Rory. Then he turned and left, slamming the door behind him.

They both smoked for a few beats, letting the atmosphere in the room ease and be replaced by the overpowering scent of tobacco.

"You shouldn't goad him Rory, does you no good."

"Yeah well, your partner's a dick head."

Kelly shrugged, "So I'm not telling you this but if you want to get out of here then play nice and don't say too much more."

"What?"

"You got wax in your ears? I said play nice. We got nothing on you. Not a thing. Well maybe drunk in public, but hell if we arrested everyone in New York for that, well. When we both come back in say you want a solicitor, you want everything recorded. We'll have no choice but to let you go."

"Why are you helping me?"

The big cop sighed, crossed his legs, "Because I don't think you've done anything wrong."

"And what about what happened, what I told you? Do you believe me?"

"Yeah, I guess I do."

Chapter 37

The Killer was still panting. He pulled off his cap and ran a hand across his sweaty brow. He was leaning against a wall outside Central Park. His chest was heaving. He checked his wound. It was open and hurt like hell.

Who was that wretched man?

Where had he come from?

Damn him- he could have ruined everything!

The Killer caught his breath, scanned the street. Busy New Yorkers passed back and forth beside him. He composed himself, planted his cap back on his head and walked steadily off towards his car, trying not to wince.

He had to find out who that man was and what he wanted.

When at the car, he felt relief; the familiar smell, everything as he had left it. He sat back in his chair and wound down the window. It was stifling hot. He could never get used to this city's heat. It was an added problem whenever he was waiting on the disposing of bodies. The horrible things stank.

He adjusted his mirror. No sign of any trouble. He had gotten away okay. But that was too close. Putting a hand to his head he felt blood. The punches had drawn blood from the side of his head. It'd probably reopened another one of the injuries that bitch had given him. He punched the steering wheel twice. Then composed himself.

What did this man want? What!

He wouldn't be able to get to the bottom of it now. But he would. The Killer would take pleasure in finishing the task of wringing his neck. He needed to get out of there, back to his sanctum solace. He turned the key in the ignition, pulled away from the sidewalk and headed for home.

CHAPTER 38

Within the hour, Rory had been sent on his way with a *keep your nose clean* talk He went straight home, straight to bed and straight to sleep. Exhaustion took him and wrapped itself around him. But he had the most unsettled sleep that he could recall. It was so disturbed, it was as if he had barely slept at all. All night he felt like he was traversing a choppy sea- at times incredibly deep, only to bob again to the surface. Then he would plunge back into the darkness again. The dreams themselves seemed bereft of any narrative. They were full of shadowy figures and dark hallways that slanted high and at odd angles. It was like living in an old Film Noir. He half expected to bump into Peter Lorre or Robert Mitchum there. But instead there were that man's eyes that greeted him, haunted him. As he stumbled through his dream world, those bulging, cold, fantastical eyes were everywhere. And so the night time went on, full of dread with a fearful tightness in his being.

When Rory finally awoke, it was only seven, but he knew that he would not get over again. Nor did he really want to. He faced the day with a weary resolve; washed, breakfasted, then called Jimmy and Dave. He wasn't looking forward to meeting them, but he knew it had to be done.

They both came for around one, accepted a cup of coffee each and sat down at the table. Rory didn't bother with any music or any alcohol. He just needed to tell them what what had gone on and let the cards fall. But they wouldn't like what they were going to hear.

"Cheers for coming fellas. I've had a hell of a few days. Dave, you in particular aren't gonna like some of this. But, it is what it is."

Dave frowned, took a sip of his coffee.

"Yesterday, I got picked up by the cops."

"Shit, man," said Jimmy, "What happened?"

Dave looked down at his coffee, ground his teeth.

Rory stroked his chin, took a breath, "So listen- I think this 'Couplet Killer' took Alice and…"

"Fucksake," interrupted Dave, shaking his head.

"There's a new plaque, alright?" said Rory, his voice louder and more determined. "I went to see it yesterday and there's a guy there polishing it. I try to talk him and he does a runner."

"Shit," said Jimmy, peering over his thin rimmed glasses, leaning across the table, "You think it was him?"

"Course it wasn't," said Dave.

"Dave, you're really starting to piss me off with your snarky remarks," said Rory, his eyes widening. He took a sip of his coffee. "Here me out okay?"

Dave shrugged grumpily.

"Go on Rory," said Jimmy.

"So I catch up with him and the fucker looks crazed, I mean, like a really looped motherfucker. Then he throws me to the ground and starts trying to choke me. I only about managed to get him off me with a couple digs. He sprints off into the distance. Then a cop grabs me, takes me in and they give me a whole heap of shit for the rest of the night. 'Course they don't believe me either, but they got nothing to charge me with and toss me out again."

"That's nuts man," said Jimmy looking anxious. He pulled out his rolling papers and began skinning up.

"Well?" said Rory, staring at Dave.

Dave had sat back in his chair, his features and stance had mellowed some.

"I dunno Rory, I don't know. All I know is I need this job. I mean, I NEED it. I thought I'd a bit of labouring work coming through too, but it didn't work out. 'Nother guy I do jobs with thought he had something coming soon as well- but nada. My split from Hard Rock- it's near gone."

"Listen buddy I'm not trying to piss on things here. I'm not crazy and I didn't ask for something to happen to Alice. And I can't ignore it."

"I still think she's just gone AWOL again."

"I don't think so."

"God-damn, you don't know for sure though," pushed Dave.

Jimmy continued to skin up, listening carefully.

"I know enough. Especially after yesterday. You should have seen this guy."

"There's a lot of nut bars in this city."

"Yeah there are, but not like him. *And*, they don't tend to try and choke you out of the blue. I need this job too, man. And let's not forget who's running this thing. It's my gig. I don't wanna fuck it up. I've been working on it and I've all the ducks lined up."

Dave blew out his cheeks. Jimmy lit up.

"I dunno what I think 'bout it all- I truly don't," he said, "But I trust you Irish- you do what you gotta do."

"Cheers Jimmy. What about you Dave?"

"Well you know what I think," he said gruffly. I just don't want you fuckin' things up. I can't afford any heat on me."

"But are you still in?" Rory said leaning over, his knee jiggling.

"Yeah, long as you don't do nothin' else, I'm in."

CHAPTER 39

Rory arrived early to meet Vicki. He walked back around half the block, smoked a few cigarettes to kill some time. The streets were crowded. Almost oppressively so. And the heat was as usual-suffocating. From above him, the beaming glass sky scrapers all around appeared to be angled so to direct the hot sun right at him. Rory slipped in his earphones and pressed play on his walkman. He'd brought *Electric Mud* with him. A Sixties Muddy Waters album, it wasn't to everyone's tastes. It was commercial, but sometimes good things are. Though thinking of himself of somewhat of a blues purist, he couldn't write off the irresistible urgency and punch of the music. Rory listened to a side, bought a can of Coke off of a yellow fingered street vendor, then made his way back to the front door of the news room. This time his welcome was noticeably warmer and he was whisked away to a private waiting area. He was given a coffee and was told he could smoke, availing of both of them.

"Rory, sorry to keep you waiting, come on through."

Vicky was impeccably dressed once again and led him through to her office with a friendly smile.

"Water, coffee?"

"No, not for me thanks, I'm grand, just had a coffee."

"Good, good. Well, I'll get right down to it. I spoke to my editor and you'll be glad to hear that he is very interested in running your story."

"Okay, great," said Rory cagily.

"Yes, but there are a few conditions."

"Sure, okay."

"If you are happy to proceed, we could even make tomorrow's edition. It would mean your committing to some time now if that is possible? I'll order in come Chinese food, some beers, and we can thrash it out."

"Okay, well yeah I'm free, but what are the conditions exactly?"

She adjusted her chair and took out a small pile of papers. She pushed her blonde bangs from over her face and set on a pair of expensive looking purple rimmed glasses.

"Right. First off, we would need to you to sign a few waivers. We would pay you a generous fee for your exclusive story. That means it would only be us that you could speak to on the record about this for a minimum of three months. Not including the police of course."

Rory nodded his understanding. She made a few lines on a page and slipped it across to him.

"This would be the figure."

Rory looked down at the page. The figure was for a thousand dollars.

He pursed his lips, "That looks fine. But like I said, it's not really the money that I'm after."

"Yes, I understand that. On that issue we are willing to make contact with our source and recommend that she speak with you. In fact, we would also cover any of her, *expenses*. However, I can't give you a personal guarantee. I don't know what she would say."

"No guarantee? I'd prefer if she was on board first."

"I appreciate that Rory. I'm afraid that our legal team could not agree to such a deal." She spread her hands on the desk, exposing finely manicured and painted nails. She smiled apologetically. "What I could give is my personal guarantee that I would *try* my upmost to arrange a meeting between you both."

Rory nodded, thinking hard. "Do you mind if I smoke?" Rory asked.

"No, go on ahead."

Rory took out his packet and slowly selected a cigarette. She pushed over a shining crystal ash tray. Rory noticed that it was Waterford Crystal.

Vicki cleared her throat, "If we proceed I also need your story to be on the record. That would be a requirement. As in, it wouldn't be anonymous."

"Oh."

"Yes. We would also want to run the story with a picture of you." She paused and tidied her sheets into a neat pile. "That is why we are able to provide you with a very good payment for your story. There would also be the option that you may wish to speak to us again. We could offer a… retainer if you like."

Rory pulled heavily on the cigarette and leaned back in the solid chair. He gazed out of the window, rush hour was starting. A build up of cars was taking over from the build up of people. Rush hour was usually more like three hours.

Shit, what do I do? I can't just let this get away from me.
Christ- what would Dave say?

"To be honest, I wasn't really wanting that much exposure. I mean… I'm just trying to find my friend."

"I get it Rory, I really do." She leaned forward, her face serious, full of understanding or something that approached it. "But I'm afraid that's the only way this could work."

"When do I need to make up my mind?"

"Well, that's the other thing. You'd really have to decide now… today."

Rory ran a hand down his legs, sucked in air through his teeth. He needed to find the best way to play this.

"Okay. So, since I last spoke to you- a lot has happened. What about if I also could tell you that the cops pulled me in about this?"

"Right, okay, go on?" Her intelligent eyes narrowed. "Why did they do that?"

"Because I had a fight with the killer."

She couldn't help her mouth drop open.

"A fight… with the killer?"

"Yep- he was at one of the plaques in Central Park. I chased him and he tried to choke me."

"Straight up? Rory, I don't wish to be indelicate- but you're sure? You'd go on the record to say this."

"Yeah, yeah I might."

"And there'll be a police report to back this up?"

"Yes there is. They mightn't see it all the same way as me, but yeah."

"Well for that, perhaps I could make that phone call now. Would you like me to do that Rory? And I could also triple our offer."

"Okay then. I'm not in any rush, go ahead and make the call."

CHAPTER 40

Rory accepted a pot of coffee and drank it all down as he waited. Within half an hour Vicki was back with him. She beamed at him.

"Well, I got her. She's agreed."

She had contacted the girl and got an agreement in principle. That was enough for Rory. That was what he wanted, it would be worth it, wouldn't it? They moved to a larger meeting room downstairs in the building, ordained with further front covers and framed media awards. They were joined by both a personal secretary and for a short while, a photographer. That turned out to be the worst part for Rory. He didn't care for having his picture taken at the best of times. Worse so in these circumstances, not knowing what sort of expression he should give, how it would be portrayed. He didn't want to have to do it, but he also couldn't make peace, not knowing what had happened to Alice. This was a clear lead and he couldn't allow it to get away from him. They worked for several hours, the secretary scribbling in long hand, while Vicki typed some notes on her Macintosh computer. Food arrived and they ate while working on. At about eight, Vicki declared that she had enough material. She then told him that she required time with her secretary to bang it into shape, ready for the morning edition. Vicki gave him a firm handshake and sent him on his way. Rory was told to call past reception on his way out, where a cheque had been cut for him. He thanked the receptionist and ventured back into the outside world.

He walked a block before getting the subway. He needed to pound the street once more and work out a little of his pent up stress. He was nervous and was at odds with what he had done, while still feeling it was something he had had to do. The rush hour commuters had been replaced by those starting on a night out. Middle aged couples passed by on their way to a show, young girls with high slits in their skirts crowded into nightclubs. A few straggling late night business people hurried for the train. Only the buildings stayed the same at night. Always there, always towering above the city. These man made creations, stretching towards heaven. He still found something unsettling about them. In the morning the whole cycle would start over again. The tallest buildings back in Belfast were only a few storeys high. There was nothing comparable here. He wondered what this city would be like if bombs were going off every other day. What if one of these huge structures were blown up? What would it to do to the place? The impact would be colossal. The city he had left behind was in flux and it would take much more of a battering before it began to creep out the other side. Rory felt a strange pining for home and made a mental note that he should phone his mother soon- maybe he would do it tomorrow. Eventually he stopped treading aimlessly, got on his train and headed for his apartment. This time sleep didn't come so easily. He tossed and turned, too hot, too wound up. He supped a whiskey. Still awake at two he had another. Finally, he slipped off to sleep around three. His sleep wasn't filled with unsettling dreams like the previous night. This time he stumbled down a black well of deep slumber. He was still asleep at eleven in the morning when there was a heavy thundering at his door.

...

Dragging himself out of his bed and through the bedroom door, Rory hopped into a pair of track bottoms and awkwardly pulled on a white vest. The hammering continued. He stumbled through the last few steps along through the living room shouting, "Just a second." He slipped the chain off and pulled the door open.

"Finally!"

Dave was standing outside, unshaven, holding a crumpled newspaper at his side. Full consciousness and a sinking feeling bubbled suddenly through Rory.

"You'd better come in."

Dave stormed in ahead of him and found a spot on the living room floor. He turned, standing coiled, his face dark and brooding.

Rory slowly closed the door and walked back into the room and balanced on the arm of the sofa.

"So, I guess you neglected to mention anything about this to us yesterday?"

"Listen, Dave- I didn't know…"

"You didn't know you were going to give some sort of…" he scrambled for the words, his tone feverish, "fucking exclusive?" He said, spitting out the final words. He folded out the paper agitatedly, "You didn't know about this?" he said prodding at the story. It was on the bottom half of the front page, a picture of Rory looked back at him. The face was serious, set.

Rory linked his hands together, feeding his fingers through and pushing down, getting to his feet. "I'll tell you how it happened, just calm down would you? I'll put on some coffee." He went to pass Dave and Dave put out his arm to stop him.

"I don't want your god-damned coffee- I want you to tell me what the hell you were thinking."

There was another knock on the door. This time it was quieter and only brief. They both turned.

"That'll be Jimmy. I rang him when I saw this, he's real pissed too."

Rory sighed and walked back towards the front door.

Opening it he considered Jimmy's expression. It was filled more with apology than accusation.

"What's up Rory? Sorry to barge in on you," he said looking past him at Dave's angry shape. "Oh. I hoped to get here first."

"Come on in, join the party," he said and ushered him inside.

"Alright Dave?"

"Jimmy."

"I'm gonna put on a pot of coffee," Rory said, striding past Dave, giving him a wider birth. He went into the kitchenette, filled the kettle and flicked the switch. His head was spinning. This was not what he needed.

"This is a fuckin' joke ay?" he heard Dave complaining to Jimmy. Jimmy shrugged, sat down on the single chair. Rory came back into the room.

"Do youse want a cup?"

Dave shook his head irritably.

"Yeah, nice one, sweet," said Jimmy.

"Before we have a tea party are you gonna tell us what the fuck you were thinking?"

Rory's patience was wearing thin, both his voice and face hardening, "I get that you're pissed. You too Jimmy. I'm sorry, I wasn't looking for all this. It was the only way they'd let me talk to the girl who was attacked and got away."

"Fucksake. You must really think you're god-damned Philip Marlowe. Or Matt Scudder more appropriately. When are you gonna see sense?"

"I'm getting a bit fucked off with your tone. You're not my keeper David, you're not bloody mother." He ran a hand through his hair as the kettle whistled in the background. "Let's all sit down and I'll tell you about it."

Dave stayed where he was, the tension in his body like an aura surrounding him. "You knew how much I needed this job. Fucksake Rory. I'm all but shit broke. And here's you runnin' your mouth off on the front cover of the god-damned Post. You've pissed away any hope of us making this job now."

"No, now hold on a second. That's bullshit anway, the job's not dead. What I did is because I'm worried about Alice. I cared about her. *Care* about her," he corrected. "And I'd do the same for the either of you."

"I wouldn't god-damned want you to. Next time I go on a fishing weekend and neglect to tell ya, I don't want you going to the press and saying I've been chopped up and fed to the mackerel."

Rory shook his head, beginning to really seethe.

"You're quiet for a change Jimmy," said Dave, turning to him, "What've you gotta say about all of this?"

Jimmy was in mid process of building a roll up. His eyes widened and he dry swallowed.

"Well uh… I mean… I'd prefer not to have this happen of course. but this is where shit is at I guess. I understand how it's happened, hear him out."

"Fucksake- I should have known you'd side with him, spineless." Dave said harshly. "You've got no balls. I told you before..."

"Ease off him," Rory warned.

Dave went on, "… here's you getting pissed on by your best buddy Rory and you say nothing. How'd you ever survive on the streets? I swear I'm blacker than you."

"Hey- quit it with that shit!" Jimmy said hopping up. His glasses quivered on his nose as he did so. "I'm fuckin' sick of it." Dave didn't flinch- his stocky frame dwarfing Jimmy's.

"It's the truth."

Rory strode across, "Fuck up with that bollox Dave, I mean it," he said, stopping inches from his face.

"Get out of my god-damned face!" Dave snarled, shoving Rory in the chest.

All at once, Rory pulled back before releasing a sharp right hook into Dave's face. It pummelled into his right cheek, the noise making a deep crack. Dave's head snapped back, his cheek scarlet. He eyeballed Rory for a moment, his right hand rolled into a fist. Rory stood tall, rubbing his swelling fist in his hand.

"Fuck you two, I'm done with ya both."

He turned and stomped back towards the door, pulled it open and strode away.

CHAPTER 41

"Can you believe that prick?"

"I know… Fucksake, lemme get us that coffee," Rory said, massaging his reddened hand.

Jimmy sat back down on the sofa, agitated, then lit up his smoke.

"Jesus. What a way to start the fuckin' day, like," Rory shouted in from the kitchen.

"Yeah," said Jimmy absently. Then he got up and came over to the kitchenette, "Hey man I'm sorry on us… like bustin' in on you. This is bullshit."

"It's not your fault Jimmy," he said stirring a cup heavily with a table spoon. "Hell- I'm sorry I hadn't said to you, Jim. It all happened late last night, I just came home to sleep a couple hours. Genuinely like- I didn't expect… that." He said, gesturing to the newspaper lying crumpled on the floor.

"I know it Rory- you a good guy. Shit- I mean it's not ideal man, but I know you know it too. You're just lookin' out for Alice." A dusting of ash blew onto his lens. He pulled off his glasses and rubbed them clean. Rory thought to himself how younger he looked without his glasses. Like a boy.

Rory handed him a steaming cup. "And Jimmy- don't listen to any of that shit Dave spouts about you not being black enough or whatever crap he says."

They walked back into the main part of the room and sat down.

"Yeah I know," he said setting his cup down, then flicking a stray piece of ash off of his rolly. "Still pisses me off though. I don't know what his problem is."

"Neither do I. Fuck 'em."

Jimmy shrugged.

"And I'll make good on my promise- I still wanna do this job. I already got one other guy lined up- just need one more now- that's all. We can still do it. You and me are tight on jobs, we just need someone for extra muscle."

"Alright Rory, man- you I know I always got your back." His face grew more worried, "But what about this story? I don't mean for the job. Aren't ya worried?"

"What d'ya mean?"

"I'm talkin' about this killer."

"You believe me then, that it's him?"

"Yeah, I guess I do. But that's not what I'm worried about. Are you not setting yourself up as a target? From the Killer?"

Rory set down his coffee and lit up his first smoke of the day. It tasted terrible.

"Yeah. I suppose I might be. I hadn't really thought about it that way."

…

Rory was alone again after an hour or so. The city was heating up and so was his apartment. He had another coffee and downed a pint of water. He wore an old lumberjack shirt loose over his T-shirt. He checked in the mirror that it concealed the '38 in his shoulder holster. It felt strange wearing it. He hadn't worn one for a very long time. He set off down the street. Hot and stifling as usual. He passed by the nearby Drugstore and Italian café' down the block. Couples sat drinking coffees over newspapers. He felt all eyes on him. He knew it was stupid, but he felt dozens of sets of eyes on him at once. He supposed a few of them might actually have been. The gun chafed against his already perspiring torso. A few streets before the subway he paused at the curb of the sidewalk as a grey sedan sat there idling. All at once the back door swung out and hands were on him and pulling him inside. As he was dragged into the back, he was pulled right off his feet. Then the doors slammed shut and the car accelerated and tore off through the traffic.

"What the fuck?" Rory shouted as he found his balance again, half seated, then pulled himself free and sat back against the leather. He took in the scene. Rory didn't recognise the man up front with the square jaw and matching shoulders. But he knew the man who had grappled him into the back seat. DI Richmond.

"I guess you're something of a celebrity now Rory," he said, turning towards Rory as he lit up a cigarette. His voice was cold, his expression sullen.

"Go fuck yourself Richmond- dragging me off the street like that? What the fuck?"

"No, you fuck *your*- self!" he raged suddenly, pointing in Rory's face.

Rory looked down at his shirt suddenly, checking that his piece wasn't showing.

"What do you want?" Rory said, keeping his voice even.

"Well what I would like is some jumped-up-Mick-fuck not to be whining in the press about how the NYPD won't look into his little fantasy. But I guess it's too late for that. As Mick Jagger sang, 'You don't always get what you fucking want.'"

"I don't remember that version."

"Shut up. Shut the fuck up. I oughtta slap you about some."

Rory knew he was trying to get a rise out of him. It would suit him well if Rory hit him a dig. It'd feel great, sure. But he knew what it would mean. Even if he had been picked up for no damn reason. There'd be a police record. Even troubles with immigration. And probably a beating to go along with it too.

"Get on with it then. Hit me or say whatever the fuck it is you want to say."

The big cop in the front glanced into at the rear view mirror and locked eyes with him. Then he looked away and returned to weaving through the mid morning traffic.

Richmond squashed his cigarette into a plastic tray in the side shelf. He licked his lips. "You know- I've been doing a bit of digging of my own. Digging about you Rory."

"That must have been a short dig. Did you have your wee bucket and spade?"

"Bit of a reputation back home- hadn't ya?" Richmond continued, his face hardening.

"Nope."

"Well, couple cops I spoke to from back that way would disagree with ya."

He made a show of taking out his notebook and flicking through it.

"I got places I need to be y'know," Rory said, adjusting his shirt again.

"Hold up," Richmond snarled without looking up.

"So what- this is a kidnapping?"

"Don't be such an asshole. Here we are, Yes… quite the record from back home."

"I don't have a record."

"Well you certainly have a file. Let me see now… ahh yes- suspected larceny, suspected armed robbery, connections with paramilitaries."

"Suspected."

"No smoke without fire I'd say."

Richmond was looking unhappier by the moment. The lack of concern on Rory's face appeared to be enraging him further.

They had passed the subway already and were turning out left now past a row of businesses- an attorneys, a realtors and a small restaurant. Rory sighed heavily, trying to keep calm- seeing they were heading now in the wrong direction for him getting his train.

"So am I under arrest for something or what?"

This time the driver locked eyes for a moment with Richmond before settling back on the road again.

"This is just a friendly warning Downey. You don't wanna piss off the NYPD. We've got our eye on you now- your card's marked."

"Any other clichés you'd like to share before I shoot on?"

"No- that'll do it for now you stupid Mick-fuck. I hope all your immigration papers are in order."

"Yep."

The car pulled up at a stop sign.

Rory grabbed the door handle.

"I best be off. I'm late for a booty call with your ma."

With that he pulled the handle and hopped out. He just missed Richmond lunging across the backseat towards him. Rory skipped between the traffic and joined the smattering of commuters on the other end of sidewalk. Richmond's eyes blazed as he pulled the door closed. The driver put his foot to the gas and merged into the traffic. Rory smiled at them and flipped the bird as they passed by the sidewalk.

CHAPTER 42

Now thoroughly hacked off with day, Rory doubled back and went down into the subway. He had decided to look in on Winston for a chat. Stewing as the train hammered along, he was a little calmer by the time he got to his stop. Rory felt better by the time he was stood outside the little antique shop. A hotch-potch of medals, ornaments and paintings were in the window. Behind them was Winston adjusting a pile of dusty encyclopaedias. He spotted Rory through the glass and gave a little wave. Rory told him about everything that had been happening since they had lost talked. Winston hadn't seen the paper yet. His usual calm expression changed to as close to shock as Rory had ever seen. He was nice about it all, the same as Jimmy had been. They drank coffee out the back, while one collector browsed a box of part filled stamp collections. And Winston confirmed that he was still up for being part of the job. That was the best part.

Rory's next stop was calling to see Crystal. He hammered on her door a few times to no reply. He lay down on the dirty ground outside and smoked a cigarette. It was blisteringly hot. Nobody else was about. Apart from some kind of rodent that he heard scurry beneath the front steps. He stretched out his legs, squatted into a corner and smoked another Marlborough. After about half an hour his patience was rewarded.

Crystal's wedges clip clopped up the stair-case, as she heaved two bulging netted bags of shopping. When she saw him her lips started to slip into a smile, before her mouth drooped down again. She stomped up the remaining steps, her eyes set.

"Crystal," he said, pushing himself awkwardly off the floor. "I'm really glad I caught you."

"Are you in-between photo shoots?" she said dryly, squeezing past him.

She set down her shopping and searched in her handbag for her keys.

"That's what I wanted to talk to you about. I…"

She located her key and slotted it into the lock. "I'm surprised you have the time, now that you're a what?" She paused for effect and jutted out her jaw, "A serial killer hunter?"

She lifted up her shopping and trod into her apartment.

"You could have told me that you thought that had happened to Alice first. Nice way for me to find out." she said, her back still turned.

"Crystal, listen I uh…"

The door slammed in his face.

"Fuck," he muttered to himself, "Who wants to be mad at me next?"

He pulled out his smokes and walked away.

CHAPTER 43

The Killer stood up suddenly, launching his full mug of coffee across the room. It smashed dramatically against the wall of his office, splattering the paint- the ceramic fragments scattering across the room. A brown pool formed where the main part lay on the gray carpet. He stood rigid for a moment, then remembered that neither of his employees were in yet. It wouldn't have looked well if they had been. Breathing in, he clenched his fists. He sat back down and re-read the article, seething.

Who in the hell did this Downey think he is?

He'll ruin everything.

The ignorant fool had somehow stumbled upon it all. Wretched meddling. Attention seeker.

He set the newspaper down, glanced at the mess, then took in a few deep breaths. The Killer closed his eyes, unclenched his fists. He could feel his rapid heart rate begin to slow. He picked up the newspaper again and carefully ripped out the black and white picture of Rory. He folded it over twice before placing it inside his wallet.

Something needed to be done about him.

Chapter 44

Fuck it.

Rory arrived into Grogan's in the middle afternoon, world weary and in need of serious libation. He took a pint of stout, suiting the Irish environment and also meaning that he would drink slower. He always considered a few pints of Guinness as equivalent to a Sunday Roast. It was part meal, part relaxant. He smoked a few cigarettes and passed the time half watching a Gaelic match on the T.V. The pub was mostly full of old men and their faces full of worry lines. He checked his watch. It was too early yet. He fiddled with the beer mat and the cartoon on it advertising Harp Larger.

What a fucking day.

He'd been on a kind of auto pilot the day before. He'd just rolled with the punches. Until he threw one today. Maybe he'd been too rash about the interview. But it had felt right. It had seemed his only chance to make any kind of progress. Reading his books was something, but he'd no other direct links to The Killer. Rory *had* to do the interview. It was the only way he could keep on his trail. But it was true that he hadn't really thought it all through. Not fully. He hadn't thought through all of the ramifications. In a way that was out of character for him. He was used to sussing out a job, working out all the angles. But this had been different. Everything about it had made him act differently. And he should have told them all before it was published. Was it Alice who had made him act this way, so obsessively? If he was honest with himself, he didn't think so. Yes, he cared for her, and that was what had started it all off. But really it was something else too. A puzzle? A mystery? Or maybe it was just a distraction. A distraction from his troubled life. Or it was just the flawed way he was. A life that had been torn apart back in Ireland and that he had tried to mend here in *The New World*. But maybe he'd just been kidding himself all along. Maybe everything was nothing more than that anyway. One big joke.

He went up and ordered a Jameson and shared a few words with the bar man. He was already roasting and that warmed him further. He didn't want to get too much of a buzz on. He wasn't in the form for it. He knew it would just make him more miserable. Stepping back outside, he searched out any shaded areas on the sidewalk and headed off to find something to eat. He killed a little time in a diner, had his umpteenth burger of the week and a diet soda. He actually managed to find himself unwind a little. Then he noticed a discarded edition of today's paper. Finally he sat and actually read the full article. He was surprised that he wasn't horrified by it. It wasn't particularly sensationalist and he thought he was presented fairly. *Don't Come Around Here No More* was playing on the radio. Against his usual preferences, he kind of liked that song. He was a minor fan of early Tom Petty, but didn't care much for the more recent and polished singles. There was something of the unashamed *poppyness*, mixed with the Eurythmics vibe and electric sitar that just worked. But he wouldn't have admitted it to many people.

Soon enough and he was once again in Vicki's office as arranged.

"Well Rory- I think we made quite a splash," she said sitting opposite him with a coquettish grin. "We've ruffled a few feathers for sure."

"Don't I know it."

"Oh?"

"No, nothing."

"I've had the NYPD Media Relations guys on for much of the day."

"Not very happy campers?"

"You bet. Not one bit."

"At least they'll maybe start taking the whole story more seriously."

"Yeah, maybe," she said brusquely, "Now, about this meeting I've arranged for you."

She ripped a page from a purple notebook and passed it across the desk. Rory turned the page to face him.

"My contact as far as you're concerned is called Susan."

"Ok," Rory said slowly.

"Yes, she doesn't want to give out her real name. She… em doesn't want the police involved."

"How come?"

Vicki licked her lips.

"Well, she doesn't want it advertised, but she has an involvement, well with some activity that isn't let's say… quite legal."

"Oh right. Drugs?"

Vicki locked her fingers, regarding Rory thoughtfully. "Yes. She's not a big player or anything. She does a little dealing. College stuff. But even so- the NYPD aren't on her Christmas Card list."

"Yeah I can imagine," Rory said lighting up a Marlborough Red. "Neither are we."

"So, she's only up for meeting you this one time. Eight o'clock tonight at 'Bongo Fury' in The Village. Do you know it? It's a music club."

"Yeah, don't think I've been in, but I know it."

Rory looked down at the piece of paper. There was nothing else but those few details on it.

"How will I know her?"

Vicki gave a sharp little laugh, like the bark from a small dog. "Oh, she'll recognise you- after today."

"Oh yeah, 'course."

"We have had to pay… a certain fee for her meeting you tonight. So, I hope you'll agree that I've upheld my end of the deal? There won't be anything else. I mean… it's just a one time thing. Of course, I'll be pleased to hear from you again if there's anything substantial later for a follow up piece."

"Yeah, I get it. Thank you. I appreciate it."

"Okay, well good luck with everything," she said standing and offering her hand.

They shook, before Rory took the elevator down and then crossed the reception area. He gripped the sheet, a pleasant feeling of excited nervousness within him. Pushing the glass front door open, he instantly recognised the outline of the figure standing with his back to him, smoking. The man turned. Detective Kelly.

"Rory, fancy seeing you here."

"Imagine," Rory said, moving to walk past him.

"Hold up a minute will ya?"

Rory stopped, stepping to the side to let the steady stream of pedestrians room to pass by. The glare of the late afternoon New York sun surrounding him was almost too much.

"I've already had a *friendly* chat with your bud today."

"Yeah I heard."

"I'm sure you're sad you missed out on."

"Listen Rory, my partner's a prick sometimes. I know it. But he's a good cop. A decent guy."

"Is he now?"

"Yeah, but like I say he's also an asshole at times."

"Yeah I agree there."

"Lemme buy you a drink. Have a talk. My partner's wrong about you. He's wrong about this case- because there is one. I can help you. We can help each other."

Rory sighed, kicked at the sidewalk kerb.

"Alright, seeing as you're buying."

CHAPTER 45

Kelly set two pints of Guinness down in front of them, with two Bushmills chasers. He'd taken them to an Irish pub a few blocks away.

"Well at least you know how to order a drink."

They were silent for a moment. Sting's new single *Englishman in New York* played quietly in the background. "Close, but not close enough," Rory said under his btreath.

"What's that?"

"It's nothing. Cheers for the drinks."

He shrugged casually. "Did your meeting go well?" Kelly asked, his face open.

Rory raised an eyebrow, "Fine thanks."

"Good," Kelly said with a benevolent smirk.

"What is it you want to talk about exactly?"

"I'll be straight with you Rory. It's about your meeting… and the one you've arranged next."

"What're you talking about?"

Rory lit up a cigarette and Kelly followed suit. Their tobacco trails wisped off and joined the mist hanging over the rest of the bar.

"C'mon Rory. Don't you think I've a couple journalists I feed stories to once in a while? Don't you suppose they tell me things too?"

Kelly took a long drag on his smoke. Rory shrugged and had a first taste of his whiskey. It was good.

"I know you had an arrangement for that story. In exchange, you get to meet with the witness- the lady who says she got attacked."

"Maybe that's right, maybe it isn't. What does it matter to you anyway?"

Kelly squinted, took a first pull on his own whiskey. "This girl, she's never come to us. She hasn't reported it. That's odd. Very strange. If it's genuine then why wouldn't she want to talk to us? My guess would be she's on the game."

"Or dealing some drugs?"

Kelly broke into a smile, "Is that right?"

"Could be," Rory said, stubbing out his smoke and lighting another.

"You see? We can help each other out me and you."

"And how would you help me?"

"Well for a start I'd keep Richmond off your back."

"Big deal."

"Okay, don't go getting worked up," Kelly said with his easy manner, "That's just for starters. I wanna find this guy. I want to nail this fucker," he said leaning closer, his face earnest, "We'll get him together Rory."

Rory bit his lip, leaned back and reached for a fresh cigarette.

"Okay, I mean… sure. I'm up for sharing information if you like. I wanna know what happened to Alice. I think that plaque was for her." Rory's eyes glazed for a moment and he supped a little more whiskey. "That's why I came to you lot in the first place. But there's not much more I can tell you at the minute."

"You could take me along to visit the girl."

"What?"

"Yeah. You could take me with you."

"I haven't even said there *is* a girl."

"C'mon Rory, you don't have to fuck around with me. You're going to meet her later. Let's work together. I know you're probably into some other shit from time to time. I know you're not exactly on the straight and narrow. But I also don't care about that. Not right now anyhow. I think you seem a decent fella, I can see you've nothing to gain by sticking your neck out over this. You're just trying to find your friend."

Rory listened, smoking silently. He found himself beginning to nod in agreement.

"Lemme get us another pint."

Rory used the time at the bar to think. He blocked out the noise of the several tables of drinkers. He ignored the gruff commentators talking over the football on the big screen. He let his mind tick over as the cloudy stout began to settle. By the time the barmaid had topped it up and formed the head, he'd made up his mind.

Back at the table, Rory set down the pint with another chaser.

"Jesus. I mustn't be as Irish as I thought I was. It's barely even dinner time- I'm still on duty."

"Maybe you don't always stick to the straight and narrow yourself."

Kelly cracked a smile. Rory sunk the rest of his first pint and Kelly did the same.

"So, do we have a deal?"

"One thing. What the hell do I say to the girl if I turn up with you? She said no cops."

"Tell her I'm your brother." He said with a wink.

"With different accents?"

"I don't know- tell her I'm your boyfriend. This is the eighties after all."

"Christ."

They shared a chuckle and Rory lit a cigarette, before lighting one for Kelly.

"I suppose I could say you're my cousin. There for moral support."

"That'll work."

CHAPTER 46

Rory was beginning to feel the effects of the early evening drinks and suggested they order some food. Kelly agreed, the drinks had been loosening him up too. The conversation had begun as guarded, but then slipped into easy and natural. It was as if these two men had sized each other up like fighters in the ring, and concluded that the other one wasn't so bad. After a helping of sausage, champ and gravy each, Kelly drove them across town to Queens. He found a disabled spot ten minutes walk from the club and displayed his police vehicle papers in the window.

"Might save me a ticket," he said shrugging as they got out of the car.

"Bloody cops," Rory said with a wink.

They walked along the sidewalk together. The evening was still bright and hot.

"So, how's that reading of yours going?"

It took Rory a second to comprehend.

"Oh that- yeah. Alright I suppose. It helps me get over when it's too hot to sleep."

"Anything interesting?"

"Well I'm not sure if *interesting* is the right word. It was certainly enlightening. I had no idea how many of these crazy fucks are out there."

"Yeah 'fraid so. World's a crazy place. A box of frogs."

They carried on in step together until the end of the block and paused at the Walk/ Don't Walk.

"But yeah, I suppose I found some of it interesting. Maybe it gives me an idea of the kind of guy this bastard is. Or might be. I dunno, I'm just an ordinary fella, I didn't go to university or anything." He shrugged uncomfortably.

They strolled on to the next block. "Yeah well, diplomas can be overrated," Kelly said, "I can see you've got something better than that; instincts. You can't teach that in school."

"Well, I dunno. Maybe. Anyway- I'm afraid I didn't have any revelations. The Jack The Ripper book was intense. I'd no idea what a sick fuck he was. One thing I noticed was it's the hundredth anniversary of the murders next year." He gestured with a hand, "Don't suppose that has anything to do with things. It just caught my eye."

Kelly pursed his lips, raised an eyebrow, "You never know. That's the shit thing 'bout being a cop sometimes. You might have all the information in front of you, it's the working out what's the minute, yet crucial part. The rest is just a crock of shit."

There was a friendly hubbub outside of the club. A green canopy hung out from the red brick of the building. Tables were set up underneath, full of drinkers. There was a steady stream of patrons coming in and out of the door.

"How the fuck are we gonna spot her here? Rory said.

"C'mon let's go in and see," said Kelly striding on out in front.

Inside wasn't just as busy as Rory had expected. There were a few empty tables. The club was large, with a dance floor in front of the stage, the bar at the side and a big seating area off from it. On the stage was a charismatic female singer with black wavy hair. She was backed by two seated acoustic guitarists. Kelly gestured the universal sign for a drink and Rory nodded. Rory commandeered a table, near to the side of the stage. He smoked in silence, his eyes searching for any flicker of recognition from anyone else. It was a few minutes later and they were halfway through their first round when she suddenly appeared at their table. Brown hair dyed darker, denims and a pretty, strong jawed face.

"Hello Rory, I'm Sharon."

"I thought it was Susan."

"Whatever."

"Please, take a seat."

She eyed Kelly with suspicion.

"Who's this guy?" She said frowning, shuffling into a chair.

"It's just my cousin. He holds my hand sometimes. 'Specially when I'm meeting serial killer victims."

She weighed it up. "Okay, I suppose," she said awkwardly slipping her hands underneath her thighs. She stared at them both, who eyes as wide and questioning as a child's.

"Lemme get us all some drinks," said Kelly.

"Vodka on the rocks with a twist please," she said.

"Coming up."

Rory and her talked for a few minutes. They passed the time well enough, before commenting a little on Vicki (She said that Vicki was a ruthless viper disguised in a power suit. Rory said that she might be right) and their respective newspaper articles. Then Kelly her drink and another round for Rory and him. Rory's head was starting to swim again with both the volume of drinks that day and the gravity of the situation.

Sharon, or Susan, took a drink of her vodka, her eyes watering as she did so. She looked down at the table, before her heavily made up eye lids flicked up again, setting on Rory.

"So, what d'ya wanna know exactly?" She gave a little cough. Her accent was broad and high pitched Brooklyn. It went right through him. Rory tried not to show it, she seemed like an alright girl.

"Well," Rory started, shifting in his seat, turning the leg of his chair towards her, "Just what happened, I mean... as much as you want to say, no pressure," he said. He suddenly felt as if he'd just paid a prostitute and asked for something off menu.

Kelly kept in the background but smiled encouragingly at her. She told them how The Killer had stopped her to ask for directions, then was acting weirder and weirder. That she tried to leave and there was a chase, how he'd pulled a gun and she'd barely gotten away. As she spoke, she appeared five years younger, with a much softer and less assured voice. Rory and Kelly both listened to her attentively, sitting forwards. Rory's knee jostled. All three smoked; the wisps appearing to join together to create a little cloud over the table. The trio on the stage were performing a stripped back and almost gothic version of In a *Gadda Da Vida.*

"Have you any idea where he came from that night? Like what way he came?" Rory asked.

"Not really. He said his car was down at the bottom, that he was just after some directions."

"Did you get much of a look at the car?" Kelly asked.

"No, I never saw it. Soon as he made to grab me, I screamed and ran for it."

"What did he look like?" Rory asked suddenly, his expression sober.

She gave an almost undetectable shiver. "Well er… he was tall, shortish dark hair, maybe in his forties. But the thing that stands out…"

"His eyes right?" Rory said, interrupting.

"Yes, right," she said slowly. Then she nodded in recognition. "They gave me the creeps. More than anything else."

"Cold and staring?"

"Yeah," she said reaching for her drink, her hand with a slight quiver, "I don't know, they seemed to almost hang out of his face. And that face- God, it was like old rubber."

"That's him," Rory declared, running his tongue over his top lip, "That's the fucking guy."

Kelly gave a brief nod, hooded his eyes for a moment. "What about his voice? What did it sound like?"

"Oh yeah, I didn't say. His voice was kinda weird. It didn't sound local. I mean- not even really American. There was a twang there, but I'd say, I don't know- maybe part British?"

"Okay, great, thank you," Rory said when they were starting to finish up. If nothing else, it had been worth it just for that. It *had* been the same guy- nobody could doubt it now. And the accent- that was something new- something he hadn't known.

She downed the rest of her drink before lighting another cigarette.

Kelly looked thoughtful, "Is there anything else you can tell us? Anything at all? It might help."

Rory gave him a sardonic look as if to say 'less of the cop stuff.'

She thought about the question, looking up towards the dim spotlights on the cream ceiling. "I don't know. Maybe one other thing- he had a strange run. I mean he was runnin' after me- but it was as if one leg was bigger than the other."

Rory nodded, smiling. "No doubt about it- that's him."

CHAPTER 47

Rory arrived home around eleven, exhausted. It'd been a hell of a day. He met a few residents he knew on the stairs and they muttered a hello to each other. A last straggler was leaving his neighbour's apartment and he stopped and chatted with them both for a few minutes. He was relieved that they didn't mention the article. Though he thought that the visitor gave him a look of recognition. Back inside his own apartment, he felt relief. It was hot and musty inside, but still he was glad to be home. On his rush to get out that morning, he hadn't opened any windows, not even onto the latch. He opened the windows now in the living room and his bedroom. He stripped off his clothes and threw on a white vest with his boxers. He let the tap run in the kitchenette and downed two pints of water. Hopefully that would stave off the hangover, maybe even just a little. He'd stayed for another drink with Kelly after Sharon had left. They had agreed it'd been worth while and Kelly said he'd keep in touch. The drink had been one too many. That and the anxiety around it all had left Rory feeling antsy and a little queasy. He couldn't face the subway after turning down a lift from Kelly. After walking a block he'd hailed a cab outside a Seven Eleven. The driver hadn't taken the piss with his route and he'd got home nice and quickly. He relieved himself in the bathroom, brushed his teeth, then switched off all the lights, except the lamp in his bedroom. Laying down on top of the sheets, they felt warm but comfortable. He pushed the window open a little further and picked up one of his True Crime books. There was the distant sound of conversation from the street below. It wasn't intrusive, it was quite soothing. He could also hear the faint sound of Bill Withers pounding the keys from beyond the wall. Lee must have been listening to a side of something before bed. At least he had good taste in music. Rory tried for a moment to think what the track was called- but he couldn't remember. Something off his first album he thought- some sort of modal jazz played by the piano trio. Rory never felt of himself as particularly lonely, but it was nice to hear music and voices from the apartments around him just the same. After a few minutes Rory realised he couldn't concentrate on the pages and his eyes were crossing. He set the book down on the floor and turned off the lights. It felt like it might take a long time to get over, but within five minutes he was fast asleep.

Awake.

Consciousness flooded back to him.

Rory opened his eyes and everything seemed much as it had been. He was still lying above the sheets. There was the same amount of light creeping in through his curtains from the street light outside, though the quiet chatter had gone. Bill Evans had also called it quits for the night.

How long was I asleep? Maybe a couple of hours.

But there was something else.

Or there had been. Something had made him stir.

He heard a creak then from the living room. He instantly placed it as being the sound of the wooden window frame. Then he doubted himself. Was he imagining things? But his heart began to quicken and he felt immediately alert, primed. There was a much greater feeling too: fear.

He eased himself upright. There was another faint noise from beyond the bedroom wall.

Footsteps? Fuck.

He gently placed his bare feet down onto the floor. Noiselessly, he padded across the room, putting his ear to the door. He had been sweating in his sleep. Beads of perspiration were across his face. His clammy feet pulled fibres of the old carpet to their soles.

Nothing.

Maybe he had been imagining things? Had he dreamed it?

Then another creak.

Jesus Christ.

He hadn't been imagining it. He sensed someone was there. And he knew who that someone was. Maybe that part was only his imagination, but all the same he was certain that on the other side of that door was something terrible, something evil. The Killer had come for him.

Urgently his eyes searched the room for something to use to protect himself, anything.

His gun?

Shit.

It was in the other room under his shirt.

What else was there? No baseball bat, nothing large. Nothing to swing.

Only the guitar. Howlin' Wolf's guitar.

"Sorry Chester," he thought to himself. He whipped it up from where it was carefully balanced between the small bookcase and the wall. He swivelled it in his hands, holding it aloft by the neck. The polished hollowed body sparkled for a moment in the moonlight.

Another creak, closer.

As an afterthought Rory silently moved back to the bed, put the guitar down, then placed his pillows under the covers to resemble a sleeping body. He picked the guitar up again and hid behind where the door would swing out to.

Rory tried to steady his breathing, tried to breathe noiselessly. He hoped that the thudding in his chest couldn't be heard outside his body. In his ears there was a sound like crashing waves. He kept his nerve.

Then the line of the light around the door darkened. Shadows moved underneath the doorway. His eyes didn't want to believe it as the handle moved down, forcing a soft click. Then the door began to swing out. He pressed his sweaty back against the cool wall and his sweaty hands gripped the neck of the guitar. The door opened fully, casting new shadows across the room. Then an outstretched gun appeared; a black handled Glock with a silencer screwed onto the end. The intruder stepped one foot into the room and Rory could see the outline of the face.

It was him; The Killer.

His heavy-lidded eyes gleamed. Rory almost leaped into the air as all at once the gun smoked with a stifled roar and a *pft, pft* came from the pillows. At least Rory's little rouse had worked. The Killer stepped fully into the room now, his face almost at right angles to Rory's.

He took another step.

Rory swung the big guitar like a bulking baseball bat. It crashed into the gun, flinging it across the room. Much of the huge f-holed body cracked across The Killer's arm, forcing out a strangled yelp. Rory jabbed him in the ribs with the headstock, using the continued momentum. Already off balance, The Killer fell backwards onto the floor. Rory heaved the guitar up again, then swung it down towards the intruder. The Killer rolled away from the bed, the guitar crashing against the floor; the bridge splitting and strings snapping in all directions. He threw the instrument half-heartedly towards The Killer and pushed off his heels to the side, striding on through the doorway. The Killer was scrambling to his feet as Rory raced across the living room floor. He flailed at the chair where he had thrown his clothes and clawed to find the gun. The only thing on Rory's mind now; getting that weapon.

Kill the fucker. End this tonight.

That's all he wanted to do. It was all so clear. *The Killer* had to be killed. Alice was certainly dead. None of this would bring her back. It wasn't about that any longer. Whether The Killer had come looking for him or not, this was already about needing to stop him. And about revenge.

Rory freed his six shooter from its holster and clicked off the safety. As he turned to look back at the bedroom, The Killer appeared in the doorway, framed in darkness. He aimed steadily at Rory, closing one of his bulging eyes. Rory dived across the room, over the sofa, as the muffled crack of three bullets thudded into the fabric. Rory leaned around the side, aimed and returned a volley of two shots. His unmuffled revolver sounded like an explosion in the silence of the heavy night. They went wide, piercing the thin sheet rock of his bedroom wall. The Killer ducked down and crawled behind a chair.

Silence.

Only for a few seconds.

A thin swirl of smoke hung in the air, leaving the unmistakable smell of cordite. Following the pounding of Rory's two shots seemed to make the silence even greater.

Rory peered over the top of the sofa, unable to see where The Killer was exactly. He glanced towards the outside door behind him, unsure what to do next.

Make a run for it?

Or make a run at him?

He'd four more bullets. He might get lucky or at least make more noise. Surely someone would call the cops. Rory reached around the side and aimed the gun at the centre of the chair. He pulled the trigger. The dark serenity was shattered once more as the bullet tore through the middle of the chair. He didn't think he hit him. He could hear The Killer scraping around the floor behind, trying to stay covered. He was filled with terror that he would rise up suddenly, marching forwards, firing off rounds. Then Rory would be a sitting duck.

Then suddenly there was a different sound. Another hammering. But at the door behind him

"Rory! Rory- you alright man?"

It was Lee from next door, beating hard on the door.

Rory changed position, down on his honkers, weighing it up.

"Lee!" he shouted, "Call the cops- he's in here!"

Then The Killer was on his feet again. He squeezed off two rounds, whizzing past Rory's head, one of them shattering the window with an almighty crash of glass. Then he knelt back down again. Taking the chance, Rory half stood now himself, moving backwards towards the door, keeping low. He slipped a hand behind him to release the lock. The Killer began to stand up again as Rory fired off his last shot, just going wide. The Killer crawled back for cover. Rory turned and flung the door open. In the door jamb was a very anxious but determined looking Lee, stood holding a shotgun.

"You alright?"

"The guy in there- it's him- he tried to fuckin' kill me," Rory gasped.

The Killer was on his feet again, moving out from beside the chair. In what seemed like one movement, Lee nudged Rory to the side and cocked his shotgun. Then he aimed and plunged off both barrels. If Rory's gun had been loud, this sounded like a Panther Tank was in the room. The bullets took a chunk out of the back wall, glasses and crockery smashing from the ricochet, plaster crumbling from the wall. The Killer had ducked out of the way now. Now he swivelled and directed his long frame back towards the bedroom door. Lee took a few steps into the room and fired another brace off at the retreating figure, who was disappearing back into the bedroom. Rory's bedroom door took a hit, as did an old watercolour on the wall. Lee kept going, cocking the gun again. Rory fell in step beside him as they jogged across to the bedroom door. They got there just in time to see the flapping of the Killer's long coat as he scrambled off down the outside fire escape.

"Police! Stay where you are!"

Rory and Lee spun around to find two cops rushing in the front door, guns drawn.

"Drop your weapons- now! Put your hands in the air!"

They both looked down at their guns with shock as if the guns had appeared out of nowhere. They dropped them and did as they were told.

"Put your hands behind your backs," commanded the second cop as he and his partner moved closer, one gun aimed at each of them. With a swift and practiced action, they each holstered their weapons before whipping out cuffs and clasping them on tightly each to Rory and Lee.

"He's getting away! The guy you want just jumped out the window," Rory panted, gritting his teeth as his arms were pulled awkwardly behind him.

"You Rory Downey?" said the first cop."

"Yeah?"

"Then we've got who we wanted."

"What the fuck?"

"I saw him too… man- son of a bitch just hopped down the fire escape," broke in Lee.

"Shut the fuck up," said the second cop, grabbing him by the chain of the cuffs and spinning him around.

The first cop did the same with Rory. "Rory Downey, I am arresting you on suspicion of murder and kidnapping. You have the right to remain silent. You have the right to an attorney…"

"What the hell? Hold off! Who am I meant to have murdered?"

"Shannon Carter. You were with her earlier tonight."

Rory's head swam. Surely this was all just a horrific nightmare.

Shannon Carter? Was that Susan or whatever she said her name was?

"Shot dead in her apartment," added the second cop, in between chewing on a large whack of gum.

"After her killer left she wasn't quite dead yet. We found her on the floor, poor fuck. She'd pulled open a newspaper and left her bloody finger pointed at a picture. A photograph of you."

CHAPTER 48

"This is bullshit."

The balding detective with the bulging and sweat-stained blue shirt shrugged.

"I don't know what to tell ya kid."

"Tell me you're gonna get me a lawyer then," Rory said, trying to keep his voice low and controlled.

"It's four a.m. son, I mean, even the rats are asleep. Lawyers, rats," he shrugged again, "What's the difference?"

Rory had talked through everything that had happened three times to the detective and his partner. His impression was that neither of them cared much for the night shift or for getting started on a complicated case. But he also sensed that they might believe him. They were at the nearest precinct, Rory and Lee had been taken their in their cuffs, processed and tossed in separate interview rooms. Rory had gone over and over every detail. What he hadn't got was much of an explanation on what had happened to Shannon Carter. He hadn't got much of an explanation about anything. The second detective was presently off in search of three more crappy cups of coffee.

"Where's Lee? What's any of this have to do with him?" Rory said rubbing a clammy hand through his now greasy hair.

"Well now," the detective continued in his broad Queens accent, "Your fella there was found spraying bullets all around the place. With a shotgun no less. And this is after us sending out uniforms to bring you in on a murder rap. He don't even have a licence for it. So, we've a bit more talkin' to do I think. It don't look good does it? I'll go check on those coffees, have another cigarette if you want to," he said, transporting his bulky frame through the door. Rory rubbed a hand over his jiggling knees before stifling a yawn. He fiddled with the cigarette carton for a moment before fishing one out and lighting it.

What a fucking day.

He didn't know what to feel about any of it. The here and now was filled with the necessity of having to convince them that he hadn't killed Shannon Carter. And to believe him about what happened at his own apartment. That could wait until after. He'd do nobody any good locked up on murder charge. Not that he thought there was anything substantial against him. But that hadn't stopped many a police department before.

And what did he think about the attack at his apartment?

Relief. For a start.

He had come through it. Part of him had been ready to accept death. Not to invite it, he was just prepared. He knew it'd have to come to us all some time and really it hadn't felt so bad. Maybe the adrenalin and serotonin had helped. But now, sitting in a stifling and foul smelling interview room in the middle of the night, things didn't feel quite so great. Or Rory wasn't feeling quite as accepting of them, such as they were. Another emotion bubbling away in the vat inside him; disappointment. Again he was face to face with The Killer. But again, he had gotten away unscathed. Rory vowed there wouldn't be a third time. He smoked at the cigarette, feeling pure frustration. Every part of him felt agitated. And what else did he feel? Fear? He certainly had back at his apartment. What about now?

Yeah, maybe.

Rory might have been too tired to know. He kept thinking about Crystal. He didn't know why. Just kept picturing her face. Was he worried that she could be in danger too? He didn't know. He didn't think she should be.

The door opened and the same detective put down a coffee in a foam cup down in front of him. A cigarette dangled out the side of his mouth.

"Don't know where my prick partner got to, here ya go. But I ran into these two guys, think you all know one another."

Richmond stepped in to the room, his clothes ruffled, his eyes red pin pricks. 'Like two piss-holes in the snow', his father would have called them. Kelly shuffled in behind him, looking even more dishevelled. His hair stood off to one side. He glanced at Rory, then his eyes settled on nowhere in particular. The detective closed the door behind him and the two arrivals took a seat.

"Well you're harder to get rid of than *the clap* aren't you Rory?" said Richmond, flinging his coat over the back of a chair. Rory rolled his eyes. The two sat down heavily and the other detective left, closing the door shut. Rory chewed on his lip, then busied himself picking up his coffee. Steam poured off the top, he blew on it, but it was too hot to drink. No point in getting scolded by third rate coffee. He plucked out yet another cigarette. His throat was dry and sore, but he lit it anyway. Richmond and Kelly did likewise.

"You had any sleep?" asked Kelly.

"None."

"Something to eat?"

"Nope."

"I'll talk to the desk sergeant after- get us all something."

"Okay you two, dinner arrangements can wait," broke in Richmond, "So Rory," he said leaning back in the uncomfortable blue plastic chair, "This time you and some spook go shooting up your apartment block, is that it?"

Rory glanced at Kelly, then turned to Richmond, "I don't know what the fuck it's gonna take for you to take this seriously. And enough of the racist shit. That guy saved my life. What is it you guys want? Has the killer got to bust in here with a knife to your wife's throat?"

"Easy Irish," warned Richmond, his jaw hard, "Let's not get personal."

"This all feels pretty fucking personal to me."

"And what about this er... Shannon Carter," he said looking down at a print out sheet, "Did you kill her?"

"Of course I fucking didn't."

"Well that here's what you would say, ain't it?" he said smiling at Kelly, as if sharing a private joke. Kelly met his partner's eyes with a blank expression.

"Why the fuck would I kill her? I just met her. She was meant to help me find the killer."

"Oh yeah, *The Killer*. Jesus. And what about the other guy you were with? Seems you were spotted with someone else in the bar."

Rory swallowed, took another long drag on his smoke. He daren't look towards Kelly.

"What d'ya mean, there was no other guy."

Now he did look at Kelly for a moment. Kelly took out a slim black comb and began passively fixing his unruly hair.

"You were seen with a guy."

"I don't know what to tell ya. The place was busy- there were lots of folks around. I spoke to a few people, others sat by our table," Rory shrugged, "I met her alone. Then she left. And I didn't fucking kill her."

Richmond blew out a plume of smoke and gave a Kelly a 'can you believe this guy?' look.

"For God's sake- the killer was in my apartment tonight. He tried to fucking kill me!"

"Says you."

"Yes says me. Lee'll tell you too. He's just my next door neighbour- he's got no axe to grand! He came in just at the right time- like I said- probably saved my life."

"The big nigger? Sure, whatever."

Kelly put a hand on Richmond's arm, he shook his head.

"Enough of the *spook* and *nigger* shit. Christ." Rory said, disgust on his face.

Richmond rolled his eyes. The PC Brigade is it? Alright then I'll focus on you, ya dirty fuckin' Mick bastard. Is that any better? You fuckin' cocksuckers getting me out of my bed in the middle of the night."

Rory sat back, rubbing his hands over themselves, restraining his temper. He knew if he lost he wouldn't be getting out of a cell anytime soon. Richmond was working himself up, whether through tiredness or frustration.

"C'mon, take a break," said Kelly turning to him, "Get us both another cup of Joe will ya?" His eyes were sharp, his voice solid. Richmond chewed it over, then grudgingly accepted the advice and left.

"Jesus- that guy is some piece of shit."

"He was out of line," Kelly said leaning forwards, slipping his comb back into his shirt pocket.

"Some fuckin' shitstorm I've fell into alright."

"Listen, I uh… I appreciate your not saying anything. You didn't have to cover for me."

Rory shrugged. "Kelly- I reckon you're a decent cop. Hell, maybe even a decent guy. I've no reason to make any shit for you. That guy- I'd chuck him under a bus- gladly."

"Well I appreciate it anyway," he repeated, his eyes glazed over, staring at the many cracks on the back wall. "So tell me about it, you've had some fuckin' night."

"I went to bed- not long after we spoke to…" Rory trailed off, "Hell- I can't believe she's dead."

Kelly shook his head. "I know. The bastard. Carry on Rory."

"Surely you've already got all this from the desk sergeant?"

"Aye, but it's better hearing it from you."

"Okay," Rory sighed, exhaustion now almost taking him over fully, "So something wakes me up- I guess it was him slipping through my living room window. I just felt it- I knew it was him."

"Our guy."

"Yeah. The only thing I can think of defending myself with is a guitar I got in my room."

Rory paused- suddenly thinking about how he's attacked the killer with a bloody priceless stolen guitar. That might be another problem.

Chalk it up.

"So I hide behind the door and he comes bustin' in with his gun and I whack it out of his hand."

"Shit."

"Yeah- that bit felt good."

They shared a smile.

"He spilled the gun and I ran in next door and grabbed my gun and all of a sudden it's like an episode of Bonanza or some shit."

"You got a licence for the gun?"

"Yeah I got one."

"Good. Shame about your buddy."

"Tell me about it. He busts in and scares him away good and proper. Now he'll be sure of a big fine and what? A suspended sentence if he's lucky?"

"Yeah, I guess so."

"Shit."

"Oh, about the guitar."

Fuck.

"You got away with it."

"Huh?"

"Just a few broken strings and bridge apparently. Must be a queer steady neck on it."

"Oh, right… happy days. Tell me- what happened to Sharon… or whatever her real name is."

Kelly's jaw tightened and his eyes grew sad. "Terrible thing. Not such a steady neck on her, sadly."

"Strangled?"

"Yeah. In her apartment. She was still in bed. Probably still asleep too before he put his hands around her."

"That's probably what he had in mind for me too. No chance to wake up."

"Exactly. Seems she had been dead an hour or two before he came to get you, so the doctor says. 'Course they'll need to be an autopsy. Boyfriend came off of a night shift and found her that way."

"Fuck. So is your partner now gonna take this all a little more seriously?"

"I can't speak for him. But sure as hell the department has to. They mightn't say they're chasing a serial killer but they've got one murder now and one attempted." Kelly fiddled with his gold plated lighter for a moment, "Only you also gotta remember that we got close to fifty murders a week in this town. That and a thousand less cops on the streets than we had ten years ago. I don't know. Like rearranging deck chairs on Titanic some days. I don't know. This guy- he's what we call an E.D.P by my reckoning. An *emotionally disturbed person*. I guess so anyways. More and more of these bastards out there all the time. Much of the time they're pretty smart. They might be mad, but they're not like *Looney Tunes* mad."

"Christ." Rory lit up another cigarette, reflecting on all that Kelly had just said. "It's not really in keeping with what we know about him is it? Or what we think we know anyway."

"How do you mean?"

"Well- if he's killed all these girls and left plaques and shit- he's gone to an awful lot of trouble before getting rid of the bodies. This time it looks like he went in to kill, then get the hell out of there."

"Yeah, you're right," Kelly said dragging a tired hand across his face, stifling a yawn, "Only I think this wasn't part of his plan. Not his original one anyways. If he's got one. This was out of necessity."

"He needed to take out the only two people who've seen his face."

"That's my take on it."

Just then the door swung open and Richmond appeared in the doorway. His face was gray and drawn. He gave the slightest of nods as his eyes ran over Rory, then they settled on Kelly.

"We got a… situation. Come out here for a second will ya Michael?"

Part 3

No Place to Go

CHAPTER 49

Rory was left alone. Alone with his thoughts. Alone with all of his many fears.

How the hell did I get into all of this?

Rory swung back on his chair, then leaned forward again, scraping his finger aimlessly over the worn table.

What's happening out there?

He clock watched. Nothing else to do. There was an ancient plastic thing on the wall, that lazily dragged the minute hand from dash to dash. He tried to reflect on the last day, the last night, even the last half hour. It was impossible. He couldn't make sense out of any of it. He was exhausted. There was no chance of gaining any perspective yet. He just needed to baton down and get through this next part, as best he could, whatever might come. He knew he had done nothing wrong and that would have to be enough. *Nothing wrong*; he smiled ruefully. Images flashed through his mind; Alice, Crystal, The Killer. He must ring Crystal again. He didn't like the way he had left things with her. Jimmy too- he would have to catch him up with it all. What about Dave?

Dave could go fuck himself.

Thirty six minutes later and the door thankfully reopened, bringing with it the sounds of an urgent hullabaloo from beyond. Kelly slipped in alone and closed the door behind him. He bounced up and down on his heels. There was an odd expression on his face, somewhere between happiness and horror.

"What the fuck- what's going on now?" Rory said, bolting upright.

"Jesus, this thing keeps getting more fucked up, I tell ya."

Kelly threw himself down into a chair and loaded up a fresh cigarette. "Son-of-a-bitch got to Vicki Gibson too."

"Shit, she's dead?" Rory said pausing; halfway through lighting his own cigarette.

"No- thank God. She's next door right now," Kelly added gesturing his thumb to the right wall. "Girl she lives with found her- she's been at the ER this last hour. Now she's here talkin' to us."

"What's she say?"

"Shit like you wouldn't believe Rory," Kelly said, his eyes wide. "Seems our friend broke into her place, shoved a hood over her head and tied her up. She didn't take too much convincing to let him on her computer and get your address."

"And Sharon's too."

"Yeah."

"Then what? He just got up and left?"

"Yeah, that's the kicker," Kelly said, excitedly sitting forward. "Why's he leave her alive?"

Rory held his cigarette and scratched his head absently with his other. "He knew killing a well known journalist would bring a lot more heat?"

"Yeah, maybe."

The cigarette smoke in the stuffy humid room now was heavy.

"What're you thinking?"

"A pattern Rory, I think he's got a pattern. You ever read Red Dragon? Hannibal Lecter and all that gruesome shit. Killer in that- fella has a pattern. Yeah he might kill other people sometimes outside of that- but not often. He'd no reason to kill her really"

"So he took what he needed and then there was no reason to finish her off. Maybe he wants her to keep writing stories too. But he needed to take us two out. That's why he wasn't worried about leaving bodies, just shooting us and leaving us where we were. We weren't part of whatever he's got going on, just two loose ends."

"Exactly. We've got him rattled. *You've* got him rattled."

"You think you can sell that angle to your partner?"

"Not a chance."

Chapter 50

The Killer tried not to slam his front door against the worn wooden frame as he strode inside. He hadn't been able to concentrate on work. He hadn't slept much the night before by the time he had crawled into bed. There were enough workers in anyway, better if he got offside. He had been close to losing his temper a number of times with them. He knew they all viewed him as some kind of oddball, but that was one thing. He didn't like showing flashes of what was underneath the surface. It was his own damn company alone now, so he could do whatever he liked.

He went through to the kitchen. It was at the far side of the house. Sometimes it was hateful living on the same site as his business. In many other ways it was essential. Anyhow, he felt the need for solitude right then, to be away from any disturbances. He sat down at the old wooden kitchen table as the kettle boiled. His awkward frame slumped over it. He had hardly changed any of his furniture since his parents had died. He had never found any of it comfortable then and he certainly didn't now. He poured the boiled water over a fresh tea bags in the stained pot and returned to his chair.

That fool. That stupid idiot. Fucking Irish simpleton.

He slammed his large hand down on the table. He clenched his yellowed teeth. The Killer mulled it all over. At least it had gone smoothly enough with the two women. But that Downey- the jammy bastard had some how managed to get away. He had a fool's luck alright. It wasn't even down to him. That big nigger had saved him. Stupid. Stupid that these idiots could spoil things. He got up and finished making his tea, fishing out the tea bags. It was almost as stewed as he was. He drank down a cup, sitting there rigid, tense all over. The sunlight cut in through the back window over the unkempt back yard. He got up and pulled the blinds across. The Killer reached for his keys, then unlocked the basement door and tramped downstairs. He unlocked the second door and stepped in. Inside was darkness and an acrid smell of bleach masking something altogether worse. He had changed the sheets and cleaned the room thoroughly since Alice had been there. He sat down on the edge of the bed. He rubbed at his temples. What would the newspapers write now? More speculation, more melodrama. It wasn't meat to get to this level yet. There was still work to do. It all had been so smooth, but now the engine was running off the tracks.

But the plan couldn't be derailed for anyone or anything. He still needed to take one more girl. Getting back to his work, would make him feel better. One more for now anyway.

CHAPTER 51

A cop car took Rory back to his apartment. It was almost half ten in the morning by the time they made it there. Rory'd been up for going on thirty hours. The beat cop opened up the temporary padlock on his front door and waited while Rory grabbed a few things. Inside was a shit-show. It still stank of cordite above the usual stale tobacco. There was furniture scattered everywhere. He gazed at the bullet holes in the walls and furniture and shook his head. The cop walked about whistling and shaking his head at the state of the place. Throwing a few things in a hold-all, Rory reflected that it was just as well he never kept anything *hot* in his apartment. Nothing except the *Wolf* guitar. Now he picked it up from where it had been placed on the kitchen surface. Not in bad shape at all. He thanked the cop and the guy nodded and padlocked the front back up before padding off in search of his breakfast. Rory turned and stood facing Lee's door, he gave it a rap. He had apparently been released a few hours earlier and Rory hoped that he was home. The door opened slowly and Lee appeared in the doorway wearing blue jeans and a black t-shirt.

"What up Rory? You another white boy you need me to plug a few rounds after?" he said with a wry smile.

Rory grinned, "Lee- you alright man? I'm so sorry about last night."

"Come on in bro."

Lee brought him inside. His apartment was a mirror image of Rory's. But it was neater, cleaner and there was an absence of bullet holes. Lee made them some coffees and they sat down on his black leather sofa. He put on a Donald Byrd 'cool jazz' LP on the turntable.

"Man, what's your apartment like? Cops have been there on and off the last couple hours."

"It's pretty messed up, I won't be staying there for a while."

"You need a place to stay bro?"

"No, no- you've done enough Lee. I'm crashin' at a friend's across town, don't worry, but thank you. And listen, I really appreciate what you did last night."

"It was nothin."

"It weren't nothin'. You damn sure saved my neck. It's pure shit they got a rap on you for your gun. I'm sorry for that."

"It ain't your fault I got no licence," he said sipping his coffee.

"Well it's my fault you got caught with it. I'm gonna pay whatever fine you get- it's the least I can do."

"No man, there no need."

"No honestly, you gotta let me pay it."

"No man," Lee said, his face determined, "I'm a proud motherfucker, it was my own fault."

"Shit, I feel real bad about it all."

"So what's the story. Is this whitey actually a fuckin' serial killer?"

Rory gave him the detail of everything that had happened over the past few weeks. The cops hadn't told him about Vicki and Rory explained all of that side of it too.

"Damn!" Lee said, breaking into a chuckle, "I sure did make that serial killin' son-of-a-bitch go runnin.'"

"You did man! You looked like a badass."

"Haha, god-damn."

Rory finished the last of his coffee, mulling things over.

"Listen, you can obviously handle yourself Lee. You won't take my money this way. What if there was a way you get work for it. And get a big chunk more with it?"

Lee clicked his tongue, "Alright man, I'm listening."

"It all depends how comfortable you'd be with… well… working outside of what's quite legal."

"Damn boy, that don't much bother me none."

Rory smiled, "Well I've been looking out for one more guy for a job."

"I'm always up for subsidising the personal training- this city ain't cheap to live in. Tell me 'bout it."

Rory took a yellow cab over to Jimmy's place. He was feeling better, despite his exhaustion. Lee had agreed to take the job. He was a solid guy and it'd make Rory feel better about the gun rap too. If he had Jimmy, Winston and Lee all in, he could still make the job work. It if all went off okay, he'd be set up at least for the rest of the year. Then he could get the hell out of the city. He was done with it.

Rory tipped the surly, chain smoking driver a few dollars and heaved his stuff onto the sidewalk. Jimmy's place was another old brownstone, in need of an overhaul, much like his own place. He'd been outside a number of times before, dropping Jimmy off, but he'd actually never been inside. Jimmy appeared at the main door as Rory gathered up his stuff. He ran over to him.

"Yo man, lemme help ya with that shit."

"Cheers Jim, good to see my man- it's been a very long fuckin' night."

Jimmy's eyes were full of concern behind his thick lenses. He leaned over and gave Rory a quick hug.

"Damn son- you gotta be more careful."

"I intend to be. Appreciate you takin' me in buddy."

"Not a problem."

They gathered up the small pile of Rory's things, Jimmy giving a high pitched whistle when he saw the tangle of strings hanging off the guitar. There was a working elevator in the building, which was already a step up from Rory's digs. And the inside of the building was less dilapidated than Rory's. They arrived at the door to Jimmy's place on the second floor. Jimmy turned the lock and they heaved the stuff inside.

"Holy Shit Jimmy," Rory said as he took in the apartment.

It wasn't much bigger than Rory's, with a similar kitchen/ diner, one bedroom and bathroom lay out. But it looked to Rory like something you'd see in an interiors magazine. The walls were painted a dark navy and there were black and white jazz prints on the walls. It was lit by a cluster of dim lamps on tables around leather sofas. In the corner was a huge television set with a massive back on it. Stylish wooden blinds hung on the windows.

"My God- this is such a cool pad."

"Cheers brother."

They set the stuff down on the hard wood floor.

"Seriously- this is sweet. You're a dark horse."

"I never wanted to bring Dave in here- he'd start all that 'you've got it easy- you're barely even black' routine."

"Fuck Dave, man," Rory said slapping him on the back and they both broke into laughter.

"Sit-down-, take a weight off man."

"I'm pretty beat for sure," he said, easing into a spongy brown leather sofa.

"Yeah man- you been up like goin' on two days. Hows about I fix us some rashers of bacon and toast? Get you some coffee?"

"Man, you've never gonna get rid of me outta here." He closed his eyes.

Jimmy set about getting organised in the kitchen. Before he'd even heated the pan, Rory was already fast asleep.

CHAPTER 52

Rory spent the next few days, keeping a low profile. From the morning afterwards, the story had gone colossal. 'The Couplet Killer' goings on were splashed across the front page of every newspaper in the city. The picture of Rory had been reproduced a number of times too. Vicki had even managed to get herself together and to write a personal feature for *The Post*. It gained them their biggest sales since The Mob Trial. The TV stations had then followed the smell of easy money too. They had been staking out his apartment and calling up his friends. Thankfully they hadn't known about Jimmy. There might weekly be a new 'big story' in the city, but for now this was it. Rory went out a few times, mostly just for some fresh air, though Jimmy had an actual working air-con. The apartment in all ways was much nicer to hole up in than his own ever was. He regretted going out almost every time- clocking people recognising him. Before it had been mostly in his head, but now it was for real. A couple of times strangers even approached him and tried to ask him about it all. On these occasions Rory mumbled something, shrank into himself and scurried away back to Jimmy's apartment. He watched crappy day time T.V and tried to keep the drinking to a minimum. It felt like a very strange period. He tried to make notes from his books and work on the job, but it was hard. For the rest of the week there were features everywhere on the story. Once the initial boom covering the night of the murder, the kidnapping and attempted murder had passed; journalists scrambled to keep it from fading. There were relatives of those involved interviewed, former school principals, co-workers. One story even involved a psychic who made various unsubstantiated and fairly wild claims. They even had got hold of a school friend of Rory's still living in Belfast. Rory barely remembered the guy though he had made it sound as if they were blood brothers. By the end of the week it also seemed like every family in New York had a missing relative who they thought had been taken by 'The Couplet Killer.' Rory found the whole thing incredibly uncomfortable. It made his skin crawl. After a few days he just had to stop reading about it. It was too much to process. He wanted none of it. Jimmy was out a lot with family and friends, going for drinks, shooting hoops. Rory hadn't realised how sociable he was. When he was there he was good to Rory, he had really come through for him. When he was out, it gave Rory time to re-group, to hide away, and to re-charge his well worn batteries. He thought a lot about Crystal and if he should call her. She'd seemed majorly pissed with him before and had made it pretty clear that she didn't want to see him. He guessed he'd fucked that one up rightly. The cops called hauled in a few more times, and now things were less frosty. He met with detectives who were part of the wider team, he wondered if it had been too much for Richmond to try to play civil. It was still unclear how much they linked it altogether and how much they believed it was all just one killer. They certainly said very little to the press, despite the pressure on them. As time went on, the intensity of the coverage faded and Rory's will to try and get back to something more normal increased.

Kelly invited him out for a coffee. They sat for two hours talking about the case. They didn't come up with much, but they both felt better for it. Kelly had been side-lined, but it didn't seem to bother him any. Rory also called the first meeting for the job including Lee and Winston. It'd gone well. Jimmy had hosted. Lee had called over a few times since the attack to meet up with Rory and had got to know Jimmy better. Lee even got Jimmy out running with him a few times.

About a week before the night of the job, they all met up again; this time at Lee's place. It felt strange to Rory to be back in his building. It had only been a few weeks, but it might well have been years. He wondered when he would want to return to his apartment, or if ever would. His landlord had been decent about it and wasn't charging him any rent while the apartment was repaired and redecorated. Rory felt in no rush. They had ordered in Chinese food and were all having a few beers. The atmosphere was easy, as if they all were old friends. At one point Rory speared a piece of his Chicken Chow Mein and looked around the room, thinking about just that. They were such a mix. Rory an Irish immigrant, Jimmy a middle class safe cracker, Lee a wiry personal trainer. And then there was Winston- decades older than any of them, sitting in his suit with a napkin carefully placed across his knees. And yet it was working. He'd particularly worried about how Winston and Lee would integrate into the group. But it worked fine, they all got along. Before their take out, they had gone over the plan once again. Rory was satisfied that everyone knew their part and how it fitted in with the rest. He was confident that they each could handle it. It was like they were preparing for an Off Broadway production, rather than a heist. It struck him how much better things were now that Dave wasn't about with his awkwardness and bad temper. And he felt a little bad that he didn't miss him in the slightest.

"You gonna eat that or just torture it a little?" Lee said, breaking Rory out of his thoughts.

Rory laughed. "If it repeats on me tomorrow I know who to send round to get me my money back."

"Lemme get a licence sorted first."

They cleared the table of plates and empty cartons of food. Lee tipped most of it into a big rubbish bag and dumped it in the corner.

"That can be sorted later. I'll brew us some coffee- you gonna make a wee number?" he called across to Jimmy.

"I can arrange that," he replied.

The four of them sat around the table as the daylight started to fade, sipping their coffees. Jimmy passed the joint on to Lee, who took a hit before offering it on to Rory. Rory narrowed his eyes on the number.

"Fuck it," he said, accepting it and filling his cheeks with smoke. He didn't smoke weed much, it didn't always agree with him.

He went to pass it back to Jimmy.

"What about me?" drawled Winston, his face filled with a dramatic frown.

Rory smirked, his eyes watery, "You want this?"

"Yeah, why not?"

Rory raised an eyebrow and passed it to him. Jimmy and Lee looked on, grinning.

Winston inhaled causally.

They all waited for him to splutter. Instead he swallowed most of the smoke down, then blew out a thin brown wisp.

"You gotta remember I hit my prime in the fifties and sixties. The shit we had then would flatten you three. I did a lot of reefer in my time."

They all fell about laughing.

"More coffee?" said Lee getting up.

"Hell, I reckon so," said Jimmy.

Just then there was a loud banging from outside in the hall. It sounded like somebody was pounding on Rory's apartment door. They all froze for a moment. Rory darted across the room and slipped on his jacket to cover up his now ever present Glock.

The banging hammered outside again. A neighbour somewhere shouted "keep it down out there!"

Jimmy, Lee and Winston all got to their feet too.

Rory put one hand in his inside pocket, while leaning in behind the door.

He opened it a crack.

When he saw who it was he audibly breathed out and naturally broke into a smile. He turned to everyone in the room, "It's all okay, back in a second," then he slipped out of the room.

"Crystal," he said softly, coming up behind her.

She had still been focused on hammering on the door, "Jesus!" she shouted, bobbing on her heels, spinning around. "Rory!"

She flung her arms around him and kissed him hard on the cheek. "You're okay, thank God."

"Yeah, I'm fine, I'm fine, what're you doing here?"

"Looking for you, ya dumb-ass, damn- I've been so worried. I been coming here every few days."

She hugged him again and Rory put his arms around her in return. He was reminded of her beautiful face, her toned, yet soft body. The familiarity of her perfume was comforting.

"I'm sorry, I shoulda called. But you were so pissed at me. I'm sorry for that too."

She straightened herself up. She was wearing a smart casual gray trouser suit. She corrected her handbag where it had become tangled below her shoulder. She took a step back and assessed Rory's appearance.

"You looking well- I'm glad you're okay. You had me real scared."

"I'm fine. Crystal- you look great. I'm sorry again for what happened. I didn't know if you'd want me to call again, then I had all this grief from the cops, the press…"

"Don't worry Rory." She wrinkled her nose, then cocked her head, "You'll smokin' weed in there?"

Rory shrugged, smiling. His eyes were a little dilated and his smile a little bit goofy.

She returned the smile with change, "You coulda just come round mine to do that."

CHAPTER 53

Rory was led by the hand into Crystal's bedroom. In the yellow cab across town they had talked quietly to each other in the back seat and held hands. He had already had a small buzz on from the smoke of the joint and the few drinks. Now he went into the dimly lit room and lay down on the bed. She went to the door and shut it tight. The room was hot. A very light breeze came in from the open window, along with the familiar hum of the city beyond. Crystal smiled coquettishly as she unbuttoned her blouse. She threw it onto the floor, leaving only a light pink bra on top. She unfastened her trousers and let them drop.

"I've never been with a celebrity before," she said with a girlish giggle.

She climbed onto the bed and straddled Rory, placing her full, warm lips onto his. Rory grabbed her close to him, overcome with desire. She bit at his mouth and he responded by nibbling at her neck, his hands squeezing her full breasts. Soon they were both naked, both hungry. Rory pushed her firmly onto the bed and climbed above her. As he pushed himself inside her, she dug her nails into the small of his back.

After a second time, they both lay back, exhausted, spent. Rory couldn't remember the last time he had felt so good, happy even. She smiled at him widely and kissed him on the cheek.

"Will I make us a little smoke?" she asked.

"Why not?"

Rory released a satisfied yawn as he stretched and lay his head on the pilow. He watched her toned, caramel coloured body reach out of the covers and lift her tobacco tin and rolling papers from the bedside table. She sat up against the headboard, placing a hardback book on her knees and began to roll up. The bed covers slipped just below her breasts.

"Whoops," she said, pulling them back up.

"It's alright, I don't mind."

"You think you're some sort of player now Irish boy?" she teased.

"Well, you know."

"Took me to bed, a bona fide A-lister tonight."

Rory guffawed, "That's me."

They enjoyed a comfortable silence as she finished rolling.

"You smoke much Rory?"

"Just cigarettes usually. I took an inkling tonight."

"You could say you've had a stressful few weeks."

"Ain't that the truth."

She narrowed her eyes as she lit the number up. The window blinds streaked stripes across her body. Rory felt a desire to remember everything about this moment.

"But seriously, are you doing okay Rory?"

"I am now."

Rory sat up and they smoked the joint, then had another. They talked about everything; the recent weeks, old stories, snippets from their childhoods. He looked at her like some exotic creature. They didn't have women like this back home. Yeah they didn't have black women, but not just that. She was something so alien to him, and so intriguing. He realised how much she had been at the back of his mind through everything. He had wanted to see her, to make things right. He just hadn't. God, he felt dumb.

They lay back together and Crystal cuddled into him. After a minute or so she asked,

"But really, you're alright Rory? I was so worried."

"Yeah- I'm pretty great," he said smiling, turning his head and kissing her head. "I'm sorry that you were, truly."

"I mean with everything that's happened."

He blew out his cheeks, "Well yeah- that's been something else. Hell- I don't know."

"What was he like?" she asked quietly, "Were you scared?"

"I was shitting myself," he said with a short laugh.

"It must have been horrible," she said rubbing his leg softly.

"Yeah, it was. And what was he like? Honestly? He was fucking terrifying. I've never seen anyone like him."

"Poor baby."

She hugged him tighter.

"Don't you worry though. It's all gonna be fine."

He didn't really believe it. It might have been the dope, but his brain seemed to have all but shut down. There was a pleasant tingling through his body. He couldn't focus and he didn't know how he really expected things would end up. All he knew was that he wanted to stop this guy. He had to. He was set on a particular path and he didn't have the desire or maybe the where with all to plot a different course.

"Alice is dead, isn't she?" she asked in a whisper.

"Yeah, I think she is. I'm sorry. I'm so sorry." He said, absently taking her hand and stroking it inside his own.

She nodded.

Her eyes were filled with sadness. He stroked them closed, then kissed her gently on the forehead.

Soon they were both asleep. Or at least Rory had entered a *kind* of sleep. His body was crying out for rest. But his mind didn't want to quite let go yet. He entered a strange and cloudy dream state. He was lost down some annoymous foggy and cobbled street. It seemed to be London, not that he had ever been there. The mist eased and revealed a figure towards the end of the dark alley. The figure held a knife at his side dripping with blood. Rory locked eyes with him. The eyes were those of The Killer. All at once the figure began racing towards him in a blur. Rory couldn't move. He stood planted to the ground in terror as the figure ran at him with the knife. It came down.

"Rory, Rory! You okay?"

He jolted upright, dripping in sweat.

"Baby, you were crying out."

"Shit, I'm sorry," Rory said with a mixture of embarrassment and disorientation.

"It's okay." She rubbed his back for a moment, then switched on the lamp.

Rory was glad of the break in the darkness.

Jesus.

He looked at the alarm clock on the bedside table- it was only one a.m.

"Fuck," he said, running a hand through his wet hair.

"I'll make us a smoke," she said, propping herself up and pulling on a vest.

Rory sat up too, rubbing at his eyes. He could tell that his subconscious had been working overtime. Not just the dream, but generally. Many a time he would wake up tired, but would have better clarity about something- usually a part of a job that he hadn't been able to fit a part together to yet. There was something in the back reaches of his mind now. But it was like trying to hold onto running water.

Rory glanced at the book she was using to roll up on, 'The Vulture.'

"Is it any good?"

"Oh- this. Yeah it's cool y'a know. I've just started it. I love Gill Scott Heron's music."

"Yeah, me too. The records were hard to get hold of back home, but I had a couple."

"I saw him when I was, like, seventeen. In the city. Man, he was so cool."

"I'm sure."

There was a heavy pause.

"Was it a nightmare about… him?" she asked before licking the cigarette paper.

"Em… sort of. I dunno- it was weird."

She nodded and lit up the number. Her face was serious.

"The whole things scares me, y'a know? I don't like that you're so involved with it all. Pease be careful."

"I know. Me too, but there's no getting away from it all now."

"No, I guess not," she said, passing the joint.

Rory considered it for a moment, then accepting it took a long drag. He passed it back.

He took in a sharp intake, then exhaled a flurry of brown. "It's the not knowing what he's gonna do next. I've seen him twice now, hell, I've shot a gun at him. But I've no way of tracking him, getting inside his head. I need a thread to pull on. He's gotta be stopped."

"There don't seem no pattern. How many's it been- five plaques, so five girls?" She shivered, "It's so horrible."

Rory stared blankly at her for a moment. He narrowed his eyes. Then he folded his arms.

"I wonder."

"What?"

He stared off into space a moment. "It's only been four plaques so far. But maybe he wants to hit five this year. I don't know- it's probably stupid- but I keep thinking about Jack The Ripper."

"I'm not passing you back this doobie. You're already too high."

"No, seriously. I don't know- I think our guy wants to link with him in some way, like he's his … I don't know- hero, role model? There were at least five that Jack murdered."

"Role model for serial killers?" She sniggered, then passed him the J.

"I don't really know Crystal. I've been reading a lot of books about serial killers and there's just something that seems to resonate about Jack The Ripper. I'm not sure, maybe it's daft."

"Like a copycat?"

"Yeah, sort of. It's been one hundred years next since the Whitechapel Murders next year."

"You think he's getting a head start on the anniversary?"

"Yeah- well maybe actually. Or he's building up to something even worse."

CHAPTER 54

Rory got over to sleep about half an hour later. They both slept soundly until Crystal had to get up for work at half seven. They had an easy breakfast together and Crystal kissed him warmly goodbye. Rory left shortly after. Outside was already warming up. The sky was clear of clouds and the many towering buildings looked off-white and grey in the unhindered morning light. The grime that was hidden during the night was now on display for all to see. Rory stopped at the first coin box he came to and dialled up Kelly. He said he'd been thinking on a few things about the case and asked was he free to meet. Kelly said to give him an hour and they settled on a Turkish coffee shop off 7th avenue. Rory took his time taking the subway across town, stopping first for a fresh carton of smokes and a bacon wrap. When he made it there, Kelly was already seated with a steaming cup of coffee and a newly lit cigarette. They chatted at a table by the window. The street outside was busy, Midtown employees on their coffee break or on an early lunch. Kelly watched the street; his eyes always observing, searching. Rory told him about his ideas about The Killer. Kelly listened attentively, nodding. He finished a small helping of pancakes and syrup and wiped at his mouth with a napkin.

"Could be something in that Rory, I sure as heck don't know what this son-of-a-bitch is at, I surely don't. You might be right. But I think you've actually hit on something more important than that." He pushed his plate to the side and lit up a new cigarette, sitting back and crossing his legs. "I think what you're doing is you're starting to try and get inside of him. Inside his head."

"Yeah, it does feel that way," Rory said. He took a sip of his coffee, registering how good it tasted. Then he lit up a cigarette, breathing out slowly. "Y'know, even just seeing him those two times.

Maybe it's stupid- but I do feel like I know him a little bit. Christ- you only gotta see those crazed eyes once and it'll tell ya something."

Kelly nodded. "I ain't see him, but from what I do know- and when I say that it's mostly 'cause of you Rory. But what I know is, is that this guy isn't your basic nutter who kills somebody on a psycho bender. This guy has a plan. I'd swear it on the bible or any other holy book you'd care to produce. He's planning on being 'round for a while. I'm just scared he's just getting started."

Rory nodded in agreement. "And still there's no official investigation?"

Kelly shook his head, making a face.

"Not really Still nobody above's buying into the whole 'Couplet Killer angle."

"What about The Feds?"

"God, I don't know. That's above my pay grade. I'm sure there are *conversations* going on, but hell they're still tired up with The Mob trials, never mind all the other serial murderers across the country. The number of confirmed cases in this state alone would terrify you."

Rory gazed outside for a moment. A teenager skateboarded past the window in a thick leather jacket, and new Nikes, fast and confident. Rory shook his head. "Yeah, it does all scare me. This guy scares me more than anything. But…" Something was plucking away inside of Rory's head. It was like a thought was trying to pick axe its way out. "I think he's only wanting to do one more this year."

"One more. I don't know Rory, he's already killed four, five including Shannon."

"Yeah he's killed five, but I think only four are part of his, well 'system.' He only killed her 'cause he had to, same as trying to kill me. It's like we talked about before- I think he's set himself this target, there'll be a plaque for every one, then God knows what he has in plan for next year."

"You mean- like copying another killer next?"

"I dunno, maybe. Or maybe this is all just showing he can do it, look what I can do. Then next year he thinks *fuck it*, and causes as much mayhem as he possible can."

Then something clicked.

"Hold on a sec," Rory said, getting out of his seat.

He stepped across the small café to the coffee bar where a large brown skinned man was carefully slicing a fresh loaf of bread.

"Yes?" he said curtly.

"Yeah, Hi. Do you have a map of the city I could borrow?"

"We just have these." The man pulled a plastic coated map from a small white stand. "Dollar fifty."

"Yeah, okay I guess, cheers," Rory said picking out the change from his wallet and giving it to him. Then he hurried back to the table.

"Okay, this may be a long shot," Rory said folding the map out onto the table. One half contained a full map of the city. On the fourth crease on the right side was a close up of Manhattan and a diagram below of Central Park.

Kelly stubbed out his cigarette and gazed down curiously at the map.

"You… uh got a pen?" Rory said, scrutinising the map.

"Sure," said Kelly passing him a biro.

"Alright then." Rory folded the map back in half and focused in on the map of Central Park. He blinked a few times, scratched his chin, then made an x. He thought for a moment, then made another.

"This one- that's roughly where the first plaque was found? And here- that's number two."

Kelly nodded, creases appearing across his forehead. "Okay."

"And just above the lake, that was number three," he said making another mark. "And here… that's…"

"That's Alice's?" Kelly said locking eyes with him.

"Yeah."

"Okay," said Kelly, "I'm following you so far."

"Good, I'm not sure if I am. Okay, right."

"I've no clue where you're going with this." Kelly said, smiling broadly.

Rory folded the map back out to full size. He made four long slashes across the map with the pen.

"This is the fun part."

CHAPTER 55

"Well fuck me," Kelly exclaimed with a cross between a laugh and a wheeze.

"Yeah- I'm pretty stunned myself. I wasn't sure it was gonna work."

They both lit up cigarettes and stared down at the page. Rory had now put four x's on the wider map of New York too. He'd split up Central Park roughly as if it represented a map of the whole of New York. There was an x put in what could be viewed as Manhattan, Queens, Staten and Brooklyn.

"You see number four- that would make it in Queens. It matches- that's where Alice lived. It all works- as far as we know."

"So if Central Park is separated like the five boroughs, he's putting up these plaques and poems to mark where he picked up his victims?"

Rory shrugged excitedly, "Yeah… I mean- it looks that way, don't you think?"

"Well, yeah- you sure do make a good case. I don't know how it'll wash with any of my colleagues, but..." He tailed off and stared at the map in disbelief.

"We're getting closer to the motherfucker," Rory said quietly.

"So if he's murdering someone in each of the boroughs, then he's only got The Bronx left. You think that's where he'll hit?"

"Yeah, I guess. Then that'll be his five, like The Ripper's canonical five. If our theories are actually correct. God knows what he'll do after that."

Kelly licked his lips, leaning back, his eyes sparkling at Rory. "And you're what, a labourer officially- that's your job?"

Rory returned the smile, slightly hesitantly. "Officially, yeah. That's what it says on my IRS returns."

"Well as far as I'm concerned, you're damn close to a police consultant the way you're going."

"I don't reckon everyone sees it that way."

"Maybe not, but fuck 'em. You'd better find yourself a Mr Holmes. I'll organise some extra patrols round The Bronx. I don't know what sway I'll be able to get. I'm not even meant to be investigating the official murders, never mind any of this. My Chief would have canaries. But I can at least manage that."

"I just hope we're not too late."

Back out on the streets, Rory felt reenergised.

One step closer.

That's all that was ever needed. Keep stepping closer, keep moving forwards and you'd eventually get to wherever you wanted to go. He leaned against the wall outside, finding a shady spot and lit up a cigarette. Two teenagers in t-shirts and shorts paused as they were walking by. They both looked high, eyes like saucers.

"Hey- you're the serial killer chaser guy!" said the first one with a giggle.

"Aww yeah," said the second, "Poirot is in Manhattan, man! Can I've your autograph?"

Rory stepped past them, then turned back as he walked.

"You're confused. You know me from visiting your mumma sometimes."

CHAPTER 56

The Killer was waiting by the side of Henry Hudson Park. He was parked in a side street from where he could nearly view the Hudson River through the trees. He was in a long, black hearse with tinted windows. He was dressed in a black suit. It was approaching ten at night and his body was rippling with anticipation. He got quietly out of the hearse and closed the door. The road was empty and dark. There were few street lights, but there was a little additional light cast from a small apartment building across the street. The Killer walked around to the trunk and pulled the double fronted door up and let it hang there. Inside was empty- a long, bare compartment covered in blue velvet. He checked his watch.

Any minute now.

The Killer took the jack from inside the car and hooked it upon the ground towards the back of the car. He started to pump it until the hearse was pushed up a few inches off the ground. He wiped his big hands down his trousers and lapels, brushing off any dirt. He pulled out a handkerchief and rubbed his oily hands with it.

He looked over at the next parking bay. In it was the green Oldsmobile that was parked there every weekday at this time. Then came the familiar sound of heels clipping along the empty street. He had been thorough this time, particularly cautious. He bit the side of his cheek, then bent down as if examining his back tyre.

The clipping heels drew nearer.

They stopped behind him and he stood up.

"Hello, good evening," he said in his most mild mannered tone.

"Hi," the girl said hesitantly. She was in her early twenties, with long black hair and intense green eyes. She was wearing a dark skirt and a blue polo shirt with the brand of the restaurant around the corner adorned on it.

He shook his head, frowning, looking down at the hearse.

She pulled out her car keys. "Having a little car trouble?" she asked.

"Yes, I mean… I think so, does that look like a slash to you?" he asked, pointing towards the rear right tyre.

She paused a moment, dangling her keys at her side. Then she moved off on her other heel, stepping to the side of him, looking down towards the back wheel.

Suddenly he whipped up hight on his heels and socked her with a right hook to her face. She cried out and stumbled back, stunned. The Killer gripped her and pulled her off balance, swinging her towards the trunk. She began to flail, her eyes a mixture of terror and steel. He punched her again, then roughly pulled her up, dragging her inside. He climbed over her, fastening a cable tie around her wrists, then around her ankles. She began to scream, a throat shredding scream. He swiftly gagged her and pushed down the rear door shut. He had a quick glance around before hopping back into the driver's seat, gunning the engine and reversing out. He kept to all of the limits as he drove across the city, and back home.

CHAPTER 57

Two days later and Rory was on his way to meet Winston at the lock up. Now into August and the city heat was even more oppressive than ever. He stopped at a street vendor and bought a paper and a cup of coffee. The coffee was bad and the news was worse. 'The Couplet Killer' was still a big story. After a few weeks of bleeding dry the events of the night of the attack on Rory and speaking to anyone who was loosely connected; the papers were now being filled with wild speculation and 'anonymous sources.' Thankfully no one else had come to any of the conclusions and he and Kelly had drawn. If they were right, the last thing they wanted was The Killer changing tack to put them further behind. Rory rolled his eyes, leaning against the shutter of an out of business Laundromat. He flicked through to the international pages. As usual there was a feature on 'The Troubles.' In the last week there had been two bombings in Belfast and the first taxi driver had been killed- shot dead in his cab. There was an editorial about finding a way forward to some kind of peace. The only way would be through all party talks. Several American politicians had even offered to host these, to accelerate the process and probably their own careers. Ian Paisley had refused to talk with the other side, so that was that for the time being. Rory shook his head. He binned the paper, then jogged down the subway steps. He had remembered to ring his Mum a couple of days before and he made a mental note not to leave it as long. Maybe he'd go visit her when things had calmed down here.

Winston was outside the lock up when he got there. He had just filled his pipe and the sweet tobacco smell drifted towards Rory.

"That's some morning Rory."

"Too fuckin' hot for me, Winston," he said, slotting the key in the padlock. He hauled up the shutter and they stepped inside. Rory pulled the light cord and they walked around to the back of the

garage. At the front was general storage from Jimmy's contact. At the
back covered in sheets was their equipment for the job. Rory showed
Winston the various tools, the amp, the drum kit. He went over what
everything was for in fine detail.

"What about fire power- you sure you don't need any more?"

"No- the guns from The Hard Rock were never fired. They'll be
fine- no trace on any of 'em."

Winston swallowed, then nodded.

Rory put a hand on his arm for a moment, "Y'know they're just
for show don't you? I've never shot anyone, Winston. And I
wouldn't. One time I had to fire a gun on a job and that was only to
get a teller's attention. I shot it straight up into the plasterboard. I
didn't even like doing that. There's enough of that shit back home."

"Sheet-rock," Wisnton said with a wry smile.

"What? Oh- whatever. Listen- it's okay if you're a bit nervous
about it all."

"Nervous?" Winston said affronted, almost spilling the contents
of his pipe, "You were still in short pants when I was pulling jobs."

"Aye- but not usually on the front lines."

"No, but I was up to my neck in it. Don't worry about me."

"I won't. I just don't want you feeling… oh I don't know."

"Alright. Anyway- things look good here. Let's go and get a cup
of coffee and you can tell me all about your serial killer hunting, Mr
Bigshot."

"Don't think I wouldn't give you a dig old man," Rory said
pulling off the light.

"Yeah and don't think I wouldn't give you one back, and
harder."

After the coffee, Rory headed home to Lee's apartment. He
figured he'd go over the plans again while he was in the right head
space. Walking towards the big Brownstown, he clocked a familiar
figure leaning against the wall, smoking.

"Alright Rory?"

"Kelly, how's it going? How d'ya know I was here?"

"I'm a cop ain't I? Listen, something's happened, d'ya wanna go for a jar?"

They walked around the corner to a small local bar. The stout didn't look up to much so they each opted for a pint of Bud.

"Tastes like piss," said Rory taking a first sip."

"What you gonna do?"

"So, what's happened?"

Kelly took a long sip, wincing, then sighed. Rory wasn't sure if it was just the taste of the light beer.

"We think there's been another girl taken."

"Shit."

"Yeah. Her family reported her missing. A nice girl- college girl, working nights in a restaurant. Name of Shelley Beckett."

"Was it in The Bronx?"

"Yeah."

"Fuck. Fuck!"

Rory slammed his fist down onto the table, causing a few glances from the quiet locals.

"We weren't quick enough. I had more patrols out but it's like the heaviest population in the city. Would have been a needle in a haystack."

"We seem to be always one fucking step behind."

"Yeah it feels that way. There's more too. She disappeared after working a night shift. Beat cops went door to door talking to the neighbours around where she worked. There's an apartment block overlooking where her car was parked. It was still there. She never drove it home. One old lady said she thought she heard a scream. She looked out her window and saw a long black car pulling out from beside the girl's car."

"She never reported it at the time I suppose?"

"No. You know what people in this city are like. We've a hard enough problem getting folk to report gun shots."

"Christ. It's fuckin' sickening. We knew he would hit there, but we couldn't do a damn thing about it."

"I know Rory, I know."

They each lit up a cigarette.

"What about the department? What do they think now?"

"Well, like you know, there still isn't even an official serial killer investigation going on. But this is being taken seriously as suspicious. For whatever that counts."

"Well, yeah I'd fuckin' hope so, like." Rory flicked the end of cigarette irritably into an ash tray. Kelly took a longer sip of his drink. U2 came on through the stereo.

"Jesus, fuckin' 'streets have no name,' now," Rory complained under his breath.

"Aww c'mon, they're okay. Have you no kinsmanship?" Kelly asked, hoping to lighten the mood.

Rory rolled his eyes. "No, not with them- they're shite. Bono's a cocky wee bastard too." Rory's leg jiggled underneath the table, "I'm gutted. Another poor girl. Bastard."

"I know. We'll get him Rory, we will. Anyway, I'd best be getting back. I just wanted to keep you in the loop." He lifted his keys and lighter.

Rory turned to him and placed a hand on his arm. "I appreciate it Michael. I really do."

"No problem. And listen Rory, I mean what I say. We're gonna catch him. I swear to God we will."

CHAPTER 58

The Killer was at the top of his basement stairs. He had a steaming cup of tea balanced in one hand as he descended the steps. He turned the lock at the bottom, then nudged open the door with his shoulder. He walked in and set his cup down on the table.

"Whoops, thought I might spill it there," he said with an incongruous air of lightness. He was in a very good mood. His eyes fell on Shelley Beckett, strapped to the bed. Her mouth was gagged and her eyes above were unblinking and terrified.

"Don't you look simply miserable?" he said, his crooked teeth breaking through into a full smile, "Don't worry- it might never happen."

He allowed himself a little chuckle. He was enjoying himself. This capture had gone smoothly. It was the last one he needed this year. He would take his time, enjoy every minute. He slowly crossed the room and gently undid her gag, then went and sat down opposite her. Her breathing was rapid, frantic. She began to cough. She strained, unable to instinctively put a hand to her mouth. He sat watching her, his face blank, save for his wild eyes. He sipped at his tea.

She stopped hacking, then croaked, "Please… let me go- I promise I won't tell anyone."

"Shush shush," he said quietly, "Honestly, you all say that. It's getting terribly old."

"Please… I promise, I'll do anything you want."

"That's enough," he said firmly. He set his cup down, tea spilling at the side. He rubbed his hands along his trousers. He stood, pulling his hunting knife from his pocket as he did so. The light glinted off it and cast a dull glare over the bare wall for a moment. As she watched him come towards her, Shelley's whole body was racked by terror.

The Wolf is at Your Door

"Now, you just stay where you are," he said with another cruel chuckle.

CHAPTER 59

Rory stayed on in the bar long after Kelly had left. Drink after drink, he tried to silence the voices. The accusatory voices in his head that told him he was never good enough. Another girl taken, Alice gone. His own life passing him by. He had seen The Killer twice and had been unable to do anything to stop him. Before he had even come to the city he had been unable to do anything to save his girlfriend from the terrorists. What a waste of space he was. It was well into the afternoon by the time he stumbled back across to Jimmy's apartment. Jimmy was having a joint, watching a Columbo T.V movie. Rory lay down on the sofa and watched it with him, accepting a draw of the joints that Jimmy continually skinned up. He dozed on and off throughout the evening before eventually pulling the blanket over himself and slipping into a heavy sleep. There didn't seem to be any dreams willing to present themselves, only blackness. He woke up the next morning with a surprisingly mild hangover. As he waited on the coffee to brew he vowed to himself that he would take it easy on the drink, at least until the job was over with. And he would try his best to focus on that and put all the killer business to one side. The job could be a distraction and besides it was too late to put it off now.

He was successful in the drinking, but he still spent too much of his time still attempting to piece together all that he knew so far of the murders. The group met up a few more times and Rory drilled them on every aspect of the job, until they were like a well oiled theatre company, knowing their roles backwards, and each other's. Lee and Winston had slipped capably into the team and Rory felt a growing optimism about the job. At least that was something.

Finally the day of the 13th August arrived- two days before the Bingo Competition and one day until the heist. Rory spent the day checking off everything in his head and visiting the lock up, ensuring everything was ready there. He oiled the tools, loaded the weapons, filled the van with gas. Rory knew that he would need to switch off properly the night before and that there was no point in being awake worrying about it all night. He had only seen Crystal a few times over the proceeding weeks and she had invited him round for dinner. He knew it was just what he needed.

"This is seriously delish' Crystal- where'd you learn to cook like that?"

She dabbed at her mouth. "My Mumma. My Mom is a great cook- much better than me."

"I'm not sure I believe that," he said, scooping up another forkful of the rich pork casserole.

"D'you cook, Rory?"

"Aye- boiled eggs and cheese on toast. Or *grilled cheese* as you guys would say."

She smiled.

They were seated at her small dining room table. She had dressed in a tight black dress for the occasion. Candles were lit and she'd put on *Astral Weeks* by Van Morrison in the background.

"I appreciate the music too- makes a boy feel right at home."

"You're a long way from home."

"Yeah- some days it feels more so than others."

"What about today?"

"Today this is the only place I want to be."

After dinner they had coffee on the sofa. Soon they were kissing, then they progressed into the bedroom. Afterwards they lay under the sheets, Crystal running a hand absently over his chest hair. Rory felt an urge to tell her a little about the job the next day. He had alluded to a few things up until then, but she only had a very rough idea that some of his activities weren't quite legal. There would be another time to tell her about that side of his life. He put the desire to one side, not wanting to spoil the moment. He also didn't want to open up his own apprehension about the next day any further.

"How are you feeling about things baby?" she asked.

He was pulled from his revue and turned his neck to look up at her.

"About the other girl being taken?"

"Yeah- just all of it. I'm worried about you- you've taken a lot onto yourself. I'm not being funny- but it's not your responsibility."

Rory shrugged, "I don't know. I just wish we could stop this fucker."

"I know. It still feels like you're getting close."

"Painfully close. Thank God for Lee."

"I know. I'll have to meet this guy and shake his hand."

She kissed Rory on the top of his head.

"It really feels like I'm circling him, y'know? I just can't get a direct catch on him, I can't hook him, I don't know."

"I guess you were on to something with the Ripper thing. I mean- it'd be a great fat coincidence- you thinking someone would be snatched from The Bronx and then that's what happens. And of course… with Alice too."

Her eyes grew heavy and sparkled. She sat up and lifted up her rolling things.

"Do you fancy one?"

"Yeah I'll take a draw. You're gonna have me becoming a druggy."

They both smiled.

"There's too many damn people in this city. I've seen the bastard… twice. But how are we meant to find him now? He could be anywhere."

"Surely that's what the cops are there for."

They shared a wry smile.

"I dunno. There was nothing about him to give anything much away. Apart from his accent. Both Shannon and Vicki said he had an

English sound to his voice." He stared off into space for a moment, "And we have zero idea what in the hell he's doing with the bodies."

"And the girl who died- Shannon- she didn't tell you much that night first, did she?"

"No, not really."

Crystal licked the paper, then lit it up. She took a few puffs, then passed it to Rory.

"What about that old lady who thinks she saw his car? She didn't get a make or model or anything?"

"No, she only saw it for a second. But my gut tells me it *was* him. There was the scream and all. She just said it was a long black car."

"Like a limo maybe?"

"Yeah, I suppose."

"Or a hearse?"

"What?"

"A hearse."

Rory started to choke on his lungful of smoke and passed back the joint.

"A hearse?" he said again.

He sat up straight in the bed.

"Jesus, Crystal, yeah it could be. Fuck."

She put on a playful grin. "Not just a pretty face, ay?"

He kissed her hard on the lips. "You just might be a bloody genius!"

"Well, shucks." She took in a long, warm inhale of smoke.

He stared through her, his mind working overtime.

A hearse.

"A fucking undertaker- that could be how he's getting rid of the bodies."

CHAPTER 60

As Crystal fixed them some breakfast the next morning, Rory trawled through the phone book. He sat in bed smoking the first cigarette of the day. It gave him his needed nicotine hit. He'd need the coffee Crystal was brewing even more than usual. He hadn't slept as well as he had wanted, and it wasn't even from fretting about the job. They had sat up late, testing out the theory. It fitted. It fitted well with all that they knew. But again, it was just another theory.

"You're a wee star, thank you," he said as she set him down a tray in bed.

"Now don't be expecting this all the time," she said, bending down to kiss him on the head.

"Thanks," he said distractedly, "Dya know how many bloody funeral directors there are in this city? Bloody dozens upon dozens of 'em."

"Oh hell, well I suppose there's a lot of people dying all the time. Gotta do something with them. But baby, I'm sorry, I'm gonna have to run. Gonna be late for the office."

She slipped on her black heels, finishing off her smart blue dress. "Help yourself to anything, let yourself out, okay?"

"I will," he said looking up at her, "God you're gorgeous, sorry- I was zoned out there. Have a good day- I'll ring you tomorrow."

"Okay, chow baby."

Rory slurped cautiously at his scolding coffee, continuing to flick through the pages. Finally, he set it down and picked at the plate of bacon and eggs she had made him. Then the thought struck him of what a truly great girl Crystal was. Beauty, brains and caring- funny, great cook. It went on. And here was he- an Irish bum barely even paying her any attention. He needed to appreciate what he had going on with her. But he couldn't think about that now. What he really should be thinking about was the job. He pushed the tray away and started flicking between the subsections again. This time he looked specifically for crematories.

What if he's not just an undertaker? What if he works where there's an on site crematorium? Perfect was disposing of unwanted bodies.

He licked his finger then turned over another page. There it was; crematories. In the City of New York there were only five registered crematoriums. He checked his watch, bit his lip. He was due to meet Winston within the hour to go over the plans one last time. He threw on his clothes and walked out to the living room where Crystal kept her phone, carrying the book with him.

He dialled the first number.

"Hello, McCartland Funeral Director's, how may I help you?" said a young sounding female receptionist.

"Yes, hello, I was hoping for some information please," started Rory, "My Aunt is very ill and sadly I fear she has not long to go now."

"I'm very sorry to hear that sir. Let me tell you about our range of services."

Rory wasn't sure what exactly he was looking for. Hell, he didn't have anything definite that he was even on the right track. He let the very corporate young lady explain their various deals to him. It didn't sound to him the kind of place that The Killer would be working in. But what did he really know?

The next call presented him with much of the same story. This time an older man with a mid western voice talked him through what their family business could offer him. He supposed this could be the one. Maybe it could even be the guy on the phone. But the fella just didn't seem the type. That and the fact he sounded a littletoo old and the place was right in the middle of a busy shopping district. It didn't seem right.

The third call kept ringing off and he couldn't get through. The girl who answered the fourth number sounded like a carbon copy of the first. Rory patiently listened through her sales pitch. He hastily dialled the number for the fifth, not wanting to keep Winston waiting. A man answered- but it was only an answering machine message.

"Hello. You are through to Granger Funeral Services. We can't come to the phone right now, leave us a message and we'll get back to you."

The voice was quiet and hollow. The accent sounded English.

Chapter 61

On a bus across town, all Rory could think about was that voice. He swung from frustration at himself for considering anything about it, to a compulsion to immediately visit the funeral director's premises. Was he just like a school kid playing silly games with his imagination? He knew that he was obsessing and that he couldn't afford to. Not today. Maybe it was just his brain trying to distract him from the anxieties to do with the job. There was nothing for it, but to put it to one side.

He bought himself a take-out coffee on the way to the lock-up to see Winston. They looked over the equipment again and Winston demonstrated that he knew his role in detail and how he would adapt if things didn't go quite to plan. In the afternoon Jimmy and Lee joined them. They talked through everything again and went for burgers and fries in a Wendy's afterwards.

At seven o'clock they pulled up in the van outside the warehouse rehearsal space of 'Run For Covers.' The band were due to arrive with their equipment at Handy's Bar and Bingo at eight. The three members should now be inside either still practicing or packing up their equipment. Winston swapped with Lee and slipped into the driver's seat. Rory, Lee and Jimmy got out and walked towards the building, watchful as they did so. They all had on dark jackets and blue jeans. Underneath, they each wore a navy polo-neck with 'Run For Covers' stitched on the right breast. Stopping at the large metal door, Rory eyes carried out a last sweep. All was quiet. There was nobody around for at least a few hundred yards. Rory nodded to them both, then all three took out black masks and slipped them over their faces. Then they all took out a gun. Each of them held an Astra revolver- known as 'The Terminator.' They hadn't been needed during the Hard Rock heist. A previous job sourced by Winston had seen Rory steal a shipment of them as they were transported between factory and wholesalers.

The ring of an electric guitar being tuned could be heard from inside. Rory hammered on the door. The flat high E string was silenced and footsteps approached the door. As it swung backwards, Rory gave it a hard kick, and it slammed against a balding, middle aged man's face.

"Nobody fuckin' move," shouted Rory, as he stepped in to stand beside the man now on the floor. Lee and Jimmy slipped in behind him, guns raised. Inside there was a guy with long hair in his mid twenties seated at a drum kit. Lastly, a thirty-something man with short black hair stood with his hands in the air and a red Gibson SG strapped across his neck. Jimmy closed the door noiselessly behind them.

"If you cooperate with us, it'll all be okay," Rory continued.

Suddenly the man on the drum stool at the rear of the room jumped up, knocking it over, and began sprinting towards the back door. Lee clocked him first and was off on his heels and running in an instant.

"Stay where you are motherfucker!" he shouted.

The man kept going.

As he reached for the door handle, Lee grappled him around the waist and pulled him hard onto the lino floor. They landed with a thud and a groan. Rory walked over to them, while Jimmy kept his pistol trained on the other two statues. Rory looked down at the man, cocked the revolver and aimed.

"You wanna get shot? We're the fuckin' I.R.A."

Minutes later and 'Run For Covers,' were tied to one another on the floor with ropes and cable ties, unable to run anywhere. Rory nodded around at the room, happy that all was as it should be.

"Now, you three sit tight and in a couple hours you'll be out of here, okay?"

The three gagged heads nodded in unison.

"We gotta turn the lights off on the way out, so I hope none of y'all are afraid of the dark," added Lee.

They pulled the doors shut before hopping back into the van. Winston immediately started the engine and they all eagerly pulled off their masks, their faces dripping with sweat.

"We in the I.R.A now bro?" said Jimmy with a chuckle.

"Well, y'know- I thought they needed a bit of a scare."

"The drummer near god-damned shit his pants," added Lee.

They all laughed nervously except Winston, who's eyes were set. He gripped the wheel hard and pulled out, handling the van smoothly around the corner and out into the early evening traffic. Then the inside of the van quietened down and the other three men each lit up a cigarette.

"Is everyone all good?" Rory asked when they were around five minutes away from the venue.

They all nodded. "Yes sir," said Winston, his grip more relaxed on the wheel now. Travelling along East 77th, he pulled up a block down.

"Okay fellas, I'll see you in a little bit," Winston said, checking his watch before getting out of the driver's door. Lee slid over, checked the mirror, then drove them in silence the rest of the way. Winston gave them a little salute as they sped away. Lee turned off along the back of York Avenue and found a space close to the mall end. If all went according to plan, that's where they would be finishing up, along with all of the cash. Lee killed the engine and then the lights. The mal, now closed for the night, was dimly lit from the rear. The small car park only had three or four cars left inside it. Nobody was around on foot and the street beyond was very quiet.

"Right, off I go then. No more dieting from tomorrow. Good luck guys," said Jimmy climbing into the back. Rory lifted the cover off one of the large wooden cabinet speakers. They had hollowed this one out and it was where Jimmy now squeezed inside and huddled himself into a ball. Rory fitted the cover back on, clicking the clasps into places over a plastic lip on each side. Lee came around the side and handed Rory a baseball cap. Now they both sported a black 'Run for Covers' cap.

"You okay in there Jim?" Rory said, a half grin on his mouth.

"Snug. As a bug," came a muffled voice from inside. Lee let out a cackle and slapped Rory on the back.

They started with the drum kit first. Taking as much of it as they could manage each, they made their way down to the side of the building and up the alleyway. They then had to carry the equipment up the outside winding metal staircase. When they got to the top, Rory hammered on the door. After a few seconds, a forty something, bulky and gray haired security guard answered the door. He wore a walkie talkie and a gun. He also wore a scowl.

"Yeah?" he said sourly.

"Hi, we're in the band," Rory said in a friendly voice, attempting his best mid-American accent. He gestured to his cap.

"Alright. How many of you are there?"

"Just us two tonight. We gotta load in, then I'll stay on a do a bit of a sound check."

"Alright then," he said still deadpan, moving to the side.

Rory and Lee struggled inside, hawking a bass drum, floor tom and several cymbals and stands. They set them down n the middle of the room.

A second security guard approached them then, walking across from the long bar. He was at least fifteen years younger than the other one, also with a walkie talkie and side arm.

"Evening fellas."

"Alright? How you doin'?" said Rory, rubbing his back, smiling.

"Fine, fine. Say- you want me to talk to security next door and see if you can bring your stuff in that way? Any easier for ya?"

"No, don't worry. Thanks- we're good," said Lee.

"You sure?"

"Yeah absolutely- this one's the heaviest anyway," Rory said making a face, "It weighs a ton. We'll be back in a minute," he said as he and Lee went back through the room and outside.

Another two runs and they had it all inside. By far the worst was lifting the speaker with Jimmy inside it. They placed it close to the office door. Rory and Lee shared another chat with the second security guard while genuinely catching their breath.

"Alright then Ror… Robert, I'll leave you to it then. I gotta get back to the kids while Ramona goes out on her night shift," Lee said, wiping sweat from his brow.

"Yeah, I'll take it from here. Ring me later sure if you need me."

Lee tipped his cap to the two security guards, then left, the surly guard shutting the door behind him. The plan was for Lee to now make it to the other side of the office wall. Around the back of the mall there was a bottom entrance that led to an internal stairway. It only had a simple padlock on it. At the top was an old store room that was hardly ever used. It was blocked off from the main part of the mall, so it wasn't much thought about and doubly he would be nowhere near the mall's own security guards. His job was to get there and once Rory started making noise with the drums and guitar, he would begin to tear down a chunk of the wall behind the venue's office. As the old building had been developed and tagged on to the newer mall at various stages, many areas weren't particularly solid. Rory's information had informed them that it was only one sheet of wood, with a layer of sheetrock on either side of it. It shouldn't take much for Lee to get through with a pick axe, saw and drill. While Lee was busy with this and Rory was causing a noise distraction, Jimmy would pick the lock of the office and go inside to start working on the safe. To give them another layer of distraction, that was where Winston would come in. That was the theory anyways.

Rory checked his watch.

More or less on track.

Right, let's get on with it.

He shoved Jimmy's speaker a little closer to the door, then went about setting up the functioning part of the PA. He grabbed a table, setting on it the mixing desk and power amp. He ran a lead over to the working speaker and poked one into the redundant input of

Jimmy's one. Rory kept a casual eye on what the two security guards were doing. The two had been pacing around the building, half heartedly checking windows and once testing the handle on the office door. In part it looked as if they were trying to keep busy to keep up appearances. They were probably intruding on a cards game. This was usually a one person security job and a quiet one and that. The night after there would be further security hired. In the mall they would have their usual one security guard, mostly in an office checking monitors and smoking cigarettes. After a while the younger guy offered to make coffee and the two went and perched on bar stools with their backs to Rory. Seizing the opportunity, Rory went over to Jimmy's wooden cabinet and tapped it quietly three times on the top. Then he flicked off the clasps. Rory walked back over towards the left hand side and began slotting the drum kit together. He checked his watch again. It was eight twenty five. Rory crossed to the two men, sidling up in-between them, his position encouraging them to be stood faced well away from the cabinet.

"Phew- I need to take a break a minute. So you reckon there'll be many in tomorrow night guys?"

The surly one looked surlier. The younger man swallowed his coffee and smiled easily. "Yeah I guess so. Be honest with ya- I'm usually only really here after closing time. Never played a hand myself."

"A night owl are you?" Rory quipped.

They continued with a brief and largely vacuous conversation.

At the other side of the room, Jimmy gently pushed open the lid of the cabinet before sliding around the side of it. Obscured by the dozens of sets of tables and chairs, he crawled the few feet over to the office door. He pulled out the necessary tools from the carefully packed utility belt around his waist. As Rory's Americanised voice carried on easily in the background, he began working on the lock. Rory tried not to look in his direction. He did glance once, his left leg and foot partly visible. In half a minute, Lee was pushing the door open and sneaking inside. The first thing he would do was as agreed.

He would screw in a new bar lock bolt on the inside of the door. It would only take him about a minute and a half to fit it with a screw drill quietly penetrating the wooden frame. But it would buy him precious time if anyone tried to get in while he was still inside. They would just think at first there was a problem with the key.

Back at the bar, Rory checked his watch again. It was one minute after half past.

Shit. They were slipping behind schedule.

"Well, better get this here sound check done- hope it's not too noisy."

Rory scuttled off towards the drum kit. Very faintly in the background he could hear a sawing noise. He immediately began thumping the rack tom over and over, then adjusting the timbre with a drum key. He continued onto the floor tom and lastly the snare. He paused in-between to judge the noise from inside the office. It was minimal. The drums echoed with a boom all over the room. There was no chance of them hearing the sawing over it. He did notice the surly guard casting an irritated look once in his direction. It was very annoying to listen to, making it even more of an ideal cover. He carried on with his tuning. Then he switched to playing the whole kit. A decent drummer, he repeated a few different grooves for a couple of minutes, stopping to make apparent adjustments here and there. He stopped and checked his watch again. Twenty to. Lee should have been through the first layers by now. He hoped they were on track. Rory set down his sticks and crossed over to Howlin' Wolf's Epiphone Casino. It had a shiny new bridge and fresh set of strings. It also sported a few new scrapes. He flicked on the PA switch and dialled it up halfway. Suddenly a drill starting up from somewhere behind the office. It was a little louder than Rory would have hoped. Rory threw the strap over his head and twisted up the guitar's volume. He couldn't think what to play for a moment.

It doesn't matter- play anything!

It was stupid, but it was like the paralysis that had happened many times when he ever tried out a guitar in a music shop. He saw the older guard cock his head, trying to identify the noise. Rory launched into a heavy and ragged blues in E. The guitar sounded huge in the room. He hit throbbing minor bar chords, then tried out a simple blues scale riff. He caught one of them nodding their heads for a moment. The tone was decent and he actually began to quite enjoy hammering out a jam on the legendary guitar. Rory kept his eyes on the two guards, still working on their coffees. He improvised some lead around the bassey chords. It began to become vaguely reminiscent of Neil Young's *Cortez The Killer*.

Rory stopped to quietly tune his guitar as the two guards crossed in front of him. His ears were ringing a little and he strained them to hear if Lee was finished drilling.

"Hey Sandy it's your turn to do a circuit next," the younger guard said to the elder.

The name might have explained a little of the older guard's gruff exterior.

"Yeah, in a minute Peter. I'm gonna have a cigarette first."

Lethargically, Sandy plucked out a cigarette and searched his pockets for his lighter.

Rory looked down at his watch again. He couldn't hear any noise, but it was best to be sure. Rory turned down the volume knob, flicked to the middle toggle and began playing another simple blues, watching the two men pull up chairs at one of the many empty tables, then light up cigarettes. He looked over at the door to the office. He hoped that the safe wasn't giving Jimmy too much trouble, but there was no way of knowing. He stopped playing again after another five minutes. He took his time slipping the guitar back into its gig bag. He strained his ears again. He couldn't detect any background noise at all.

Good.

Sandy finished his cigarette, crushing it into the glass tray. He stood up and straightened down his shirt and trousers.

"I won't be much longer now guys," Rory shouted over with a little wave. He busiest himself adjusting leads and the two microphone stands.

Abruptly there was a hammering on the outside door.

"You expecting your buddy back?" Peter shouted over, still seated at the table.

"No, shouldn't be. Just me now and I don't have much left to do."

The two guards apparently subconsciously patted their holstered weapons and hurried off towards the main door.

Chapter 62

Right on time. Good luck Winston.

Rory could only hear snippets of the conversation. Then in staggered a very frail looking Winston.

"I'm terribly sorry about this, if I could just have a quick look. There's no damn drug stores still open 'round here."

"It's no trouble, come and have a look around," said Peter.

"Thank you, son."

Winston started to slowly make his way around the various tables, searching. For a moment, it was safe for him to turn his head and catch Rory's eye. His face eased into a mischievous smile and he gave a wink. Rory tried not to smirk and turned away, switching off the PA.

"You sort out your fella here and I'll do a circuit now," said Sandy to Peter, "You got the office key?"

"Yup, here you go."

Sandy headed towards the office door, jangling the keys in his hand, searching for the right one. Rory stopped what he was doing and watched him, his mouth suddenly dry..

"Ahhh, ohhh."

Winston made a meal out of a stumble and half fell, half knelt down onto the floor.

"Hey, you okay there?" said Peter, jogging over to him and puting an arm around his back. Sandy pocketed the keys and crossed to assist in helping Winston to his feet.

"Let's get him over to a booth," said Peter. They helped him down into a seat.

"Dear me, thank you fellas, I don't know what's come over me."

"I'll get him a glass of water," said Sandy half-heartedly.

Rory crossed over to the booth. "Everything okay?"

"Yeah, this gentleman here has misplaced his heart medication. My partner's getting him a glass of water."

"Hey- I saw a bottle of pills sitting by the back of the stage earlier."

"Really?" said Winston eagerly, propping himself up, "What colour's the bottle?"

"A little yellow bottle I think. Here, lemme get them."

Rory hurried over to the stage and grabbed the bottle of sugar tablets he had placed there earlier.

"Are these them?" he said, rushing back.

"God, you're a lifesaver. Pass them here please son."

Sandy arrived with the drink and Winston threw back two tablets before taking a large drink. Rory subtly looked at his watch. It was almost nine. If all was going to plan, then Lee and Jimmy would be packing up the money into three back-packs and transferring them through the hole in the wall, over to the mall side.

"How you feeling now sir?" asked Peter.

"Oh, much better, thank you. It was just one of my turns. I think it was all the worry over losing my pills. I'll be fine, really."

"Did you drive over here?" asked Peter.

"No, I took the bus. I'll be alright though, now I've got my pills," he said pushing himself heavily up.

"I'm about done here, I could drop you some place if you like," Rory said.

"Well… if you're sure it wouldn't be too much trouble young fella? Thank you."

No bother at all."

Rory finished making a meal of tidying up leads and checked there was nothing else he needed to take. All was quiet from the room beyond. He swung the guitar over his shoulder and got ready to leave.

"Here, Pete- this is the right key ain't it?" called Sandy from outside the office. He was twisting the key in the lock. Rory's stomach flipped and his eyes darted to Winston, where he was hovering by the door.

"Hold on a sec and I'll take a look," called back Peter, "I'll just see these gents out first."

Winston thanked them again and Rory put a protective arm on his shoulder as they slowly made their way outside. As soon as the door shut behind them, they hurried down the metal steps.

"Young fella?" said Rory.

"Yeah- to me you're young."

Rory grinned. "C'mon- we haven't got much time."

They jogged around the side of the building, went round the back and over to the van. Darkness has begin to properly set in. Rory placed the guitar carefully in the back of the van and Winston ducked down and climbed in beside it.

"If all's well in there, the three of us will be back in five minutes, with bags brimming with bills."

"Good luck Rory," Winston said, lying down out of sight.

Rory put a hand to his concealed gun and crossed the car park again, carefully checking all around as he went. There was nobody about and even less cars left in the car park now. He checked his watch again. A quarter after. If everything had gone smoothly with Lee and Jimmy, they would be waiting in the little store room, the bags filled up with cash. He pulled open the bottom door that Lee must have left ajar and padded up the stairwell. He got to the top and peered round the corner. In front of him he could see the large hole torn from the wall and beyond he could see right into the little office. He eased past a pile of boxes, buckets and mops and squeezed around the corner, searching for Jimmy and Lee. Then there they were. They were sitting silently on the floor, backs against the wall. Their eyes met his own, both with a mixture of anger and fear. Rory's mind was running away with him when the sound of a gun cocking combined with the feeling of cool metal pressed against the side of his head.

"Don't move."

Chapter 63

"Hello Rory," the voice said dully.

"Fuck," Rory said, scrunching his eyes closed tight.

He opened them again, tightened his jaw, looking ahead at Jimmy and Lee.

"I think you know what I came for."

"Yeah," Rory said absently.

Rory turned his neck ninety degrees to stare into Dave's self-satisfied face.

"You are some piece of shit, Dave."

"*I'm* a piece of shit?" Dave repeated with a rueful smile, "You're the one who fucked things up. I'm meant to miss out on the job? I don't think so. Just the way it is."

"Just the way it is?" said Rory, pulling his head away from the gun barrel, "Oh, right- so it *had* to be this way? You *had* to come and rip us off? You're the one who ran out on the job."

Dave scratched at his day old stubble with his free hand. "If you hadn't fucked things about, then we would have been altogether in this still, all nice and cosy." His voice was dripping with distain.

"Well I obviously didn't fuck things up too much- did I? The job still went fine. Things were going pretty bloody swell until you turned up."

"Well, that's life Rory. You always were too soft for this game. Both of you were," he said, casting a dismissive glance at Jimmy. "You stole it from someone, now I'm stealing it from you. So, I already have these gentlemen's weapons. Kindly pass yours along… handle first mind."

Rory grudgingly did as he was told.

"You two- stand up," Dave ordered. He looked cagey now, agitated. "Nobody try anything smart," he said taking a step back towards the office. "Anybody fuck about and I'll put a bullet in 'em."

Rory and Jimmy shook their heads in disgust. Lee waved a dismissive hand to show he understood.

"Cocksucker," he said under his breath."

"Just give me a reason Sambo. The three of you go down first, carrying the bags. I'm gonna have my piece in the front of my jacket pocket. I sure as hell don't mind ruining a good coat to keep this here dough. Then I'm driving outta here in your van. Then you can do whatever the fuck you all like. I don't have to hurt you. No point in comin' after me either- I'm leaving the city and I won't be back. My Mom passed- not that any of you fucks would care. I won't be coming back."

"I'm sorry to hear that," Rory said, his voice hard, "But it don't mean you need to rip us off Dave. Maybe we could split it with you."

"Maybe you could split it with *me*?" he said incredulously. "Get fucked. I'm having the lot. Right, now- shift yourselves before these security guards come through and we all get pinched."

Lee and Jimmy shuffled around and headed towards the stairs. Rory's mind raced through all of the options. His only advantage was Winston. Dave didn't seem to know about him yet. But Winston would only know something was wrong once it was too late. Rory picked up the last bag and followed them slowly down. Jimmy and Lee both turned to look at him on the stairs as they went, giving him a questioningly look. Rory looked back at them with no answer to offer. Jimmy looked especially pissed.

"Fucker," he said under his breath.

Rory continued to strain his already ragged mind. He didn't want anyone getting shot. It wasn't worth it. His principal was always to avoid anything like that. But if the chance presented itself, he'd make a move. Once they were at the van- that would be the most likely play. But it would depend on Winston too. He didn't want Dave to get antsy and shoot someone by mistake. Dave was no killer either.

Whatever was going to happen, it would be over in the next few minutes.

Lee pushed open the outside door and stopped. The fading evening light crept up the dark staircase.

"Go on. Keep going," shouted Dave from the top steps, beginning to make his way down, "Don't be trying anything funny."

Lee moved out, holding the door with his foot. Jimmy joined him, holding the door then for Rory. The three of them walked steadily though the car park, the white van sitting impassively across the way. Dave strode out the door behind them.

"C'mon, move it," he hissed.

The four made their way in silence, all scanning around them, as innocuously as possible. All was quiet. No sign of any movement at the Bingo Hall. If the plan had worked well enough, the guards would still be searching for a different key for the office lock. As they neared, Rory strained his eyes. He couldn't see Winston. He was probably still lying down in the front. Lee and Jimmy stopped at the back door of the van. Rory sidled up beside them. The three stood at the rear, holding the bags. They all turned towards Dave. Only a few paces away now, Dave marched on, one hand inside his bulging jacket front pocket.

Then suddenly there was the whisper of a dull thud and a bloody hole opened up in Dave's chest. He staggered, looking down at himself, his expression of frightened incomprehension. Then a second silenced shot took away half of his face and he fell to the concrete, already dead. The three others looked on, aghast.

From the undergrowth behind them, The Killer stepped out into the fading sunlight and growing moonlight. He looked directly at Rory and smiled.

CHAPTER 64

Then there was silence.

"Fuck me," Jimmy whispered, breaking the reverie.

The Killer walked towards him, a Glock 38 outstretched in his hand.

"Stay where you are," The Killer commanded. His eyes blazed in the dim light.

"Is this who I think it is?" said Lee fearfully, his eyes darting to Rory.

"Yeah."

Jesus, fucking Christ.

Rory couldn't believe all that happened in the last ten minutes. All had been going to plan. Like clockwork. Now they had been robbed, their robber killed. They were unarmed and at the mercy of a serial killer.

The Killer continued to walk towards them, in that lobbing and threatening way of his.

The voice.

It was the first time Rory had heard him speak. Except it wasn't. It was the voice he had heard on the answering machine that morning, he was certain of it.

"You don't appear pleased to see me, Rory."

The Killer stopped a few feet from the group.

"It'd be fair to say I'm a little surprised," Rory said.

This is it. This is how it ends.

Rory felt a terrible sadness that because of him they would all surely die.

"There's enough money here to last you years, it's yours," Rory said.

The Killer made an *o* shape with his mouth and moved from one foot to the other.

"How terribly kind. I will accept it. But that's not what I'm here for. Aren't you wondering how I found you?"

Rory shrugged.

"You and your friends weren't difficult to find. I've been seeing a lot of you all lately. Waiting. And now here we are."

"The cops are onto you. Don't make it any worse. Take the money and go," Rory said. He did his best to sound together, but his voice was low and cracked.

The Killer sighed. "Open up the van and put the bags in the back."

"They know about the latest girl. They know you're hitting each of the boroughs. You think you're some kind of modern day *Ripper*."

"Is that so," The Killer said, uncertainty creeping into his voice. "Hurry up."

Rory took a step backwards towards the van and tapped the door twice with his hand.

"The back lock is broken. We'll have to put them in the side," he said, raising his voice a notch.

"Alright. Do it… slowly."

"C'mon, do as he says," Rory said, turning to the others. The three of them moved around the side of the van. The Killer stayed where he was, training his gun on them.

The screech of tyres unexpectedly filled the air.

With Winston suddenly behind the wheel, the van shot backwards towards The Killer. It crashed into him, launching him off his feet. The van stopped abruptly, and The Killer rolled across the loose concrete, spilling his gun. Lee launched himself upon him before he was able to get back on his feet, slamming a right hook into his jaw. The Killer fell back again onto the asphalt. Then his long, wiry frame bounced back up again like it was attached to a yo-yo. The van hadn't done him much damage. Jimmy ran over too and the three of them grappled with each other. While this was going on, Rory was running for the gun. Winston hit the gas and lurched forwards, beginning an arc around the car park to face the scene head on. The Killer pushed the two of them off him before yanking out his hunting knife. He lunged at them with it, slicing across Jimmy's left arm. Over to the side, Rory now had the gun. He raised it and squeezed off a shot over their heads. It lost the usual impact due to the silencer. Jimmy stumbled away, Lee staring shocked at the fresh cut on Jimmy's arm. The Killer paused, then scrambled off to one side. Winston was now tearing back across the car park towards them all. The Killer made off back into the undergrowth. Rory aimed and shot off another round at him. It went wide. The Killer disappeared through the trees and off over the fence. Winston pulled up towards him, the van lights on, engine purring. Lee had an arm around Jimmy, looking at his wound as he helped him along. Rory rushed over to them.

"Are you guys alright? Jimmy- shit- are you okay?"

He placed his hands gently on to Jimmy, inspecting his arm. The cut wasn't too deep, but was bleeding quite badly.

"I'm okay," Jimmy said weakly, though his face was pale. Rory pulled off his t-shirt and wrapped it tightly over the wound. Jimmy winced.

Suddenly the first storey door burst open and the guards immerged, weapons drawn.

"Shit!" said Lee.

"C'mon, get in!" Rory said to them urgently, ushering Jimmy inside. They all clambered in through the passenger door of the van.

"Get in, quick" said Winston, flinging the door open, his face full of worry.

"Hey, stop!" shouted one of the guards behind them.

"Stop or we'll shoot!" shouted the other.

They raced down the first two steps.

In the van, Rory heaved the door shut and the tyres spun again.

"Stop!" came another shout.

The van shot off, Winston beginning a new arc to head back around towards the exit.

A shot rang out and sent up a cloud of dirt beside the back left tyre. Winston pulled the wheel, the van skidded, then took off towards the rear of the carpark. Dave's body lay alone off to one side.

"There- just go through it!" Rory shouted, pointing at a section of the fence where the top plank was broken.

Winston put his foot down, speeding towards it.

Bang!

Another volley came their way, obliterating the back window was an almighty smash.

"God-damn!" Lee shouted.

They all ducked down instinctively. Winston kept his foot to the floor as they crashed through the fencing, skidding over the debris and screeching across the black top. Winston paused for a moment, everyone breathing heavily. Steam rose up from the hood. He nodded at Rory, then turned the wheel and haired off the way they had first come.

CHAPTER 65

There was no conversation until Winston had driven them a few miles at speed, before joining the traffic and slowing down to a legal speed.

"Is this the way your jobs usually go?" said Lee mirthlessly.

"No, not exactly," said Rory lighting a cigarette and putting it between Jimmy's teeth. The he lit one for himself. "Sometimes they go badly," he added, attempting a loose smile.

"Thanks. I'm alright," Jimmy said, Rory's worried eyes on him.

Lee lit up a cigarette as well.

Rory lifted a spare shirt and pulled it over his head.

"Can I bum one of those?" said Winston.

"Sure, 'course" said Lee, passing him one across. "That was some driving you did back there old timer."

Winston blinked, giving a little nod. "Well fellas, thanks for having me along," he said, the cigarette chomped between his lips, "I think I'm gonna retire now."

A further ten minutes and they were pulling the van into the lock up. The journey had been filled with nervous chatter. Once inside, the atmosphere eased some.

"The plates are fakes, there shouldn't be a problem with the van," Rory said thoughtfully, "Apart from the obvious, I think we're away clean enough."

Rory had pulled the shutter down and they were all seated inside the van, the darkness illuminated by a fresh cigarette each.

"Yeah, there must be a thousand white vans in this town," said Lee.

"I guess you're right," Jimmy said, nervously fiddling his cigarette between his fingers on his good arm. He winced a little from time to time, thankfully the bleeding had seemed to have stopped.

Rory stubbed out his Marlborough on the dash. "Guys, can you two make sure that Jimmy is okay?"

"Yeah, of course… but…" started Lee.

"Winston, if you still can take the money as planned, put in your shop safe? Lee, would you take Jimmy to his place and stay with him tonight?"

"Rory," said Winston slowly, fixing him a look, "Don't do anything stupid."

"I won't. But I need to finish this thing. Finish it now."

"Rory, what are you gonna do?" said Jimmy, propping himself up, the fabric creaking underneath him as he moved.

"It's better you all don't know. I've got to try something, it mightn't work out. And I won't go alone. But listen, you three look after yourselves and hopefully I'll look in on you later tonight. Jimmy- I'm really sorry you got hurt."

"It's not your fault. None of it."

"It doesn't feel that way," Rory said, taking out the gun, checking it and returning it to his pocket. He opened the door and climbed out.

"Take care, you three. You all did good."

"Rory, can one of us not go with you?" Winston said urgently.

"No, it's better this way."

Rory walked two blocks, before stopping at a payphone and going inside.

The call was answered on the fifth ring.

"Kelly," came the gruff response.

"Michael, it's Rory Downey."

"Rory, what's up?"

"Now, that's a question. I've got something. Something big. But I gotta insist it's on my terms."

"Go on, let me hear it." Rory could hear the click of a lighter.

"I can't tell you how, maybe I can tell you later, I don't know right now. That can look after itself. Okay. He came for me tonight."

"What? Shit. Are you alright?"

"Yeah, I'm okay," he said with a sigh, then licking his lips, "But he got away. I think I know where he's gone. I got an address."

"Aright so far, I hear you."

"Only, it has to be just the two of us. I can't tell you anymore about it. There could be trouble- for me, for some others. I wanna go now. And I need to know now. Are you in?"

There was a long pause. Rory could hear him inhaling at the other end, a gentle and muffled wheeze.

"Of course I'm fuckin' in."

Chapter 66

Rory had given him the address of the corner of a block another mile away. He trusted him, but still wanted to hold back the address of the crematory. When he made it there, Kelly was already parked up, his car idling. Another smoke was between his lips, the smoke escaping out the crack in the window.

"Thanks for coming so quick," Rory said, hopping into the passenger seat.

"It's alright, the missus can watch *Cagney and Lacy* well enough by herself."

"I really think I'm on to him this time. The slippery fuck can't get away every god-damned time. And I know I need you with me, Michael."

"You know I wanna get him as much as you do. But I'm not looking to kill him, I wanna bring that sick fuck in and see him behind bars."

"I don't much care either way. He came for me again tonight. People got hurt. The only thing I want is nobody else getting hurt because of me. I don't want you getting hurt either. If you don't wanna do it this way, I understand, that's fine and I can leave right now."

Rory stared at him, trying to read his taught expression. Kelly stubbed out his cigarette in the plastic ash tray. "I'm here aren't I? You don't need to go worrying about me; I'm the cop- you're the civilian." He smirked. "I'll have a lot of explaining to do whatever happens."

"Alright, thanks. Let's get going then."

Rory gave him the address and they set off across the city. Then he filled him in on his whole undertaker theory. It turned out that Kelly liked it. Twenty minutes after and they were entering the

Meatpacking District. Now lit was less of a hub for food production, an area of decline and in need of a new purpose. As they approached the address on West 18th, they passed countless disused warehouses and dundering in factories. Speckled in-between these shabby buildings, were small pockets of domestic houses and apartments, and a pizza shop here, a Seven Eleven there. The overall impression was that of a grim and dirty suburb. It was one of the murky undersides that would never be seen near a travel brochure. Rory had mixed feeling about much of the city since he had lived there. On one of only a few visits to Forty Second street, he had had similar feelings there in his head and stomach. Better known as 'The Deuce,' Forty Second street is home to a heavy concentration of porno shops, grindhouse cinemas, dive saloons, loan sharks and prostitution. No stranger to the rougher side of life, it had left him with a nauseated emptiness in his stomach. Maybe he just hadn't been brave enough to try any of the cuisine on offer. Whatever it was, this was how he felt right now.

As Kelly began searching out for street numbers, Rory checked his gun one last time, flicking the safety off and on again.

"Looks like it's right along up there," Kelly said gesturing towards the back of a red brick building, a hundred yards away. He pulled over onto a disused gas station forecourt and switched off the engine. Kelly chewed at the side of his mouth.

"You ready for this? I can always just go and check it out myself."

"No fuckin' chance."

"I thought you'd say that. You've got a gun then," he stated, gesturing to Rory's pocket.

"Yeah."

"Is it registered?"

"I don't know. It's the Killer's."

They started along the dusty sidewalk, more one giant pot hole than a path. The rest of this half of the street all looked to be abandoned. A quarter of a mile away they could see lights on in what looked to be a few residential houses. Apart from that, nothing.

They approached the drive to the property. There was a wooden sign, with faded black lettering declaring it to be 'Granger's Funeral Services.'

"Christ," Kelly said with a shake of his head.

He snapped his service revolver from its holster and they both started along the gravel lane. There was no barrier or fence across the entrance. Once they were twenty yards in, the street lights weren't much use. Ahead of them was the main building. To the left was a small wooden clad house. To the right was a barn. All were in darkness. Kelly moved off towards the barn first, beckoning for Rory to follow.

Right come on now Rory, stop shitting yourself.

Rory pulled out the revolver, flicked off the safety and jogged behind him.

They were quiet as they made their way. The ground was old and worn black top, overgrown with weeds at the sides. The barn loomed higher then either of the other two buildings. It's corrugated iron roof glistened in the moonlight. The rest was in shadows. They circled around the outside, staying close to the sides. Kelly rattled a side door, but there was no give in it.

"I haven't even got a fuckin' warrant," he whispered more to himself than to anyone else.

They moved further around to a large window just above eye level. Rory stood on his tip toes and rubbed at the glass. It was hard to make out anything at all. Kelly did the same, then pulled out a long, thin torch and switched it on. The glare made them squint before picking out dark shapes from inside. Much of it was empty, save for cobwebs and dirt. There was a car with a grey tarpaulin covering it. At the other side was an ancient tractor that looked to be untouched for decades. Apart from that was just an assortment of poorly stacked boxes, work tools and household junk.

"Let's move on," Kelly said, locking eyes again with Rory.

"Alright."

Kelly flicked his torch off. They kept low, moving quickly around the side. Rory took in the large rear of the main building; it had more of an industrial warehouse styled roof and a very tall chimney. They couldn't see much through the side window. They approached the front and what appeared to be a run-down reception area. Again, it was all locked up. This time all the torch picked out was a narrow waiting area with thick wooden doors blocking the view into the rest of the building.

"What d'ya reckon?" whispered Rory.

"'Nothing much we can do here. Let's try up at the house."

"Okay."

Rory's stomach gave a little unwanted flip as they crossed the drive area.

"No cars about, maybe he's not here."

"No sign of any hearse," Rory agreed.

All the curtains were pulled shut around the house. They all were identical faded, floral drapes. They climbed up the front wooden steps, onto the narrow veranda. The door was old and not very thick. There was a large section of glass in the middle. The pair stood and caught their breath, looking all around, listening. Kelly glanced at the house, then looked square at Rory.

"In for a penny, I guess."

He swivelled the gun in his hand, holding out the handle. He cracked the glass hard with the butt of the weapon. It gave in with ease, falling away onto the ancient mat inside. Kelly reached in cautiously, pulling his sleeve down and flicked open the lock.

CHAPTER 67

Inside was almost complete darkness. With the curtains drawn and the absence of artificial light, the only real illumination was from Kelly's thin torch. They went slowly from room to room downstairs. They managed to avoid stumbling over any of the old, bulky furniture as they crept through each area.

Nothing.

Kelly gestured to the stairs and they crept up one at a time. Two minutes more and they had cleared the upstairs. All they had found were the sparce and dated rooms of a presumably single man. They went silently back down the stairs and paused in the hall. Rory gingerly pulled back a little of one of the drapes and scanned the outside. All was as it had been. They returned to stand in the kitchen at the rear of the house.

"Do you still reckon it's him?" Kelly said, patting his pockets for his cigarettes.

"Yeah, I really do," Rory said, his voice sounding hoarse and removed, "It just feels right. What about you?"

"Yeah. It's the place alright, I'd bet money on it."

He drew out a cigarette, after setting the torch down onto the work surface. His expression was far away.

"We haven't looked in the basement yet."

Rory chewed on his lip and nodded. "Where's the door do you think? Somewhere over that way?" he said gesturing backwards.

"Yeah, past the alcove we checked. I don't think that's another outside door. That might be it."

Kelly squeezed the unlit cigarette back into his trouser pocket, picked up the torch and led them both to the alcove. Rory tried the handle. It was locked.

Then they both froze.

There was a noise, something slight, something strangled.

"Do you fuckin' hear that?" Rory said.

"I hear it."

It came again. It sounded like very faint groaning. Possibly a woman.

"Here, move back a little," Kelly said, pushing Rory lightly with the torch. He raised his leg and gave the lock on the thin door a solid kick. Then another. There was a splintering sound. He gave it a hard shoulder charge, and it at last it cracked open.

"Jesus," Rory said as they hurried down the rest of the stairs after him.

Outside the door, the noise was very clearly the muffled cries of a woman.

"It's okay- we're gonna get you out of there," Kelly shouted, "This is the police."

Then to Rory, "I won't be able to kick this one in. You any good with locks?"

"Not me."

"Alright then. Go back up a couple steps there."

Kelly shone the torch on the lock and braced the gun over his wrist.

"Ma'am? I need to shoot out the lock," he called, "Nothing to worry about, but if you can please stay back."

He squinted, then shot off a round into the wood around the lock. Smoke emanated away from it. He craned his neck down, inspecting it.

"Gonna need another one," he said absently, before stepping away then drilling another round into it.

"That oughtta do it," Rory said, peering over Kelly's shoulder at the splintered wood.

Kelly gave it one hard kick and the door flew open.

"Fuck me," Rory heard Kelly mumble as he leaped into the room. Rory followed closely behind, anxiously taking in the macabre scene.

A girl strapped to a bed.

He forced vomit to stay down as for a moment he had the misplaced hope it might be Alice. It was stupid, but what did that matter when it came to feelings? He still felt sick as he stumbled towards the girl strapped to the bed. She was trying to lift her head up, her eyes glowing. There were visible cuts across her arms. But none more prominent than the slash from alongside her left eye, down to her jaw. It wasn't deep. He had been toying with her.

The sick fuck. Poor girl. Had he done the same with Alice?
Indignant fury raced through Rory.

She made a kind of grateful whimpering noise as Kelly spoke encouragingly to her, quickly untying her bonds. There was a terrible stench in the room that Rory couldn't place. Whatever it was exactly had been partly masked by a putrid smell of fading bleach. Rory found himself gently untying the twisted rag tied around her mouth. She breathed shallowly, then savagely; gasping for fresh air. It wasn't quite what her body needed and she gagged and coughed on the stale air. Finally, she was untied and Kelly supported her body as she struggled to sit upright.

"Where is he? Is he here… Did you get him?" Her voice was raspy, frantic. She was shaking all over, goosebumps speckling her arms.

"Not yet. No, he's not here, it's okay, we're gonna take you home." Kelly said soothingly.

Her troubled and quivering face tried an unsuccessful smile.

"When was he last here?" said Rory, carefully patting a hand to her arm, avoiding any of the lacerations. She winced anyway, pulled away.

"I…I don't know, most of the day?" she said, her voice croaking with dryness.

Rory hurried across the room and took a sniff of the jug of water. He poured some into a tumbler and brought it to her. She tried to take it from him, but her arms shook too violently. Rory held it to her lips and she drank it greedily down. It was followed by a hacking flurry of coughs.

"He t… t… told me he had something to do and then he would f… finish things. Finish… me?" Then she broke down into a hysterical bout of sobbing. Her tears flowed dry.

Then all at once the three of them froze.

Outside came the clear sound of tyres on gravel, then an engine switching off.

"Shit." said Kelly.

"Oh my God," Shelley whispered, trembling again uncontrollably.

"We've gotta get her out of here," Rory said, his voice clipped, urgent.

"C'mon, lemme help you" said Kelly, supporting her to her feet.

She faltered, unable to hold her own weight. Kelly helped her up more, half leaning on the side of the bed. Rory lifted his gun off the table and checked it, moving towards the doorway. Kelly continued to struggle to get her on to her feet. Again she stumbled, almost falling altogether. He looked to Rory, his eyes full of worry.

"It's alright. Keep helping her," Rory said, his voice strong, "I'll take a look."

"You sure?"

"I'm sure. Just look after her."

Rory held the gun out, in one hand, his elbow tucked in. His arm was as steady as granite. He paused at the foot of the stairs.

Silence.

He moved out, angling the gun, pointed at the top of the stairs. Cautiously, but steadily, he climbed the staircase. He cringed as he made a creak halfway up. He stopped again, his breath rapid.

He felt a burning sensation in his ears.

Rory continued on.

At the top, he kneeled down and inched around the corner.

Bang!

A shotgun blast.

He sunk backwards, shaded by the alcove wall as a hole was blown out of the wooden floor to his side. He stretched around the corner and fired off a round. He had removed the silencer and the blast echoed all around the bare house, though it wasn't a patch on the roar as the shotgun returned fire.

Kelly came running up the staircase, his revolver out, leaving the girl in the basement. He held the gun around the corner, plunging two rounds across the room. Then he strode out, firing again, his torch searching for The Killer. Rory moved out behind him, aiming, keeping low.

There he was; ducking for cover behind the living room sofa.

The torch picked out his huge, hooded eyes. He swung the shotgun as he stood, plunging two shots towards them. The first blew a chunk out of the kitchen wall. The second glanced Kelly's gun arm. He fell, injured, dropping his weapon, rolling back around the alcove. Rory seized the opportunity, standing and steadying his aim. He fired from a solid stance, absorbing the kick back. The bullet struck the shotgun in The Killer's grip, showering and cutting his hand with shrapnel. He cried out and fell to the floor. Rory looked back to check on Kelly. He was holding his bleeding arm, but was okay. As Rory turned back, The Killer was launching himself at him, his hunting knife drawn. They fell to the floor, The Killer frantically stabbing the knife at him. Rory dropped the gun, desperate to avoid the slashes. One sliced his arm, but only shallowly. Using the frenzied attack to his advantage, Rory pushed him off him for a second, allowing him to pull back and launch a crushing right hook into The Killer's jaw. He cried out again; guttural, an animal. Then he was back on him. Rory's other arm took a slice as he grappled for the knife. In the background, Kelly attempted to get to his feet, weak from his gunshot.

The Killer made gains, the knife inching closer towards Rory's throat. The Killer's eyes bore into him, gleaming with rage and excitement. Rory could feel his strength leaving him.

Then there was an almighty *whack* and the knife fell away and The Killer rolled away from him. Rory looked up to see the girl stood shaking beside him, panting, her teeth bared. In her hands was an unsanded two by four planl of wood. Rory picked up the knife and scrambled to his feet. Behind, Kelly also managed to stand, pulling himself up from the wall.

The Killer rose again, despite his many injuries, as if shrugging off a fly. He cradled his injured hand. His face was crazed, his body electric. He was now completely unarmed, but so were they. He let out a strangled scream, much louder than any of the gunshots had been. Then he turned and fled out of the doorway.

Chapter 68

Rory glanced back at Kelly, his face full of questions. He bounced on his heels.

"Go. I'm alright. I'll get the girl and call for back up from the car."

Rory nodded, grabbed up the gun and raced out of the door. Outside, The Killer was unlocking the hearse. Rory aimed, but missed, shooting a hole through the side window; glass shattering all around. The Killer feinted to the side and ran off towards the gates. Rory pursued him, breaking into a run. The Killer tilted his head and clocked Rory before putting his head down and forcing his long legs into a stride. He bolted off in Chelsea direction.

The Killer raced off through the industrial area, Rory half a street behind. It was now early morning; most sensible New Yorkers safely tucked up in bed. The Killer skidded round a corner, clutching his wounded hand awkwardly, though it didn't seem to be slowing him any. Rory shoved the gun down the front of his jeans and focused on the run. He almost toppled a filthy old woman with a shopping cart as he slewed around the corner himself.

"Sorry," he shouted behind him.

The Killer was striding out ahead now, past a row of derelict retail shops; nearly free of the Meat Packing District.

Rory felt his exhausted body slowing, then tensed his legs, commanding them to keep going. But it was his lungs that were weakening fastest. He was already panting hard and his chest burned. He cursed himself for smoking every last god-damned cigarette that had ever met his lips. It had been five minutes flat out running and they both were tiring, the gap between them much as it had been.

Come on you sack of shit- keep going!

Rory pressed on, trying to ignore the pain everywhere. The Killer pulled off right and Rory found they were now passing through the edge of the harbour. In the distance was The Hudson and beyond it, Jersey. He bit his lip and kept going. He refused to acknowledge the pain.

Rory thought of Alice, then had a pining for Crystal. He thought of his dead girlfriend, under the ground in Ireland. Somebody had to do something about people like this; killers.

Somebody had to something about The Killer; this Thomas Granger.

He thought of Dave also- dead on the black top. It was more than he deserved. Jimmy, Kelly; each hurt by this man. Never mind all of the girls. Where were they now? Burned probably and their ashes scattered anonymously with some other poor soul. Maybe they would never know.

The Killer looked back, his face dripping with sweat, like a melting Halloween candle. He bolted across 11ᵗʰ avenue, careering around a yellow cab. The angry driver sounded his horn. The Killer paused a second; his face frantic, looking all around him. He had no gun, no knife now. He ran on.

Rory skidded to a stop at the side of the road, as a huge articulated lorry rattled past towards the harbour. He doubled over, his shirt soaked, his legs aching, taking a second. He begged his body to offer him up some proper breaths, something to fill his lungs. Then he pulled out the gun and jogged across the road.

The Killer was now only twenty yards ahead. He was running towards one of the piers. There was a five foot gate. He clambered up it, grunting as he did so, his wounded arm twisted. Rory arrived just behind him.

"Stop! You've nowhere to go."

The Killer ploughed on. Rory stuffed the gun in his jeans again and scaled the gate, jumping down the other side with little trouble. His vision was blurring, his legs burning. Now The Killer was barely running at all. He hobbled on, his long frame huddled over itself; that strange gait of his accentuated. He was all out of options. Rory could feel the change. The power was drifting towards him. Rory still had some strength. And he had the gun.

The pier was empty, save for a few small boats tied up at the side. There was noise in the distance, somewhere a ship was being loaded up- perhaps dozens of them. But here it was just the two of them. The moon seemed to hang just above them, as if on a pulley string, over New Jersey too and over the gently bubbling Hudson River.

The Killer hobbled on towards the very end of the pier, like he had forgotten about the chase altogether. Rory, now yards away, drew his gun and slowed to a walk. Thomas Granger stopped at the edge of the pier, staring off across the river.

"Stop. You've nowhere to go," Rory said, no need to shout any longer. He clicked off the safety and aimed the gun at his back.

Slowly The Killer turned to face him. He swayed, clutching his mangled arm. His long coat flapped in the breeze around his spindly legs. His eyes had lost their intensity, but still appeared inhuman. They now gazed into Rory's. What they wanted to say, Rory didn't know.

"It's simple. Come with me now or I shoot you… again. It's over." Rory said clearly. He had managed to stop panting. He licked his lips. His arm was straight and steady.

The Killer craned his neck and looked down into the simmering Hudson below. Then he turned back to gaze at Rory.

"That girl," he said, his voice rasping, but still cavernously deep, "The one you knew. She was one of my favourites. She didn't go out easy."

"Quiet. Step over here and give yourself up."

"She didn't *die well*. Not well at all."

"I said shut the fuck up!"

The Killer took a cautious step backwards, then a second. He was now teetering on the very edge.

"Don't do it," Rory said, his fingers turning red as he gripped hard on the gun.

"See you around Rory," he said, raising his arms above him, allowing himself to tip slowly backwards.

Rory pressed down on the trigger and the gunshot resounded throughout the port. A bleeding hole appeared in the chest of The Killer as he continued to fall backwards. Rory would later swear he saw a smile begin to form on his face as he did so. Then there was a pause, then a splash as Rory ran to the end. He stared down and watched The Killer's body sink down into the river, a trail of red bubbling above him. Then it disappeared completely, as if it had never been.

Rory continued to stare, searching for any sign of life. He dropped to his knees, exhausted. He continued to watch.

After a few minutes his ears pricked up to the distant sound of sirens. He rubbed sweat from his eyes. Maybe they were on their way, maybe from Kelly's call. Or they could be going to any number of incidents across the city- some perhaps just as rotten a scene as this one. He pulled himself off his knees, looked at the gun, then launched it high in the air and into the river. It was swallowed up, just like its owner had been. Rory stretched out his back, rubbed his hand over his face. He searched his pockets and found the battered carton of smokes. Rory fired up a Marlborough Red, then he turned and walked back towards the city lights.

END.

Printed in Great Britain
by Amazon

87746539R00147